MW01008514

for my eclectic doc
Dr. Ingelmo -
- thank you

Our Mothers and Daughters

Short Stories by Diane Thomas-Plunk

Diane Thomas-Plunk

DEDICATION

For my mother, Martha,
and all the women who have been daughters or mothers,
those who will face the challenge of being both, or,
greater yet, those who mother the motherless
who were never their own.
And to Linda Sheriff Raiteri for her unfailing insights and impeccable guidance.

CONTENTS

Dedication	v
Preface	vii
Cassie's Chair	1
The Ravine	6
The Family Pratt	16
Such a Good Girl	21
Foster Caring	33
Kith and Kin	53
Family Circle	57
Abduction	65
Hear No Evil	75
The Pinch	81
Runaway	91
The Suitcase	95
Grace's Story	98
Hospice	104
The Walk	114
The Call	121
The Bus Station	124
Greener Pastures	134
Mother Knows Best	149
Angels With Only One Wing	156
Camp	168
Revival	176
Decisions	183
Tardy	193
Juvie Hall	201
Nearly Departed	209
The Envelope	216
End of Days	230
Vanished	238
High Tide	241
Sisterhood	253

CASSIE'S CHAIR

When Cassie sat down, it was for sure a serious sit. It didn't matter if she sat on the front steps, the back yard swing, a dining room chair pulled to a window, or the corner of her classroom. She just sat.

Dad blamed Mom. Mom hovered and coaxed. First, second, and third grade teachers warned and suggested that Cassie see a doctor, maybe several kinds of doctors. Dad dismissed their concerns and continued to avoid Cassie. In his opinion, Mom should just do a better job. She could pull Cassie out of this, if she only tried. Most of the time Cassie pretended that she didn't hear them argue. Other times she simply sat motionless for hours. No one knew why she seemed to go away when she entered her fugue state.

Mom had secretly taken Cassie to the family doctor who found nothing out of the ordinary. He thought, however, that it would be useful to refer her to a neurologist, but Mom declined. Her husband would find out, and be angry.

When Cassie wasn't sitting, she was a regular girl with blonde, curly hair who read storybooks and played with her dolls. She chatted with Mon about the stories she read and did her little chores. She giggled. She played games. Her normalcy made Mom sad as if *this* was the unnatural child.

Only one person treated Cassie the same whether or not Cassie was sitting. Her best friend, Felicia, lived across the street and two doors down, so it was easy to see Cassie when she chose the front steps for her sit. Felicia would grab a coloring book and crayons, or maybe a doll, or sometimes their homework assignment, and run down to Cassie's house.

Felicia sat next to Cassie on the porch steps. "You're right, Cassie. We have to do our homework now. I try not to do the arithmetic. I don't like it. I'm glad you do, or I'd just make marks on the paper and turn it in. Of course, Miss Murray would send home a bad note to Mama then, and I'd be in trouble at home and school. So you save me from a spanking."

Cassie gazed off into the secret world only she inhabited. Her breathing was even and slow. Her face was expressionless.

"Here's our first problem. Fifteen take away seven. I don't have that in my head. Here's how I do it." Felicia opened her notebook to a clean page and made fifteen well-spaced dots. "Now look at this. Watch me, Cassie." Felicia carefully put a strike mark through seven of the dots as she counted them out loud. "Now we just have to count the remainder. That's what Miss Murray calls it. The remainder. One, two, three. See. There are eight dots left. That's the answer, Cassie. We did it." Cassie still drifted.

The girls did arithmetic problems until Mom came out to the big porch. "Felicia, it's our supper time. Cassie, you come in now."

"Ma'am, Cassie's not back yet." Felicia looked embarrassed. She took her friend's hand.

Mom closed her eyes briefly as she drew a deep breath. "Okay then. Felicia, would you like to stay to supper? I'll call your mother, if you'd like."

Mom would move Felicia into their home, if she could. Coming to the dining room table with pink and purple sunset lights probing the bay window, Dad looked suspiciously at Felicia. As much as Cassie made him uncomfortable, Felicia caused discomfort times ten. He wondered what must be wrong with her that she saw nothing wrong with his daughter. Maybe she was a witch. He gave a polite nod to Felicia, but didn't speak to either child. He said a perfunctory blessing for the meal.

Plates were passed and served and handed about. Felicia sat to Cassie's right. Mom tried to make lighthearted chatter. She had been pretty and perky at one time, a real head turner, but the last few years weighed hard, and it showed. Dad never looked at her in the same way anymore. He looked like a man searching for the exit door.

"S'cuse me," said Felicia. "Cassie likes more potatoes than that, please."

Mom took back the plate extended to her and added more mashed sweet potatoes.

Felicia smiled. She put a fork in Cassie's hand and helped it scoop a bite of potatoes dripping with sweet butter. She slightly lifted Cassie's arm, watching her friend take the bite.

Dad roughly shoved away his plate and stomped out the back door. Mom looked from her husband's departing back to her daughter's glazed eyes, then to Felicia's beatific smile. The women remained at the table while Felicia prompted Cassie's intake. As they reached the end of the meal, Cassie brightened, reached for her glass and swigged down the remaining milk.

The three cleared the table. Cassie took dishes to the kitchen. Mom walked Felicia to the door.

"Thank you for staying."

"Sure thing." Felicia started down the porch steps before Mom stopped her. "Felicia, how is she at school? How do the other children treat her?"

"Most everybody likes Cassie good enough. She's fun, and she's the prettiest, you know. Some of the bad kids make fun of her, though, when she goes away. They think she's spooky."

"Away? She's just unconscious. In some sort of trance. Why do you say *away,* and why do they say *spooky*? She's just a sick little girl."

"No, ma'am. She goes someplace else. She likes it there, too. You want her to like it here better, but I don't know if she can. I wonder what she sees when she goes *there*, but she doesn't tell. Gotta go." Felicia hopped over the last step and ran across the yard, yelling behind her a thank-you for supper.

When Mom returned to the dining room, Cassie had finished stacking dishes in the kitchen. She was speeding through her arithmetic homework.

"You're very good at arithmetic, aren't you, baby?"

"A little. It all seems like I've had this assignment before. Isn't that funny?

Where's Daddy?"

"I think he went for a walk. You and Felicia are very close friends, aren't you?"

"Yes, ma'am. Oh." Cassie put down her pencil and dug through her notebook. "You gotta sign my permission slip. Next week we're going to St Louis cemetery. You know that's where all the people are buried on top of the ground in little house things. That's where the witch Marie Laveau is buried. Won't that be cool? You could be a chaperone and go with us."

Mom shivered. "I'll take the permission slip and look it over, but I don't know if this is a healthy field trip for young children." Mom sat down next to her beautiful child. "I talked to Felicia about you being sick."

Cassie laughed.

"No, it's not funny. Don't you know, baby, that you sometimes ... lose time?"

"I have to finish the problems, Mom."

"Right. Go ahead. I have some ice cream when you're done. Then, we'll need to get you ready for bed."

"Can I have a story? Will Daddy tuck me in?"

"I'll read your story when you get in bed. Finish up here, and we'll get your dessert before bath time."

Dad came in the back door while Cassie worked on the arithmetic.

"She wants you to read the bedtime story," said Mom.

"I can't anymore. She ain't natural."

"Is that your considered opinion, or is it the booze you consumed at the bar? I can smell it."

"Don't smart off at me."

"She's your little girl. You need to start acting like a father!"

"Actually, I been thinkin' on that. I don't think I could've made what's sittin' in there."

There was little choice between Mom's horror at Dad's words and her fury at them. For the first time in their many years, she slapped him so hard that his head snapped back. Moments elapsed in mutual, hate-filled silence. Right now, this moment could never be taken back. Almost in unison, they both growled, "Go to hell."

"I want you out of this house first thing tomorrow. I never want to see you again." Mom turned sharply and left the room.

Later, when Cassie was snuggled in bed, she smelled like fresh lilacs and honeysuckle. Her hair wasn't quite dry, and it clumped in dainty swirls about her head. Her cheeks flushed. Her eyes sparkled. *How could this child possibly be something wrong?*

"What story do you want, baby?"

"Snow White. She eats the bad apple and goes to sleep. Goes somewhere else. Then, the prince kisses her (*giggles*), and she comes back. I like that story."

"Do you know why you like that story?" Mom braced for an answer.

"It's just a good story. That's all."

"My baby, do you know that you sort of go to sleep sometimes when you're really awake? That we all seem to lose you for periods of time?"

Cassie turned pages in the storybook.

"Please listen to me, Cassie. I don't know what happens or what to do about it, but, if you do go some place else like Felicia thinks, I want you to know that I need you to be here. With me. Please. I love you so much."

Cassie smiled in the most all-knowing way. A way that chilled Mom even before the child spoke.

"Funny. That's just what my Mom in the other place says."

THE RAVINE

The rain was so heavy, and the reach of the headlights so limited that the illusion was created that the car was perfectly still, and it was the road that flew by like a movie backdrop. Clare Levy shook her head periodically to help her re-focus on the road ahead. The windshield wipers slapped at the downpour, but couldn't poke a hole in the curtain of water. Clare leaned forward, straining to see the difference between the center line and the shoulder. They were on their way home from the lake house, driving on a worn, two-lane highway. Clare's back cramped from the strain.

"Are we all right? Can I turn on the radio?" asked seven-year-old Ivy.

"Shh, don't talk now."

"But, I'm tired of this." Seven had become a whiney year for Ivy.

"Quiet! Not now."

The car began to shimmy, then fishtail. The tires hydroplaned, and the car headed for the shoulder where it took flight.

Clare cried out, "No, no, no, no."

Ivy screamed.

It only took seconds before the car tilted to its right. It slammed onto the downside of the hill, and made a complete three-sixty rollover. Once again right side up, it slid scarily down the embankment. If Clare had been able to listen, she'd have heard the sounds of underbrush and small trees banging against and under the lurching vehicle. Twenty feet down from the highway, the car slammed against a tree large enough to stop it.

Clare thought she might have been unconscious, but there was no way to measure how long. The torrential rain still assaulted the car, and its aggressive, drenching fingers pushed through cracks in the windows, and dripped inside. The world was inky black. She felt herself pressed against the seatbelt harness in a slight forward tilt. She wanted to unfasten it, but didn't know if they were through sliding, or if there might be a drop-off or other hazard in front of them. Ivy was silent and still. Clare twisted to reach for her, but yelled in pain. Her left leg, ankle to hip, must be badly injured.

Deep breaths, woman. Breathe through the pain. Think about labor. Yeah, that didn't work either, she told herself.

She reached again for Ivy, but without twisting her torso. Ivy didn't respond.

She's unconscious. She's not dead. Dear God, don't let her be dead.

Clare tried to think of what to do, but passed out again instead. The next time she woke, it was to Ivy's crying, a blessed sound – all things considered.

"Baby, sweet girl, Mommy's right here, It's going to be all right."

"My head hurts. My tummy hurts," Ivy whimpered. "The belt hurts. Take it off."

"Ivy, not yet. I think we should wait a while. I know it doesn't feel right, but we'll just wait. We had an accident, and we need to wait a bit. When it's light we'll know better what to do."

"The rain's on me. I want to go home, Mommy."

"Me, too, baby. Me, too."

Ivy fidgeted a while, and then became quiet again. The rain had given way to a light sprinkle, and the blackness eased into a dismal ash gray. The sun would be up soon, and that would make everything better. Rescuers would be able to see them.

Clare tried to remember where her purse might have landed after the vicious ride into the ravine. She attempted to reach forward to feel the floorboard under her legs, but her hip screamed again. *Breathe, breathe.* Reaching to the passenger floorboard was out of the question. To do that, she'd have to move her leg and hip again. Maybe Ivy could do it when she came to. Careful to hold her torso rigid, Clare reached over the center console into the back seat. She could only feel around slightly to the left and then right. No purse. She wished she'd been one of those people who always had their cell phones attached to their bodies. There wasn't going to be a way to locate it.

Clare turned the key in the ignition. The engine didn't turn over, but clicking it again, she was able to turn on the headlights. Maybe the light would attract attention. In reality, however, she knew there was little traffic to attract on the road that had thrown them into the ravine. She'd turn them off when the sun came up to prevent draining the battery.

I didn't have to leave in the middle of the night. I didn't have to leave in a rainstorm. I still could have walked out on Ted if I'd waited until morning. And now, look what I've done. All because of my temper, and his infidelity.

Clare remembered that Ivy should be kept awake in case she had a concussion.

"Ivy, sweetie, wake up. Talk to me."

The child groaned quietly and opened her eyes. "Why don't we get out of the car?"

"We're kind of stuck. We went off the road and slid down here, but we'll be all right."

"Is Daddy coming to get us?"

"I don't know, but someone will for sure. We'll just wait for them."

There wasn't exactly a sunrise. The light just grew brighter through the mist and fog. Now she could see that the car contorted into a crescent on Ivy's side, with the tree as a fulcrum. About ten to fifteen more feet down the leveling hillside was a ribbon of water that probably didn't exist in the dry season. The car wasn't going to slide any more due to the strong tree pinning them in place. They could unfasten the seatbelts.

"Blood! It's blood!" yelled Ivy.

"Where?"

"My head. I put my hand here – where it hurts – and it's all red." Ivy began yelling.

"Easy, Ivy, easy. I want you to unlatch your seatbelt and open the glove compartment. There should be paper napkins in there. Get out some."

Ivy's crying slowed, and she did as directed.

"Good girl. Now, gently put one of them up to your head. See if you can feel where it's cut, and wipe it off."

"You do it."

"I can't. I'm so sorry, but I'm stuck over here. I can't reach that far. You're a big girl. Go ahead."

Ivy used three napkins to sop up blood. She threw the soaked ones onto the floorboard.

"Ivy, fold up one and hold it to where it hurts. If you can press it against your head, you might stop the bleeding."

Ivy followed instructions. She only cried slightly, but sniffled loudly.

"I'm thirsty, Mommy."

"I didn't put any water bottles in the car," said Clare. "Let me think ... okay, put your hand where the windshield's cracks let rain drip inside. Wipe your fingers on the rainwater, and then suck it off your hand. That's the best I can offer right now."

"That's lame."

"You're right, but it's all we've got right now. Look, I'll do it over here."

Clare hadn't tried to use her left arm. It was sore, but now – to lift it – was excruciating.

Using her right hand, she captured a few drops and licked her fingers. "See, that worked." Her voice trembled in spite of herself. Her left arm pulsed painfully.

Ivy followed suit.

"Ivy, how's your head?"

"It hurts. There's blood in my hair."

"We'll get it all washed clean when we get home."

"When will we be home?"

"I'm not sure. We'll need to wait a while. How's your tummy?"

"It hurts, too. Everything hurts. Make it stop." Her voice was weak, more tired than panicked.

"I'd give anything if I could make it stop. Maybe you could help. Do you think you could lean forward and look at the floorboard in front of you? Is my purse down there?"

Clare cringed at Ivy's hurt noises as she bent forward.

"Not there," said the child, settling back into her seat.

"I don't want to hurt you, but I need to ask a really big favor – something that could help us."

"It hurts. My whole body."

"I know. I'm so sorry. I'd do this if I could, but I just can't move. If it's not awful, can you crawl onto the console and look all over the back seat and floor for my purse? I need my cell phone to call for help. Or anything else you see that could be useful."

"Will you call Daddy to come get us?"

"Yes. Sure, I will. I'll call for someone to help us. Do you think you can get over there to look?"

"It hurts too much." Ivy threw down another bloody napkin and folded yet another to hold against her head. She cried harder.

"I understand. I don't want you to hurt worse, and you're the only one to make that decision, but this is so important, baby. It could help us get out of here."

So this is the kind of mother I've become. One who sends her injured child to do the hard work. If we live through this, I'll be arrested for child abuse – and deserve it.

Ivy started trying to move, making noises that sounded more angry than pained. She positioned herself over the console.

"There it is," Ivy exclaimed.

"Can you get it?"

Clare saw drops of blood from Ivy's head wound dotting the console.

"I think so."

Ivy stretched over and down, grabbed the purse, and cried out. She threw it onto her mother's lap causing the impact to reverberate through Clare's hip and thigh. She managed to hold in the scream that wanted out.

"Here's a sweater, too." Ivy tossed, and it floated toward the dashboard. Clare caught it.

Ivy fell back onto her seat and sobbed.

"I'm so sorry, sweet girl, so sorry, but so proud. You did an important thing. I can make a call now to get someone here to get us out. Here. Put the sweater around you."

With her only good hand, Clare rummaged through the purse. This was certainly a reminder not to carry so much junk in there. She threw trash over her shoulder and into the back seat. The phone! There it is.

She put the phone on her lap and, in doing so, uncovered a bottle of aspirin in the bottom of the purse.

They may be out of date, but maybe not. She grappled with the lid, but got it off and retrieved a pill.

"Baby, put this in your mouth and chew it up. It won't taste good, but it might make you feel a little better."

"Eww! Gross!" Ivy's face scrunched up.

"Try to get some of the moisture from the window again. I'm so sorry."

Can I ever stop saying sorry?

Clare managed two more from the bottle and put them in her mouth. Her face scrunched up, too.

She fastened the purse and put it within reach. One-handed, she wiggled the cell phone out of its case.

I will forever more be sympathetic to disabled people. I didn't know how hard it would be to have only one arm.

The phone was in her lap, and Clare was punching 911 when she saw that there was no signal.

Of course. Why would I expect this to work? Just one more nail in our coffins. Now what?

The day dragged on. Clare heard a car up on the road and banged on the horn button. There was no reply.

She stroked Ivy's arm and soothed her when the child became agitated. They were both hungry, thirsty, and in pain. Clare encouraged wiping the remaining raindrops, but the sun was drying them up.

"I'll check my purse again," said Clare.

Digging through the refuse, she found a couple of sticks of gum and a lip moisturizer.

"Hey, Ivy. Put some of this on your lips. They won't feel so dry. And then – look. Gum! At least it will taste good."

Ivy smacked her gum for a while and relaxed enough for a nap to sneak up on her.

It was about dusk when Clare felt something bump her side of the car. She looked out the side window, but saw nothing. Another thump toward the front of the car woke Ivy, and they both saw the tawny, muscular body of an adult mountain lion. Ivy began a scream, but Clare grabbed the child's arm.

"Shhh. You must be quiet. Be very still," Clare insisted in a stage whisper.

The mountain lion moved forward, away from the car. Something else attracted his attention. Down the twist of a stream, Clare saw the young doe and her fawn. She held her breath as the lion crept forward and paused.

"Ivy, close your eyes. Now."

The lion bolted forward. Mom and fawn sprinted toward the woods. The lion was faster. Clare heard the rustling in the trees and then the tiny scream, no doubt from the fawn.

Of course, Ivy had not closed her eyes. The next scream was hers.

"He'll eat us next!" she yelled. "He'll come back here and get us." She was near hysteria.

"Baby, baby, he won't. We're in a car, so he can't get to us, and I don't think they like people anyway. We're safe. I promise."

"No, we're not! We have to get out of the car. We have to go up to the road."

Ivy started to stand in a crouch, but grabbed her midsection in pain and fell back.

Through her tears, she reproached her mother. "It's you! Your fault. You won't take me home. I want Daddy."

They both cried.

"It is my fault. I shouldn't have left when it was raining so hard. I wish I could go back and make a different choice, but I can't, baby. I know someone will come to help us. I really know that."

"The lion? Will he come for us?"

"That much I know for sure. He's not going to hurt us."

Clare prayed that she was right. She heard another vehicle on the road and snapped her headlights on and off and did it again. The car kept going.

As night settled over them, there was little to do but continue waiting. There weren't any more raindrops on the windows, and there was no more gum. Exhausted by pain and emotion, Ivy slept again.

Clare felt herself on lookout duty, listening for cars on the road and trembling at the sounds of crunching grass near the car that, in her mind, belonged to the lion. She tried to maintain guard duty, but exhaustion finally caught her, too, and she slept.

Clare was awakened either by the rising sun or the man's voice from the top of the hill.

"Anyone down there?" he yelled repeatedly.

A lightning bolt of exhilaration shot through Clare. She honked the horn again and again, hoping that she hadn't been dreaming.

"Mommy, is someone there?"

Thank God. She heard it, too.

She honked and yelled, "We're here! We're here!"

"Lady, I'm a deputy sheriff. Are you the one with a little girl there?"

Clare rolled down the window as much as the diminished electrical system would allow.

"Yes, I'm Clare Levy. My daughter is Ivy."

"Okay. I just called for county rescue teams. We'll get you out. Your husband has sure been looking for you. Hold tight."

Clare took Ivy's hand and kissed it. "We're going to be all right. Thank heaven. We'll be all right."

This time their tears were of gratitude and relief.

After a wait that wasn't as long as it felt, Clare and Ivy heard multiple vehicles arrive at the side of the highway. A couple of them sounded big.

A man's voice shouted. "Clare, Ivy, I'm here. Ivy, Daddy's here!"

"Daddy, come get me!" Her little voice didn't carry up the hill.

Then it was the deputy's voice again. "Ma'am. The rescue guys will take over now, but Mr. Levy and I will still be here. They're going to send down a man first to assess the situation and determine how to proceed."

"We've seen a mountain lion in the area," Clare shouted back.

"Good to know."

A man rigged in a safety harness and a long rope attached to something at the hilltop made his way to the car. He questioned Clare about their injuries while determining their abilities to cooperate with the extraction team.

"Ladies, we'll get you out of here as quickly as we can, but it won't be fast," he said. "We have to take it step by step to do it safely. You're obviously brave women. This will just be your last challenge before we get you to the hospital. We're going to take the roof off the car, and we'll get the steering wheel out of our way. I'm going back up now, and we'll get started. It will take a bit of time, but we have two ambulances coming. We're going to take care of you."

"Please ... get my daughter out of here first."

"Yes, ma'am. Will do."

The groan of metal being assaulted not only kept the lion at bay, but also encouraged the women to slam shut their eyes and frequently hold their breath. Ivy was the first to be lifted out and strapped to a stretcher. Two rescuers guided the stretcher as they climbed the hill. Ivy called for Mommy's help for the first half of the journey until she heard Daddy calling to her from the road. Finally at the highway, Ivy was transferred to an ambulance.

Ted yelled down to the car. "Clare, I'm going to ride with Ivy. I'll meet you at the hospital. I'll be waiting for you."

"Yes, go! I'll see you there. I'm all right."

I think everything will be all right now.

THE FAMILY PRATT

When Newton Pratt carried his young bride over the threshold of their new, little house, it was the happiest day of their lives. The house wasn't big, but there were two bedrooms, one of which Willa anticipated fixing up for the children they hoped to have.

Newton was a good catch. He wasn't a drinker, a carouser, or a gambler, and he attended church pretty regularly. Although young, he already had a job at the shoe factory where he expected to move up into higher paying positions. He'd also done well for himself by courting Willa. She was petite with long, dark hair, and bright, hazel eyes. She sang in the church choir, and delighted Newton by singing little snippets of tunes as she went about her regular activities. Willa loved parties. She seemed perpetually happy. Newton couldn't help smiling any time he was in her presence.

The young couple set about establishing the routines of married life. Willa sent Newton off to work each day with a lovingly packed lunch and a kiss. With no babies yet, there wasn't a lot to keeping house, but she had a good vegetable garden out back. Willa prided herself and delighted Newton by setting hearty suppers on the table every night. Their social life centered around church. Willa's mother lived just a few miles from the new Pratts in east Warren County, and was grateful for her daughter's good marriage.

In less than two years, Willa cried over two miscarriages. Newton tried to comfort her, but, feeling helpless, he took her to stay for a bit with her mother.

"Newt, don't fret," said Willa's mother. "It's something hard for a man to understand. You done right by lettin' her stay by me for a while."

He kissed his wife good-bye, and left, shaking his head.

"Ma, I'm a failure. I can't get done what dogs and cats do with not a thought," moaned Willa.

"Daughter, we can't question God's plan. You're a good, Christian wife. The babies will come when it's time."

Willa stayed for a week with her mother, and ran anxiously into Newton's arms when he came to pick her up. She was grateful to be with her husband, but Newt thought some of her glow was gone.

As Ma predicted, the next three pregnancies took. Two boys and a baby girl in between. The house was full and happy. Willa easily managed the busy household, and sang to the children as they went about their days. Newton's co-workers ribbed him about yakking on and on about his perfect children and wife.

When baby Jacob was only one, the oldest boy came down with pneumonia. The country doctor shrugged. He could only give Willa directions for home remedies to treat the boy's symptoms. There was no penicillin as the U.S. entered the 1900s. Junior liked the peppermint tea, but not so much the salt water gargles. They made him choke and spit much of it out. Willa hadn't the heart to insist. When he rested, she could tend the other children. Newton could see her wearing down. As Junior worsened, Willa sent Newton to sleep on the davenport, and put the little boy in her bed, so she could care for him in the night without waking the household. She sat with him in the bathroom running steamy, hot water in hopes of opening his tortured lungs. She put cool towels on him when his fever raged. She piled on afghans, and held him close when he had chills. But both Willa and Junior lost the battle.

They buried him on a soft, spring day at the Pleasant Valley Baptist Church's graveyard. Willa took to her bed.

"Darlin', we have the two other children, and I got to work. Can't you git up? Just even for while I'm at work?" Newton pleaded. Willa turned over in bed with her back to him. So, he took his case to Ma, and moved her in. She let Willa stay in bed crying for two weeks, then she called a halt to it.

"Git up now, girl. You're a grown woman with two other young'uns that need their Momma. They're grievin', and so's your husband. Are you listenin' to me?"

"Leave me alone, Ma. Just leave me alone."

"I'll do no such a thing," Ma insisted. "I'll stay for a spell longer, but I want my own bed back, and I want you to act right." Ma pulled back the sheet, and yanked the pillow from under Willa's head. "Get up, I say."

Slowly, Willa mostly returned to her previous self, but every Sunday after church, she went out back to Junior's grave where she talked to him, and cried.

Jacob was a rambunctious three-year-old when he caught the measles. The doctor immediately ordered their five-year-old girl, Opal, to her grandmother's house to prevent her catching the contagious disease. He assured that some children ride through the danger and survive.

Willa and Newt darkened the children's room where only Jacob lay, and, once again, Willa treated fever symptoms. The fever ran high. Headaches worsened. Jacob was confused, but, after all, he was so young. When he stopped breathing, Willa screamed, and wouldn't let go of him. Newton and the doctor were finally able to disengage the small body from Willa's arms. He was buried next to his brother. Willa was never the same.

Opal was a pretty little thing, and as busy as any five year old. One day when she was dancing on the front porch, she stepped too far back, and took a tumble down the two steps to the porch yard. She let out a yelp, and cried at the little bump on her head. Willa was beside herself. She examined the child from head to toe, put cold rags on her head, and sat with the child for the rest of the afternoon to watch for any physical changes.

"Momma," Opal whined. "I want to go play outside."

"No, you stay in here where I can keep up with you."

Newt got home from work, and, to Willa's dismay, he laughed at her. "Woman, kids get bumps and scrapes. She's fine."

"I ain't havin' no more children. This is the one I got, and this is the one I'll take care of," snapped Willa.

The first time Opal joined her mother in the kitchen, and took up the knife to cut onions, Willa gasped. She took the knife away from her. "You go to the living room, child. Practice that crochet stitch I showed you."

Opal turned six, and loved school. "Look, Momma. I can write numbers, and I played jump rope at recess."

Willa stood with Opal every morning at the end of their lane to wait for the school bus. She was there in the afternoon, waiting for the bus to return the child safely. Willa went to school to talk with Opal's teacher, and told the veteran teacher that Opal was a sickly child, and shouldn't have too much activity at recess. The teacher considered Willa, and, because the woman was so earnest, she kept Opal inside at playtime.

A few times in the second grade, mothers of Opal's classmates invited the child to their house to play after school. Willa made up excuses. The invitations eventually stopped coming. Opal never knew she'd been invited.

Newton paid a call to Willa's mother.

"Ma, I don't rightly know what to do," he said. "I know Willa's troubled by all the babies we've lost. It lays on my heart, too. But she's bein' more than a mother hen to Opal. I don't think it's right, but she won't listen to me. Tell me what to do."

"Son, I don't rightly know what to say to you, but I'll go over, and have a talk with her."

It didn't go well.

"Daughter, I went around back, and saw your fine garden. You're raisin' them up good. How 'bout your Opal? She comin' up good, too?"

"Of course, Ma. I watch over her. And it's time to go down to the road for me to wait for the school bus. You can come with me."

"Willa, that child's in the third grade now. Don't you think she can get off the bus, and walk straight up this little way to the house?"

"Sure, she could, Ma; but it don't hurt for me to be there."

"Maybe it does."

"That don't make a lick of sense."

"Willa, she's got to grow a little. And that's up to you. I know you fear her dyin'. I know you think you'll lose her like you lost the other babies, but you can't let that fear squash that little girl."

"We're done talkin', Ma." Willa stood with that new, hard look that had begun creasing her face. "This one's gonna be fine. This one's gonna grow up if I have to lock her inside this house. You can't stop me from protectin' my only child. No one can."

Opal graduated from high school, but never had a date. Momma kept all the nasty boys away. They only wanted one thing. Daddy got Opal a job at the shoe factory, but it didn't last long. Opal went home to help Momma take care of Daddy 'cause he was sick. And then Opal just stayed. She stayed with Momma for many years until the older woman had a stroke and died. Opal lived by herself in the little house until she was very old.

Momma had succeeded.

SUCH A GOOD GIRL

"*Clouds swarmed the late-afternoon sun, and the Oregon sky grew sapphire where still revealed. Cops gathered like bright-eyed crows in the lengthening shadow of the fire tower.*"

"I think you've read her to sleep again." Cynthia, the three-to-eleven nurse, approached the bed, and smiled at Valerie sitting in a straight-back chair next to her mother.

"It worked, didn't it? It's Dean Koontz, her favorite author. Mom loves the word pictures he paints. She enjoys it when she's *present*, and I guess it does no harm when she fades."

"I agree," said the nurse as she leaned down for a closer look at her patient. "Your visits do her good even if she's not clear-headed. I like it that you leave her notes when she's not been clear during your visit. It's a great way to let her know you've been here. I've given that tip to some of our other families. I hope you don't mind."

"Of course not. Share it with whoever you choose."

The whirr of something vibrating drew the attention of both women. The nurse touched the pocket of her lab coat.

"No, it's me," said Valerie as she reached into her open purse, and pressed her thumb to the iPhone while glancing at caller ID.

"Hi, baby."

"Where are you?" growled her daughter's voice.

"Well, I'm at Gramaw's. Why?"

"Because you're not here at my play. I shouldn't have even expected you."

"Oh, Avery, I'm so sorry. Gramaw was agitated, and I've been calming her. I got distracted. I'm so sorry. I'll leave now and get right over to the school."

"Don't bother. It's intermission. I have to get back on stage, and it'll be over before you can get here. Just forget it. Oh, that's right. You already did."

The call disconnected.

"Damn. I've blown it again."

"Don't beat yourself up. You can't be everywhere. Everything's under control here. Go on home," said Cynthia.

Valerie leaned down, and kissed her mother's creased forehead. "I'll come tomorrow at lunch, Cynthia. Good night." She stroked her mother's hair before leaving.

It was 11 p.m. when Avery strolled through the front door. Valerie jumped to her feet, and met the girl in the foyer.

"Where on earth have you been? I've been worried sick."

Unrepentant, the teenager boldly met her mother's eyes. "Mrs. Pierson took some of us for pizza to celebrate. *She* was actually at the play because *her* daughter was in it. Odd behavior, huh?"

"There's no cause for sarcasm. I told you what happened. Told you I needed to be with Gramaw. I'm sorry I missed your play. I can't be two places at once. I was worried because you didn't even answer my calls or texts. I didn't know where you were or if you were safe. You need to let me know where you are, Avery."

"What difference would it make? I guess you would have known if you remembered today that you have a daughter. Maybe you should let *me* know where *you* are." Avery brushed past her mother, and started up the stairs.

"Going to your room is a good idea. You have school in the morning. We'll talk about this tomorrow night."

Avery shrugged as she continued upstairs.

Caught between wanting to punch the wall or cry, Valerie went to the kitchen instead and refilled her wine glass. Back in her favorite living room chair, she punched speed dial for her younger sister.

"Yes, Val."

"Caller ID takes all the fun out of making calls, Sooz. Remember when we used to make crank calls when we were kids? 'Is your refrigerator running? Better go catch it.' We thought it was hysterical. Can't do that now – caller ID."

"I know how to get around ID, and still make crank calls, but that's neither here nor there. The good thing, though, about caller ID is that you know I willingly took your call. It's late, Val. What's up?"

"Everything's up including my blood pressure. Hey, I need your help with Mom this weekend. I need to spend some time with Avery. She feels neglected, and probably rightfully so. She's developed quite the attitude. Okay, she's a pill. If she were smaller, I'd spank her."

"I'm pretty booked up already," said Suzannah. "What's the deal? You and Avery can spend time with Mom, and still do something else. By the by, we pay nicely for Riverview care and all their activities. Mom doesn't exactly lack for stimulation, Val. Hate to say it, but a lot of the time, she doesn't know anyone's there anyway."

"Well, that's just cold. So much for loving concern. Maybe what she *lacks* is her younger daughter, Sooz. I really need to free up some time. I want to take Avery away for the weekend. She's acting out, and I need to focus on her this weekend to start getting things back under control. Give me some help, okay?"

"You think Mom can't do without us hovering over her for two short days? Hey, I do my part. I pay my share for that fancy nursing home. I should move in there myself, and let them fuss over *me*. Besides, she's out there close to you in hot-shot suburbs-land. I'm all the way downtown."

"Don't poor-mouth for me. That's a pretty nifty loft you have with a river view. And we were together when we chose Riverview. Always thought it was an odd name since it wasn't even near the river. But I've got work, and Mom, and Avery, and I need a break – at least this weekend. Spend some time with our mother, please – both days. Maybe I could run up to Nashville with Avery for an overnight. You don't really have any responsibilities, you know. You could do this."

"Val, just because you kicked out your rotten husband, and you're flying solo over there, don't get judgmental about my lifestyle. I have a big job, and private clients as well. I have a full, busy life, and I'm not hooked into being the Good Daughter like you are. You need way too much approval from Mom. Everyone else, too. You always have. Being pulled apart like this is something you created."

"Jesus Christ, Sooz. You are completely selfish, and you don't even know it! If you won't help out for Mom's sake, do it for yourself. She's going to die, you know, and then how will you feel? What regrets will you have?"

"Ding, dong, the witch is dead."

"God, Sooz. Surely you don't mean that."

"Maybe. Are you unconscious? Do you not remember how hard she was – is – on us? How she berated us? Criticized us when she wasn't ignoring us? Our home wasn't exactly Ozzie and Harriet. I think Dad died just to get away from her. I chose to distance myself. You chose to keep begging for her approval. It's sick. I keep hoping you'll get over it, Val. And now you tell me that you're letting down your own daughter to be what you think is a good girl. My God, Val, the circle is never ending."

Then, Suzannah hung up. It seemed to be a night of Wallace women hanging up on Val.

On Friday morning, Valerie got up particularly early to make Avery a "take-out" breakfast from packaged croissants, scrambled eggs, cheese, cilantro and some cayenne powder. It didn't break Avery's freeze.

"I'll be home by six tonight, Avery. We'll order in Chinese, and talk about some things. I want us to make plans," said Valerie.

"Whatever." Avery hoisted her backpack and headed for the door. But she had the croissant in hand.

That morning, Valerie had two important meetings. The client in the first meeting frowned and trashed the campaign proposal from Valerie's team. Next, she had to meet with the principals of the ad agency where she was a division manager. They already knew about the earlier failed meeting. They presumed lack of preparation was the cause and particularly blamed the poor work of one of her team members. She defended him and knew she acted too defensive. *Just shut up and take the flack*, she thought too late.

Just after twelve, Valerie hurried from the office for a short visit at the nursing home. She swung through the drive-through lane of a fast food place. She ate on the way, arrived at twelve thirty-five. Upon entering the room, it was obvious that Betty Wallace was present. Valerie crossed the room with a grin and kissed her mother's cheek.

"You smell like onions," said Betty.

"Sorry. I guess I do. I ate a burger on the way."

"You know that's not healthy. You need more vegetables. And some salads considering how snugly that skirt fits. Do you have the clean night-gowns for me?"

"The service here does that for us, Mom. They should be back today."

"Well, they're not here yet. I don't want strangers handling my delicates. I want you to do them from now on."

The back of the bed was raised to its highest point. Betty Wallace sat as straight and dignified as if on a throne. Her white hair was smoothed into a severe bun. Her bed jacket was immaculate. Hands folded properly in her lap. Her gaze piercing. Once again, she was her formidable self. All creatures in her vicinity might cringe in fear.

"Why is it only you who I see? Where are lovely Suzannah and our precious Avery?"

"They've been here, Mother, and they'll be here again soon. Maybe I'm just lucky that it's me you remember most."

"Maybe I remember because you don't take care of business."

Valerie kissed her mother's forehead and smoothed the delicately crocheted, blue and silver afghan across Betty's lap. Val had commissioned it from a folk artist in north Mississippi who created stunning pieces.

"Stop fussing, child. Where's my lunch? You know they bring the most dreadful fare. I can't imagine who they think I am that I would tolerate that garbage."

"Tell me what you'd like to have, Mother. I can get a change in your menu, or I can require that they order in some special meals once in a while. What do you think about that? We'll make a list next week of what you'd like, and I'll take care of it."

Valerie looked out the door, hoping to see the lunch cart.

"What are you looking out there for? I'm right here. Do you plan to spend any time with me?"

"Of course, Mother. I was just looking for your lunch. I'm going to need to get back to work really soon."

"I want you to read to me after I've eaten. And you should improve those menus as soon as possible. And you must gather my delicates to take home to wash them yourself – by hand, of course. Daughter, you need to use more blush on your cheeks. You'll never get married again looking so pale and tired."

"Mother, I do my best." Without thought, she began picking at her fingernails, just as she had as a child.

"Oh, dear. I made you pick your nails again. Shame on me."

Betty's smugness disappeared as a cloud passed over her eyes. The frightened vulnerability that appeared always broke Valerie's heart.

"It's okay, Mother. I'm here now, and your little Sooz will be here this weekend. Avery and I will stop by Sunday evening. Look, here's your lunch coming in, darlin'. This nice lady will help you with it."

Betty looked from Val to the aide entering with the lunch tray. She took Val's hand and squeezed it hard. "Where is Denise? I want her."

"I'll go look for her, Mother," said Valerie of Betty's deceased sister.

"Ma'am, are you all right?" the aide asked Val.

"Fine, just fine. Please help her with lunch." Valerie turned and left.

Her cell phone rang on the way back to work. She didn't reach it in time, so the caller was left with voicemail. "Hi, Val. Okay. You win. I'll be there for a while on Saturday and Sunday. I'll see that her highness is all right. Have fun with our beautiful Avery this weekend. I'm doing this for her, not our mother."

Every once in a while, something goes right.

Valerie arrived home at 6:15 p.m., but there was no Avery. She kicked her not-so-sensible high heels across the living room, and slammed her briefcase down on the foyer table. She was instantly on her phone, first leaving a voicemail for Avery, then texting her. No response to either. She paced. She remembered a hidden pack of cigarettes she'd tucked away for emergencies after she'd quit. She dug it out along with a book of matches and stepped onto the patio, leaving open the French doors to the living room, so she'd hear Avery come home. The cigarette tasted terrible, and made her dizzy, but she knew she'd get past that if she just kept smoking. It was 8 p.m. when Avery sauntered in.

By that time, Val's patience had evaporated just like the smoke from her cigarette.

"Where in God's name have you been? And why the hell can't you answer my messages?"

"You said that *you'd* be home at six. You didn't ask if *I'd* be here." Avery turned toward the staircase, but Val grabbed the strap on her backpack and slammed it across the foyer.

"Oh no, you are *not* going to play this game with me. March yourself into the living room, and put your butt in the chair. Right now. We're having a talk."

Stunned, Avery did exactly as directed.

"My dear daughter, I know that circumstances have interfered lately with your life and the way you want life to be. Circumstances have interfered with my life, too." Valerie's voice shook with barely controlled anger. "There's always my job. That's what keeps a roof over our heads and food on the table, in addition to the goodies you want to have. Also, I have responsibilities as your mother. I want to be involved in your life and activities. You bring me great joy. But I'm also a daughter to a sick, old lady. Your Gramaw needs me the most right now. To be her daughter, I've neglected my own daughter. I own up to that, and I'm truly sorry. You and I need to be patient with each other.

"Here's what I want to do. I've made arrangements for your Aunt Sooz to check in with Gramaw over the weekend, so you and I can go away – spend girl time and relax. Get re-acquainted."

"Something will happen," said Avery. "You'll have to work or the nursing home will call."

"Nothing will happen," said Valerie. "This weekend is for us."

The girl wasn't yet convinced. "So, we'd just stay home?"

"No, I thought we'd go up to Nashville. We'll leave early tomorrow. It's an easy drive. I can score tickets tomorrow night to the Opry, and there are scads of antique shops and delightful tearooms. We'll spend the night in an extravagant hotel and maybe get massages. It will be great. What do you think?"

"BOR-ING."

"Really? Okay. If we go to Nashville, tell me what you'd want to do – or any place else close by. You tell me."

"Honest? If we really go out of town, and you really want to do what *I* want ... Coaster Kingdom!"

"Coaster Kingdom?"

"Omigod, Mom, are you totally out of it? It's new and just outside Nashville, and it's only the coolest. It has the best rides anywhere, totally. We could do that boring stuff if you just have to, on Sunday, but I would so love to hit the rides at Coaster Kingdom. Would you really take me? No one in my crowd has been there yet. That's what I want to do."

It was the happiest Val had seen Avery in ... who knew how long? If it was roller coasters she wanted, then that's what she'd have.

The ride to Nashville was quiet. Avery immediately plugged in to her MP3 player, and stuck buds in her ears. She listened to her music throughout the three-hour drive. Checked into an exclusive, downtown hotel, the women set out for Coaster Kingdom by lunchtime. Valerie choked at the admission fee and cost of food and drink, but it was worth it if that was the cost of re-connecting with her daughter. Avery laughed and pulled her mother along like when she was a kid. It was a great adventure.

As Avery loped along toward a ride that looked like a demon-possessed pirate ship, Val went to a nearby bench inhabited only by a well-dressed, elderly lady.

"Your daughter looks like a yearling colt," said the woman.

Valerie sat and smiled at her. "Sometimes teenagers forget to act sophisticated. I'm enjoying watching her be a child for a while today. Do you have children or grandchildren here today?"

"No. Sometimes I just come to watch the young people. It's a lovely way to spend an afternoon, and well worth the price of admission."

As the insane pirate ship began slowing at the end of the ride, Val rose to walk toward the ride's exit. She felt the woman's hand on her arm, and looked down at the swollen knuckles, tissue paper skin, and bulging, blue veins. She shivered and looked into the woman's eyes that momentarily looked like her mother's.

"Peace."

"What?"

"Make peace with yourself."

Val wordlessly pulled away, and met Avery bouncing out the exit gate.

Valerie looked back, but the old woman was gone.

"Awesome! That was just the best. I screamed so loud that my throat hurts. Thanks, Mom. This is the best. I can't wait to tell all my friends. You have to come ride with me now. You just have to."

"Baby, I'm not a roller coaster kind of gal, but I love that you're having a terrific time."

"No, c'mon, Mom. We'll do something calm. Look, there's the ferris wheel. That's good for old people, isn't it?"

Val looked up at the tallest ferris wheel she'd ever seen.

"Are you serious?"

"No big deal, Mom. It's just a boring ferris wheel. Let's go."

It was at least two stories tall, maybe three. They boarded and rose slowly and jerkily into the sky, stopping and starting to admit new passengers and unload others. With passengers exchanged, the smooth ride began. Val's hands were clammy, and her stomach churned. She stared straight ahead, trying to ignore the height they reached. On the second revolution, just after they topped the crest, the metal machine groaned and stopped. Their carriage swayed. It seemed to be suspended in space – way out in space.

"Wow, look. I can see all the way to downtown Nashville." Avery leaned over the side, and the carriage jiggled.

"Please! Be still."

Avery started to laugh. "Oh, Mom. Look at the stars. Look at the lights. We're just swinging above it all." Avery tilted back and forth to rock the carriage.

"Stop!"

Avery finally noticed her mother's white-knuckled grip on the safety bar. Mom was holding on as if she'd fly off if she let go. Her jaw was clinched, and her eyes were wide.

"Oh, my God. You're really scared, aren't you? We'll get started real soon. They're just letting someone off again, I'm sure. We're fine." Avery put her warm hand on her mother's cold one. She leaned close, and smelled of funnel cake.

But the carriage didn't move.

"We're stuck. We're stuck all the way up here, and they can't get us down," said Val.

"Mom, Mama. Sometimes they have a stall. Nothing's bad wrong. Look how pretty everything is from up here."

"No thanks. I think I'd die if I looked down."

"You're afraid of heights. I never knew. Gosh, I'm sorry. Why didn't you say so? Why did you get on this with me?"

"Because you wanted to, and I wanted your day to be perfect. I thought I'd be okay."

They were quiet for a while. Val gasped when a breeze briefly rocked the carriage. She thought she might cry. That or throw up.

"It's okay, Mom. I've got you. You're safe. Can we talk while we sit here?"

"If you don't move again." Val's eyes were riveted straight ahead.

"Well, I love Gramaw and all that, but sometimes I see her being real mean to you. Why does she do that?"

"That's just her way. She has high expectations – always has."

"Do you have high expectations for me?"

"Baby, I have high *hopes* for you, and I have faith in you."

"But you're always there for her, taking her bad-mouthing, never talking back, doing everything she wants. Aunt Sooz doesn't act like that."

"We each have our own way of dealing with problems. You and I have been struggling with just that lately, haven't we?"

"I've been a bitch. And I think I've been jealous of the attention you give Gramaw."

"I'm sorry you've felt that way, and that I've been too busy to notice. I've been trying to balance a lot of things, and you've been getting the short stick. It always feels like I'm cheating someone no matter what I'm doing. Can you help me work on this?"

The ferris wheel sighed, and the carriage proceeded about ten feet and stopped again. Valerie's hands on the safety bar were slippery with sweat, but she couldn't release her grip.

"God, I hope we live through this," she whispered.

"Mom, can I go with you sometimes to visit Gramaw? We could do it together."

"Absolutely, Avery. I appreciate that you want to."

"Yeah, but you'd appreciate me more if I hadn't made you get on this ride, right?"

Valerie would have seen the girl's teasing grin if she'd felt secure enough to turn her head.

"I'd laugh if it wouldn't make us shake." Valerie almost smiled.

The ferris wheel began its descent as if nothing had ever been wrong.

FOSTER CARING

The elegant, oversized front door should have been a tip-off to what awaited on the other side, but Dooley would never have guessed. The foyer, more like a hotel lobby, might be thirty-five feet wide. The marble floor stretched back to what looked like the length of a football field. Two-thirds of the way back from the entrance, a broad staircase reminded her of the one in *Gone With The Wind* except that this one actually went somewhere other than a backdrop. Gleaming, carved doors adorned each side of the foyer and led who knew where. In the center of the foyer was a round, marble-topped table with ornate metalwork legs that looked so much like honeysuckle vines and flowers that Dooley expected their cloying scent. In the movies and magazine pictures, the table would support a jumbo vase and overflowing flower arrangement. On this one, however, there were backpacks and a baseball cap. Nothing here made sense.

Particularly the woman who'd admitted them and now stepped in front of Dooley. She was surely more than six feet tall, square jawed and broad shouldered. Her short, curly hair and lace collared, print dress were insufficient to contradict the overall impression of an NFL linebacker in drag.

The social worker was supposed to take Dooley to some old lady's house for yet another foster care placement. *What the hell are we doing here?* she wondered.

"Mrs. Brewster, this is the girl I told you I was bringing," said Miss Price, the social worker. "Her name's Dooley McDougal. Like I said, she's fourteen and a habitual runaway. Good luck."

The Amazon in lace smiled and her face transformed. Dooley couldn't remember the last adult she'd trusted, but the sweetness that she saw in this woman's face warmed her heart. She maintained her guardedness, but felt a glimmer of gratitude for being here.

I'm probably wrong. Something's not right here, Dooley told herself.

That's about when she noticed the little girl clinging to Mrs. Brewster and standing nearly behind the woman.

"Dooley McDougal – it's almost musical," said the woman. "Welcome to our home, Dooley McDougal. The precious child peeking around my skirts is Twinks. She's a part of our household, and she likes to stay close."

At hearing her name, Twinks retreated completely behind Mrs. Brewster. Although Twinks was tiny, her deep brown eyes were so large that she must constantly look surprised.

"Though I don't actually have eyes in the back of my head, I'd be surprised if you don't see two other young ladies creeping down the stairs to see who's arrived. Are they there, Dooley McDougal?"

"Yeah."

"Well good. Miss Price and I will go in the study to complete the paperwork they insist on. Reena, I'd like you and Patty to take Dooley upstairs and let her settle in."

Mrs. Brewster eyed the tight, low-slung jeans and the too-tight tee shirt that clung to young breasts that were certainly not constricted by a bra. The shirt pulled up just enough in the back to hint at the tattoo spanning her thin waistline. Through the shirt was also the outline of a hoop piercing the girl's navel.

"And, Reena, you'll want to get Dooley some more appropriate clothes and underwear."

Miss Price handed Dooley the pillowcase containing all of Dooley's possessions.

Mrs. Brewster, with Twinks seemingly attached to her, led Miss Price to one of the doors. Dooley, faced with newness and insecurity again, looked to the girls on the staircase for direction. She needed them for now, but she didn't trust anyone young or old. Eventually, everyone turned on you.

The older of the two spoke. "Come on, new girl. You're not going to believe this."

Dooley was already in disbelief.

Patty, who might be ten or eleven, laughed. "Don't pay any mind to Reena and that 'new girl' stuff. She's just messing with you."

"Maybe I don't like being messed with." The hair on the back of Dooley's neck

bristled. She'd been in shelters and foster care before. They were barely better than her family's home where she'd barely escaped. Her antennae were sensitized to bullies, and she could take care of herself. That's what she told herself.

"Chill, new girl. This isn't the kind of place that any of us has been before. Nobody gets hurt here. Nobody needs to be afraid. I'm just playing with your head. Up the stairs we go."

Just like she'd expect from the movies, halls broke off to the right and left and straight ahead of the second floor landing. The trio turned left and proceeded down a wide hall with age-old portraits and artwork adorning the walls. They stopped at the first door. Before Reena could open it, Dooley's attention fixed on the arrangement directly across from the door. There was a wide, overstuffed chair upholstered in brocade with a matching ottoman. Next to the chair was a side table bearing a cascade of books and a cork coaster. The burnished brass floor lamp stood slightly behind the chair and table and wore a blue, green and red Tiffany lampshade. Pretty, but odd.

Reena noticed Dooley's averted attention. "You'll see, new girl." She was beautiful when she grinned at their new sister. "Welcome to our home."

Reena opened the door dramatically, and the trio plus the pillowcase went inside.

"Good God!" said Dooley.

The room was huge, easily thirty-five by forty-five feet. Each of the four corners was dressed out as a distinct bedroom. Individual areas featured a three-quarter bed, throw rug, nightstand and lamp, chiffarobe, and a small desk with lamp and chair. Each of the bedroom areas, furnishings and accessories, was decorated in a different color scheme. They were red, blue, green, and yellow. In the center of the room were two large bookcases placed at right angles to each other and sagging with the classics and newer mysteries and fantasies. There was another desk and computer that Dooley would learn had many blocked areas. It was only available for a few hours per day. A half dozen beanbag chairs dotted the area.

"What the hell is this set-up?"

"Come on in. You're red. I'll explain while you put up your stuff," said Reena. She lowered herself to the desk chair while Patty sat cross-legged on the bed, and Dooley put her few belongings in the chiffarobe. Reena observed that they'd surely need to go shopping for her.

"Here's the deal. First off, we call her Ma Brewster or just Ma," explained Reena. "We don't cuss, and we say ma'am. Got it? This mansion – or castle from my point of view – has been in her family for generations. They had tons of money and maybe she still does. I don't know. No matter. I know she doesn't take us in for the allowance she's paid. She just believes it's the right thing to do. She only takes four girls because that's the number she thinks is what a family should be. She also thinks that's how many she can get to really know and help.

"This room was a ballroom sometime way back," Reena continued. "See the fancy floor? That was for dancing. She thinks we'll do better if we're all together, but still have our own space. This way, we can know what's going on with each other and give support, but still be to ourselves when we want. She's good people, Dooley. She's smart about helping us. Like I said, no one will hurt you here."

"How long have you guys been here?"

Patty looked at Reena and dropped her head.

"She's told me it's okay to tell," said Reena. "Patty's been here about six months. They found her digging through a dumpster for food. Her parents were deliberately starving her. See, she looks good now. Ma took her to the doc and put her on a good diet and supplements. She still takes some medicine I don't understand. Me, I've been here nearly a year and a half. That makes me the senior member of the clan."

Dooley looked at the swell beneath Reena's tee shirt. "So you weren't knocked up when you got here?"

"No. I settled in okay, but then I rebelled against rules I thought were caging me in. I started sneaking out, doing bad stuff, and this is what happened. I wasn't so smart after all." It was a sad smile on Reena's face as she patted her belly. "I didn't tell Ma until I was showing and had to tell. I was sure she'd kick me out, but she didn't. She took me for a doctor's appointment like she's been doing ever since. We've talked about what happened and why, but she never shamed me. My real mother would have kicked my ass. She did kick me out a long time ago, and I wasn't even preggers back then. Not being pregnant was only luck, though. Mom's boyfriend of the moment was getting to me I don't know how many times a week. Maybe he was shooting blanks. I don't know, but good ol' Mom didn't believe what I told her about him. Wouldn't do anything to help me. She needed him more than she needed me, so she told me to hit the road, and I did. I went through a lot of shit before I turned up here. It's a good place, Dooley. Take your time, and you'll see."

"How far along are you?"

"I'm twenty-two weeks now. I have a doc appointment tomorrow."

"What's twenty-two weeks mean?"

"I'm a little more than halfway there, maybe twenty weeks left. Look at me. I'll be ginormous by then. Patty's gonna have to put my socks on for me.

"Patty, go get some jeans and a decent tee-shirt for the new girl – some pj's, too," directed Reena. "Later, I'll take you to supplies so you can pick out undies and a bra, for God's sake. You gotta get those tits in a harness."

Reena turned to Dooley after Patty left the dormitory room. "Don't say anything, if you see her steal food at meals. She brings things up here and stashes them in her chiffarobe. We have to clean them out from time to time. We pretend we don't know that she does it. She still fears that someone will starve her. So, what's your story, kid?"

"I don't have a story, and I'm not a kid. You're barely older than me. Sixteen?"

"Fifteen. The pregnancy ages me."

"So, what's the story on the little girl hanging onto Mrs. Brewster?"

"Twinks? All we know is that she's seven. She's been here I think three months now. Ma hasn't told us what happened to her, but it must have been bad. She doesn't talk at all and is scared all the time. She doesn't like to be away from Ma. She's sweet, but she's kinda spooky. I mean, we all *know* we're messed up, but we're working on it. Twinks is just a scary mystery. By the way, no one's going to force you to tell your story, but you'll feel better when you can trust someone enough to share."

Ever cheerful Patty nearly skipped across the converted ballroom and put clothes on the red and white bedspread.

"I bet you'd like a shower, Dooley. Grab your pj's and I'll show you the bathroom. We'll have night snack pretty soon, so the pj's will do."

On the wall between the red and the yellow corners was the door to the bathroom. The interior had been obviously converted for use by several girls. Two, large walk-in showers with frosted glass doors were on the left wall along with open shelving that housed stacks of fluffy, white towels, hand towels and wash cloths. The dirty clothes hamper was there, too. To the right of the door was a row of slatted doors that, upon inspection, led to toilets. The wall between showers and potties afforded a lengthy counter with four washbasins and a wall-to-wall mirror on the wall above them. Along the wall next to the entry door were two upholstered benches. Whereas the dorm room was excessively colorful, this room was crisply black and white art deco. It was beautiful. It was not like any bath and pee room Dooley had ever seen. It gleamed. The starkness of *2001 Space Odyssey* came to mind. Dooley liked old movies.

"Okay, new girl, you see where everything is. Dump your dirties over there. Here's your jammies. Take your time. Patty and I are going to change, and then we'll be with the beanbags until you're ready to go down for snacks. Can you freakin' believe I'm reading a book on pregnancy and child care?" Reena laughed and started toward the door.

"Are you keeping it?" asked Dooley.

Reena looked sad or fearful or both. Her hand automatically went to the baby bump. "I don't know. I just don't know." She left the room so fast that it was as if she'd never been there.

Dooley stood quite still, looking around the large, beautiful room uncertain and uncomfortable. She went to the door and pressed her ear against it. She held her breath. There was no sound. No breathing or heartbeat on the other side. The voices she heard were distant, from the far side of the ballroom. Good. No one was spying on her. She heard music and imagined the residents of the mansion in ball gowns swooping around the room with their beaux, hiding their blushes behind feathered fans. Then, she flipped on the door's lock. She examined both showers. She chose one and sat inside on the bench for ten minutes, thinking and listening before collecting her courage enough to disrobe and turn on the water.

All alone, no one could see the welts and scars on her upper back, the backs of her legs and butt. She always hid her abuse.

The hot shower was amazing. In the last shelter, she'd been afraid to get naked and into a shower. She looked through scented shampoos and soaps and scrubs that were available on a shelf. The aromas relaxed her and encouraged a long-forgotten smile. She wanted to sing, but didn't want the others to hear. Her jagged-cut hair was cleaner than it had been for months.

When she emerged and slipped into the pink cotton pajamas, she felt clean in more than a physical sense. It was a first step away from a year of running and abuse. Maybe she'd be safe here. She started toward the door and stopped, pulling up her pj shirt to unclasp the belly button ring. She tossed it into the dirty clothes hamper. It was just one of many things these people didn't need to know.

Outside in the big room, Patty was at the computer table, and Reena sat in an easy chair. It had been moved in to accommodate her pregnancy awkwardness. They were both in similar pajamas and slippers, but of different colors.

"Patty, you updating your facebook status?" asked Dooley, looking fresh and childlike.

"No, we're not allowed facebook or Twitter or any of those. Just not good for us yet. Too much trouble to get into," said Patty.

"Good God, has the Nazi brainwashed you?"

Both Patty and Reena stiffened. "Back off, smart ass," Reena snapped. "She's not a Nazi. That just shows how stupid you are, new kid. There's lots you don't understand yet. Ma is helping us get back to where we should be – where we *want* to be. No one ever taught any of us how to behave or respect ourselves. That's how we got screwed up. So shut your face till you learn something." Reena marked her place in the book and stood. "C'mon, baby Patty. Let's go to snack. You can come, too," she said as an afterthought to the newcomer.

Dooley followed down the grand staircase, around to the left and back down the hall, knowing she'd screwed up big time, not knowing how to fix it. They probably hated her now. She never used to care what anyone thought. But now, maybe she did just a little. Dooley followed the girls through a door on the right that opened to a spacious, eat-in kitchen. Again – like nothing she'd seen. How many surprises could there be in this house? The shiny, stainless steel appliances, including two refrigerators and double ovens, might have been in a fine restaurant. The back wall, above counters and around appliances, was glass block. It would provide glorious sunshine in the daylight. In contrast to the modern equipment, the oaken kitchen table and chairs must have been in the family for generations. It was round, allowing for no head of the table just like King Arthur's, and would seat eight. Little Twinks was already there, looking angelic in a long, cotton nightgown. By virtue of deduction, Dooley knew that Twinks inhabited the yellow corner of the dormitory. Perhaps she needed the light of day more than any of them. Twinks smiled at Dooley.

Ma, clad in a long, frilly white robe, busied herself about the kitchen counters. The warm aromas of the room were so good that Dooley thought she could just eat *them*. Reena and Patty went to Ma, so Dooley did, too.

"Look at all the beautiful young ladies," Ma said to the trio. She poured hot chocolate for the girls to carry. Ma loaded a heaping platter of hot apple turnovers. Reena carried mugs. Patty carried the dish of turnovers. Individual plates were already on the table.

Once situated at the table, Ma asked, "So, Dooley McDougal, what have you learned so far?"

Too many pairs of eyes stared at her. Dooley studied the turnovers. Studied her napkin. When the silence became unbearable, she responded. "They love you. They say that no one gets hurt here."

"That's a good start. They're important truths. I hope you'll learn to trust and let us into your life. No one will push you, but know that we're here. Now, pass the turnovers, Patty."

Cocoa was sipped. Turnovers were munched. Ma said, "We have rules here, Dooley, and we have chores. Nothing is punitive, but every member of a family must work together for the well-being of the household. Clara is our beloved housekeeper and cook, but the house is large and each of us must be responsible for sharing in the upkeep. Does that make sense?"

"Yes, ma'am." The other girls smiled at Dooley. It was clearly the right answer. Even Twinks smiled between sips and munches. Patty disappeared a turnover into the napkin in her lap. Everyone ignored it.

At the end of snack, Dooley followed suit as the other girls, even Twinks, picked up dishes and carried them to the sink. Patty wiped crumbs from the table. Ma cleared the cooking utensils.

"We've rinsed and stacked, Ma," said Reena. "We'll wash in the morning. See the list on the chalkboard, newbie? That's the list of duties, and guess what, new kid? You're already on it." Reena laughed. "We'll check it at breakfast and show you what you need to do. It will be fine. We'll help you."

Maybe she doesn't hate me after all, Dooley thought.

The entire group walked upstairs, and Ma tucked in each girl, whispering special messages to each, and kissing each child's cheek. She withdrew and switched off the lights.

Dooley lay in her red and white bed, looking to the windows and the moonlight that sifted into the big room in a sparkling shower. She didn't trust the goodness of this odd place. Something had to be wrong. It must be a trick. Something bad was going to happen. She lay still and listened. An hour or so passed. When the breathing from all corners became soft and rhythmic, she quietly crept out of bed and slipped into the new jeans, tee shirt and shoes. She threw her few belongings into another pillowcase. She periodically paused to listen for movement in the house, but hearing none, she tiptoed to the door, not knowing where she might be going.

Stepping into the hall, quiet as any ghost that might inhabit the mansion, she saw Ma comfortably settled into the big chair with Twinks curled in her ample lap, soundly asleep. There was a mug on the cork coaster. Ma put down the book she was reading and smiled.

"Good evening, Dooley. I've been expecting you."

Dooley stood, frozen in place. This would be where their goodness would morph into something evil. She was in for it now.

"Don't be afraid." Ma moved her long legs to one side of the ottoman. "There's enough room. Sit with me. We won't wake Twinks. She sleeps like a rock once she's with someone."

"Why did you expect me?"

"Sometimes new girls have trouble settling in. Before we've become worthy of their trust, they're suspicious. I understand. Sometimes in the first night or so they want to ... take a walk. So, I thought I'd just do some reading here and be available to chat if you want. I'm reading *Little Women* for probably the twentieth time. Have you read it?"

"No, I don't read much."

"I think you'll like it. We home-school here, and I'm refreshing myself because we're going to use it for reading and writing exercises. It's the story of a mother and four daughters and how they struggle, but work in unity. I think it will describe many values for us to discuss. Tell me what's on your mind, Dooley."

"Am I a prisoner? Are you the warden sitting guard at the door?"

"Oh, no, dear girl. I'm here to be close to you for this very reason. There are no locks on our doors. You could leave any time you want, but I hope you won't. It's dangerous out there. I'm not a warden, but I *am* here to guide and teach – if you'll permit me. I'm also here to protect you. Each of you girls has already had more difficulties than a child should experience. "

"What if I walk out? Walk out right now. What would you do?"

"First, I'd give you time to sit at the gate at the end of our property and ponder your decision. I'd be looking out a front window. Hopefully, after a time, you'd choose to come back. If time went by without your return, I'd have to call your social worker, and then, after more time, I'd have to notify the police that you were missing or a runaway. I would get in the car and look for you. I would do all those things for your safety."

Dooley stared hard and deep at Ma with the face of habitual wariness.

"What happens to girls here?"

"Good question. Girls who come here may stay as long as they want or as long as it's beneficial to them and the household. I want desperately to help all my girls, but every once in a while there's a child who's beyond my help – one who needs other assistance that I can't provide. My heart breaks when that happens, but she must go someplace else that can give her what she needs. If girls want to stay here through university, I'm happy to be a part of that."

"Why? What's in it for you?"

"Well, you're blunt, Dooley, but that's to the point. It wouldn't be difficult for anyone to imagine that I stood out as a child. I grew to my height and bulk at an early age. It wasn't enough that I was self-conscious, I guess. Other children laughed at me and tormented me. High school was just as bad or worse. I was still an oddity in college. A woman isn't supposed to look like I do. I was thirty-five before my first date. I couldn't believe my good fortune when he fell in love with me and proposed. We were only married ten years before he died and left me alone in this big, old place. After two years of grief and isolation, I came out of myself and knew that other girls like me didn't fit in either, girls who'd had family or legal problems. I knew that I had the patience and love to offer sanctuary and structure to other outcasts like me. That's why I'm here and why you're here as well as the other girls. Sanctuary. The girls I take are deemed to be beyond traditional approaches. I believe in each of you, including little Twinks who needs so much nurturing. What's in it for me? Watching girls like you learn to trust, blossom, and learn your own worth. So, tell me what you think now, Dooley."

"I'll think about it. 'Course I'm not afraid. I haven't been afraid in a long time, but it all seems too good. I don't know what happens when the masks come off."

"Give us a chance, Dooley." Ma touched Dooley's arm affectionately. "Now I must ask. Have you been cutting your own hair?"

Dooley automatically fingered her scraggly locks. "No, ma'am. I was in a shelter a while back. Some girls ganged up on me and cut off most of my hair. A little piece of my ear, too. I ran out as soon as doors were open the next morning. I couldn't go back. There were too many of them for me to fight."

"I understand. I'm taking Reena to the doctor in the afternoon, so why don't I take you for a haircut and a little shopping in the morning? What do you think?"

"See, it's a bribe right off the bat."

"No," said Ma. "It's just something you need and that I think you'd enjoy. Is that all right?"

"And what do you expect in payment from me?"

"Nothing. Not now. Not ever," said Ma.

Dooley couldn't make eye contact. She just shrugged her shoulders. She watched Twinks sleep.

"She never talks?"

"Never. Maybe you could go put back on your pajamas, get some sleep and see what tomorrow brings. You don't have to make a decision tonight. Or you could walk out the front door. I hope you'll stay."

"I'm too tired to leave now. I'll go to bed," said Dooley. Looking at the sleeping child, she said, "You gonna hold her all night?"

"Not tonight. Maybe you'll help me put her to bed."

As Ma picked up Twinks, Dooley turned off the Tiffany floor lamp and opened the dormitory door. Dooley threw her pillowcase into the chif-farobe again and got into her pj's while Ma tucked in Twinks. Ma crossed to the red corner.

"We'll help you get acquainted with the house and its expectations, Dooley. Never fear that we'll ask too much of you. Relax, dear girl, and I'll see you at breakfast." Ma stroked Dooley's hair and smiled. Dooley was asleep before she saw it coming.

Dooley awoke the next morning unsure of where she was, particularly because of the haunting, classical piano music that filled the room. She sat up, confused, and saw Reena padding toward the bathroom door with Twinks in tow.

"It's Debussy – Clair de Lune. It means moonlight. You'll learn stuff like that in our school. Funny that moon music is our wake-up call, but that's a lot better than a bell going off, don't you think? C'mon. Let's all get dressed. I'm hungry for breakfast. Patty! Get up!" Reena yelled across the room. "Not gonna tell you again!"

In the kitchen, Ma and Clara were preparing breakfast with mouth-watering smells.

This is just like a scene from a movie or TV. Dooley thought. *Don't get sucked into this fantasy*, she warned herself.

Ma was wearing a pink dress with a ruffled hem. She grinned broadly as her brood clambered in. She and Clara were swarmed, receiving and giving morning hugs and kisses, an unfamiliar practice for Dooley. She gave Ma a bright smile instead. She introduced herself to Clara. The previous night's busy work taught her to fall in with the other girls setting the table, carrying bowls and platters of breakfast fare, and filling glasses with juice. Twinks again was plastered against Ma.

Dooley was sure she'd get big as a house if all the meals were that good. She'd never been anywhere that provided this much good food. For sure, not at home.

"Dooley, dear, after you ladies clean up, we'll go do our errands. Girls, you have an assignment sheet on your school table that you should get started on. We may not be back by lunch, so Clara is in charge. Reena, we go to your doctor in the afternoon. We all okay with that?"

Ma was a soft-spoken general in a frilly dress. Who knew?

The kitchen crew swung into action with apparent good spirits. The table was cleared; dishes were washed and dried; counters scrubbed; and floor swept. Even Twinks had a little job, though she looked uneasy while not hanging onto someone. Dooley pitched in, following the lead of Reena and Patty.

"Dooley McDougal, the car's ready. Are you ready to go?"

Dooley dried her hands, smoothed her new tee shirt and hurried to follow Ma out the front door. It had been dark when she'd arrived the night before, so Dooley was surprised at the circle drive providing entry and exit through iron gates at the edge of the property about a city block away. She laughed at the car sitting close to the expansive porch.

"Ma, you don't have a driver?"

"I like to drive. No reason to pay someone to take that fun from me."

"No offense, Ma, but this car is old as dirt. You live in a mansion, but own a heap that you drive yourself? Who's crazy now?"

Ma laughed at Dooley. "This car and I are old friends. You see, I like to keep my friends with me." She winked at Dooley, and they drove down the long drive.

The first stop was at a small salon a few miles away. Everyone knew Ma, and greeted her warmly. One of the younger stylists took Dooley's hand and walked her to a shampoo basin. An hour later, Dooley and Ma left the salon wearing big smiles. Only a girl with her first good hair cut could understand the boost in Dooley's confidence.

Next stop – a boutique at the end of the block. Again, Ma was greeted as an old friend. A few of the shoppers, however, eyed Ma's oversized physique and its contrast to the frilly dress. *This is why she understands damaged girls,* Dooley thought. She glared at the offenders and flipped them off when no one was looking. Neither Ma nor the shop clerks paid attention to them. So they looked at clothes, everything from the undies out. Dooley nearly hyperventilated. She'd never owned that many clothes ever and absolutely not that many new ones. She remembered Julia Roberts in *Pretty Woman* striding up Rodeo Drive loaded down with bags and packages of new clothes. Not that she thought she *looked* like Julia Roberts. She wore one of the new blouses as they left the shop.

Lunch was at a deli in the shopping center. "Every place we go, everyone knows you," Dooley said in between bites of her burger.

"Chin," Ma whispered, pointing to her own chin. Dooley dabbed off a glob of mustard. "Well, as I told you, dear. I like to keep my friends. Friends help each other, and it's good to do business in the same places – places where you have friends."

Dooley thought about that all the way back to the mansion, though she hadn't had many friends until now.

"They're back!" It was Patty's voice. The three girls poured out of the schoolroom. Clara appeared from somewhere. "You're beautiful!"

Most of them ooo'd and ahhh'd over Dooley's hairdo. Twinks smiled and gratefully attached to Ma. "Let's go upstairs and see what you have in the bags," said Reena. "I'll be right back down, Ma. Dooley, you have kitchen duty this afternoon."

Dooley's face was still flushed with excitement when Ma and Reena drove away. Patty went about her task, and Twinks took to following Clara. Dooley checked the chart. She was to peel and cut up potatoes for dinner. She rolled up the sleeves of her new blouse and set to work.

Mid-afternoon, Patty went into the kitchen and found it empty.

"Dooley," she called as she opened the pantry and laundry room doors. "Dooley, where are you?"

Stepping onto the back porch, she spotted thin strands of smoke gracefully dancing up from underneath the porch. "Dooley, you fool. Any idiot can tell you're down there smoking!"

"Okay, okay. I'm busted." Dooley dug a shallow hole in the dirt with the heel of her shoe. She buried the cigarette butt and started up to the porch.

"Where's Twinks? I can't find her anywhere," said Patty.

"Well, you should have walked right over her in the kitchen. I conned her into cutting up potatoes, so I could sneak a smoke while Ma was gone."

"Idiot! We don't let Twinks have sharps!" Patty turned and ran back into the kitchen. Potatoes were in a bowl on the counter, but there was no knife. At the same time, she heard approaching footsteps. Ma and Reena were home. Patty ran into the hall, heart pounding.

"I can't find Twinks! She has a knife. Dooley gave her a knife."

"I didn't *give* it to her, and I didn't know not to. I just didn't know."

The general took over. "Everyone calm down. Clara and I will take the upstairs. Reena, you check the front of the house. Patty, you and Dooley search the rooms back here. Remember, everyone, she's tiny enough to be hiding under any table. Check closets, everything. Let's go!"

Dooley was afraid and shamed, but also angry that no one had told her something so important. She knew they'd make her leave.

"I'll check all the service rooms and closets," said Patty. "You take the cellar." She started away as Dooley stood, motionless as Lot's wife, staring at the cellar door.

"I can't go down there," she whispered. "I can't. I won't. Not anymore." Her voice quivered and grew louder. She trembled as if she were freezing. "Don't make me go. I'll be good. I promise I'll do anything you want. Don't make me go down there again. Please don't hurt me anymore! I'm begging." Dooley was crying, and the crying became animal-like keening. She backed away from the door as if it might sprout arms and pull her through. "No, no, no, no."

Patty ran back to her and embraced the older, trembling girl. "Shhh, shhh, baby Dooley. It's okay. I'm here. No cellar. You don't have to go down. I will. Shhh, baby girl."

She guided Dooley away from the cellar door and the overpowering flashback of something horrible.

"Look at me, Dooley. Pay attention. No cellar. Ever. But we're looking for Twinks, remember? I need your help. Can you help? You take the rooms back there. I'll check downstairs."

Dooley's spirit returned from her own hell to the back hall of the mansion. She nodded. "Twinks, yes." And began her inspection, still trying to gather herself. Patty flipped on the cellar light and went downstairs. It was only minutes until she was running back upstairs, screaming for Ma.

"She's down there! In the cellar. She's hurt," she yelled as she ran up the hall to the foot of the staircase. Everyone came running. Ma went downstairs, and Clara stood at the cellar door with her arms around Reena and Patty, both of whom were crying.

Ma yelled up to them. "911! We need an ambulance! Clara, bring down something for tight bandages."

Reena ran to the phone.

Ma knelt next to Twinks. Both the child's arms bore deep slices from wrist to elbow. Blood ran from one cut to the next like tributaries to a great river. There were no tears in the child's large eyes. She looked calmly at Ma and said her first words. "It hurts."

Paramedics re-wrapped Twinks' arms and loaded her into the ambulance. Ma followed in her ancient car. Clara said that she'd stay as long as needed. Clara, Reema and Patty sat in the living room, intertwined like a pretzel in comfort for each other. It was Patty who finally bolted upright.

"Where's Dooley? Where on earth is Dooley?"

Another, less frantic search ensued. An hour later, she was found crouching behind boxes of canned goods in the pantry, exhausted from sobbing.

"It's my fault. All my fault," she kept repeating. "Twinks could have died. Maybe she *is* dead. Is she dead?"

Clara stayed with Patty, and Reena walked Dooley upstairs.

"You need to rest, baby. You're not to hide again, do you understand? It was an accident. Just a bad accident. We love you, Dooley. Lie down for a while. I'm sure they'll fix up Twinks."

Reena sat with her until she was sure that Dooley was dozing.

It was well after dark when Ma returned. Twinks would be all right, she explained to Clara and the girls. Patty told everyone about Dooley's flashback at the cellar door. Patty started crying again, and Ma went upstairs.

Dooley sat on the side of her bed. She didn't raise her head when Ma entered the room. Her pillowcase was once again packed. She'd put on her old clothes.

"I put all the new clothes in the chiffarobe. I can leave tonight if you want. I was just waiting to hear about Twinks before I leave. I know it's my fault, and I can't take it back. Will she be all right?"

Ma sat on the bed next to her and took Dooley's hand.

"It's not your fault, Dooley."

"But I broke rules, broke your trust. I sneaked out for a damn cigarette and handed her the knife. I *handed* her the knife."

"No one told you. We should have. And, if truth were told, it's all *my* fault, my vanity."

Dooley finally looked up, and Ma could see the girl's eyes swollen from crying.

"Twinks suffered greatly before she came here. She didn't talk because she'd shut down, wouldn't let anyone really in to that secret place where her misery lived. Somewhere inside her, I think the feeling was that if she didn't talk about it, her past abuse didn't exist. We loved her. *I* loved her dearly, and I thought that our nurturing would be enough. I can see now that it was arrogance on my part. I should have known that what I could give wasn't enough. I don't have the expertise. That's what she'll get now."

"You mean not here?"

"No, she'll be in the hospital for another day, then she'll go to a special place, a good place I'm familiar with for extremely troubled children like her. Maybe some day she can come back."

Dooley shook her head and cried some more. Ma rubbed her back.

Dooley said, "So, do you want me to leave tonight or in the morning? Have you called the social worker yet?"

"I haven't called Miss Price, and I don't plan to. You just got here, Dooley McDougal. Don't give up on us so soon. We're not giving up on you. I know that you also have deeply buried hurts. We'll work on those when you're ready. My little friend, progress doesn't always come in a straight line. It may jump forward, take a few steps back or halt completely for a spell before moving forward again. But if we have trust and faith in each other – and in ourselves – we can move beyond almost any obstacle. We'll prop up each other, as each of us needs. We're a family. I believe this with all my heart. That's why I do this. What do you think, Dooley? Will you try with me?"

"I don't know. I guess I can try. Okay, I guess if you'll have me, I want to stay. At least for a while. I'd like to have a home."

"You'll always have a place here."

KITH AND KIN

The once-grand house drooped in urban shabbiness, as did the neighborhood. At the turn of the century, the area had boasted Memphis' carriage trade in graceful French Victorian homes. There were glossy, black carriages, liveried servants, ships' captains, and cotton traders, ladies in velvet and silk who owned twenty pairs of gloves, elaborate parties, and spoiled children. Since then, the gentry had moved east. In the first wave of change, houses remained neat, but haggard. They were occupied by large, noisy, extended families, multiple families, or elderly remnants of the past who were just hanging on. In more recent years, some beauties were leveled for cheap apartments. Others became boarding houses for the downtrodden. And some remained in old families who loved them despite their decline. Seraphina's house was just that.

Her family had occupied the now-weary house for decades. Seraphina's grandparents were the first generation to move in. They'd only been married a few years and were exuberant at the purchase. The house happily welcomed the next generation when Seraphina's father was born, and then when her parents married and joined the household. It was where her parents took her straight from the hospital and where the newborn would be showered with love. When the divorce came, Seraphina stayed with her father and grandparents. She grew up in the drafty home she loved dearly. She bounded up and down the dramatic staircase, hid in the pigeon-filled attic, and occasionally peeked into the spooky basement.

Today, white wicker sentinels no longer stood post on the porch, and a downstairs shutter shed slats like fish scales. The upstairs balcony sagged dangerously. No matter. It was always home.

Seraphina, now an adult, approached the front door for her weekly visit. No need to fish for keys. It was never locked anymore. There was no need. Once inside, her dog plopped to the entry hall floor and yawned. His mistress didn't need him here. Tendrils of peeling wallpaper caressed her hand as she trailed her fingertips along the wall before reaching the living room door. She entered with anticipation, and the room illuminated. There sat grandfather as he always did, staring out the large window framed with ragged drapes. He wore the usual pajamas and that ratty bathrobe. Seraphina always thought it looked like a horse blanket. His emaciated body barely made a bulge in the garments. His white hair needed trimming. His parchment cheeks were carpeted with white stubble. And still he stared, catatonic, through his clouded eyes. Once they had been blue, and he'd taken her on the bus to Court Square to buy bags of hot peanuts and feed the nearly tame squirrels. Long ago.

"Gramps, it's me. I came to visit you. Will you tell me hello?"

No acknowledgement. She dabbed her eyes while she sat for ten minutes by the mute figure. Giving up, she went back into the hall. She passed her grandparents' expansive bedroom and stepped in momentarily. Memory and ritual served her well. There against the double windows to the east was the old, pedal sewing machine, the one that, in conjunction with Gram, had produced beautiful dresses for Seraphina and her favorite dolls for most of her young life. As a teenager she'd wanted trendier things, and she hadn't realized the disappointment that caused Gram. The machine had been idle for some time, and Seraphina smiled as she wrote her name in the dust.

Back in the hall, she saw her father come out of his room.

"My radio doesn't work."

"I'm sorry," said Seraphina. "What were you listening to?"

"The same thing I listen to every afternoon. My opera." His impatience flickered through the hall.

"Try jiggling the selection knob. Where's Gram?"

"I think I heard her in the kitchen."

Seraphina looked down the hall and glimpsed her grandmother before the old woman disappeared. Most likely into the kitchen. When Seraphina arrived, Gram was scrutinizing the pantry, hands on her meager hips. A foot tapped to a melody only she could hear.

"Hi, Gram. What are you doing?"

"I'm fixin' to make biscuits."

"Then I'm just in time. I'm starving. What else are you making?"

"We'll have ham and gravy. Like you grew up on."

"Red eye gravy?"

"Didn't I raise you right? Of course not. It's white gravy, child, like I make every time you come."

"Gram, I stopped in the living room, but Gramps won't talk to me. Why does he just sit there?"

"There's not much tellin' with him. Obstinate old fool. He can just sit for eternity for all I care."

"I'll check on Daddy and his radio. I'll be back."

Seraphina stepped into the hall and the old house inhaled deeply and exhaled roughly. It was dark, then light as she entered Daddy's room.

She perched at the foot of the iron bedstead opposite Daddy's worn easy chair and smoking table, which also held his prized radio. She heard the clattering, clanging and kitchen cacophony of pots and pans that Gram produced. No wonder the neighbors leave the house alone.

Seraphina asked, "Is it working yet?"

"No. It just sits there mocking me. Not even static."

"What opera was going to play today?"

"Aida. One of my favorites."

"Why don't you tell me the story of Aida?"

"Don't patronize me," he snapped. "We saw that together when you were a child, and you've heard the story many times. You could tell it to me if you wanted, but you won't."

"Daddy, are you pouting?" She laughed.

He laughed, too in his melodious baritone that filled the room and rattled the windows with its own music.

"Daddy, why does Gramps just sit looking out the window? I can't get him to talk or do anything."

"I don't know. That old man and I gave up on each other long ago."

"I love you so much, Daddy."

"I know, baby."

"Sometimes I miss you terribly."

"I understand. That's why I'll always be right here for you, any time you need me. I know this house gives you light, and that's important, good for you. We'll be here whenever you want us." His aura turned to beautiful, soft colors. "I'm tired now. Go to your Gram."

Seraphina returned to the kitchen, but Gram was no longer there. Reluctantly, she retreated back up the hall to the front door. The German Shepherd alerted and rose as his mistress approached. She scratched his head.

Seraphina took the handle of his harness and opened the old, front door.

"Gandy, forward," she commanded the guide dog.

As they departed, the house was cold, dark and empty once again.

FAMILY CIRCLE

Geneva Spencer Warner stalked up the wide staircase with the ferocity and stealth of a lioness. Her alligator pumps only skimmed the plush carpet. Her tawny hair barely swayed with the smooth ascent. The upstairs maid fled at the sight. At the top of the stairs, Geneva pivoted to the right without pause. She strode down the hall to the last door on the left and barged in without invitation.

"Channing Spencer Warner, get dressed. Do it now."

The girl sitting on the window seat continued staring out the window. Channing sat scrunched up, her arms around her legs, her cheek resting on her knees, her face turned toward the Warner's ample lawns. The oversized sweater encased all but the girl's head and bare toes that dug into the soft cushion. She was unmoved.

Geneva pushed down her anger and walked across the room to sit on the side of the canopied bed. She waited quietly until her youngest child finally turned her head. The girl's face was pale. There were bluish shadows under her eyes.

"Listen carefully, child. You will *not* sit this out. I have retained the most exclusive designer and seamstress in Memphis to construct your ball gown and day dresses. They will be splendid. We have an appointment. You need to pull yourself together now – I mean *right* now. Am I clear? We must leave momentarily, so stop this foolishness. You look awful."

"I have a cold, and I'm not doing this anyway. I told you so. It's 1958, for God's sake. The debutante thing is antiquated, elitist, meaningless. It's your world, not mine. I simply won't do it."

"Oh yes, you will." Geneva's eyes narrowed to glittery, green slits. "You will not shame your family, diminish our position in society. It's expected, and you must learn to live up to your social obligations. You're from a fine family line, not white trash. Obligations come with that heritage. Now get ready. We have much to do, and you'll be going back to school before we know it."

Geneva rose to leave the room.

"I'm not going back to school either."

"Of course you are, you irresponsible, ungrateful, rebellious whelp! I will not allow this. I will not permit you to ruin your life. You are going to have the best deb season in this city, and you are going to graduate from Sophie Newcomb. These advantages are costly, but we do them gladly for you. In return, you need to show respect."

"Look at me. I'm not you, and I'm not going to be your Barbie doll because you think all this was taken away from you. I just won't."

Geneva froze. No one talked back to her. No one told her ugly truths. And this particular accusation was painfully true.

Geneva had come of age in the midst of the Great Depression. Her family managed to keep her in Miss Hutchison's School for Girls through high school graduation, but there was no elite women's college like Sophie Newcomb for her. Geneva went south to Mississippi State College for Women, which had just enough prestige to ward off embarrassment. The family had strained even to handle MSCW, but it was important for appearances.

For clans like the Spencers, family fortunes were being drained just to maintain the façade of pre-Depression glory. In the South, however, the dwindling funds of a "good" family did not also diminish their social standing. It was a throwback to the post-Civil War "genteel poor" who had lost everything except their good names. Like European royalty in exile, a prince was still a prince and, in Memphis, a Spencer was still a Spencer.

Geneva's coming out ball in 1933 wasn't really a ball at all. She was certainly a debutante, but in the most modest fashion. Still, she comported herself with beauty and elegance, and only those who knew her best might have suspected her great disappointment. She'd looked forward to her coming out since she was old enough to watch the big girls getting ready for their coming out. They were giggly and glamorous in their white ball gowns. Geneva knew that one day she'd have her turn. But she didn't.

Memphis' Cotton Carnival, born in 1931, was produced by downtown merchants to stimulate business activity in those uncertain times. The Mardi Gras style event featured a King and Queen and royal court, all from the city's prominent families. There were secret societies and various formal events. Others could attend the grand parade, the carnival, and the arrival of the royal barge on the big Mississippi River. Considering her excellent breeding and good looks, Geneva knew she should have been chosen Queen in 1934, but, instead, she grimly watched her less beautiful friend take the spotlight while Geneva was given a smaller role in the court and a much less spectacular gown. She told herself that the choice was based on which families still had money, and that made her angry with her father. Cheated again.

When the big Maid of Cotton competition was initiated in '39 drawing beautiful contestants from throughout the cotton-producing states, Geneva saw it as another title that she might have earned. But by then, she was married and had her first son. There was nothing left to grant her the glory she deserved. Three strikes, and she was out.

At least she'd married well. Laurence Edwyn Warner was a handsome up-and-comer, the son of a moderately successful cotton merchant. Everyone said he was going to be somebody, and marrying a Spencer was a good move on his part. He inherited his father's company and grew it into the most influential business on Memphis' Cotton Row. Besides having a knack for making the best deals buying and selling cotton domestically, Larry became the first to identify new overseas markets for the South's greatest resource, King Cotton.

Her lineage and his increasing wealth bought the family superior social standing. That status also guaranteed entry into all the right clubs and the most distinguished Carnival secret society. In time, Larry was named King of Cotton Carnival, an honor that always went to a prominent businessman. The Queen was always the college-age daughter of a well-placed family. Geneva's sons were pages in their father's court. The wife of the King was called The Forgotten Woman, a title meant to be humorous. Geneva pasted on a proper upper-crust smile, but found no humor in her nearly invisible role. She gritted her teeth as she watched her husband center stage at extravagant events, parading his stunning, young Queen. She chose to disregard the smiles Larry gave the virginal Queen. Geneva remembered being that young and lovely. She hoped her husband did.

When Geneva finally gave birth to a daughter, Geneva swore that the baby would be groomed to make up for all the wrongs she'd suffered. She was a sufficiently good mother to her two sons, but, aside from her social obligations, she made sure that Channing received every preparatory advantage: Private school, stylish frocks, dance lessons, equestrian training, and even "charm school" for mentoring in social graces. Geneva wanted her daughter's success so desperately that she never asked Channing what she wanted.

"There's nothing wrong with parents wanting their children's lives to be better than their own," Geneva said.

"I tried to please you, Mother. We all tried, but you poisoned this house with your ambition and bitterness. It was you versus the rest of the family, and the rest of us have quit playing the game."

Geneva returned and sat on the bed. She reached to the bedside table, opened the bottom drawer and pushed aside clutter until she located the ugly ashtray, cigarette pack, and lighter. Channing finally registered an emotion.

"Don't look surprised. Of course I know you smoke. I know everything that goes on in this house."

"Do you really, Mother?"

Geneva lit a cigarette and exhaled slowly. She leveled a cold, hard gaze at her daughter.

"And I know what's really behind this bad behavior of yours. Do you think I haven't heard you slamming into the bathroom in the mornings to vomit? Do you think I haven't noticed that you suddenly have some breasts to be proud of? And do you, my dear, think you're the first deb to find herself in this awkward situation? There's more than one way to fix this. We can take care of it."

"Awkward situation? Are you serious? Okay, I'm pregnant. That's a lot more than *awkward* and much more important than your silly society crap."

"Society rituals are what will define your life – and ours by reflection. They're the framework of our community. So, who is it? One of those Tulane boys you met down at Newcomb? Or did your high school beau, Rob, go down for a visit – and a little more?"

Channing turned away her face again.

"It makes a difference, daughter. If it's Rob, he's from an acceptable family, and we can announce your engagement when deb season is over. It would likely be a decent marriage. A woman can exist in a decent marriage. Of course a marriage would mean you've given up any chance for Carnival Queen. It infuriates me that your irresponsibility has destroyed my plans for you – after all I've done, and you can't even keep your legs together." Geneva angrily stubbed out the cigarette and calmed herself.

"So, all the better that we just visit a doctor I know. How far along are you?"

"Don't you have any feelings? This isn't about you. How about giving me your attention, your surprise, anger or even motherly support. And I don't believe that abortion doctors exist in your exclusive, snooty world. Why do you think I want to get rid of the baby anyway? Or marry Rob. Have you considered that I might have plans of my own?"

"Oh, child, girls will always get unexpectedly pregnant, and there are always willing doctors to take care of this for good girls. There are now, and there were in my day. These situations can't be allowed to ruin lives and reputations."

Channing rolled her eyes and shook her head.

"In *your* day? I doubt that you knew anyone in this situation back in the olden days."

"Daughter, your generation thinks it invented sex. If you hadn't been so busy trying to hate me, you'd have known that I'm human, too. I had a life before I married. I never thought you'd need to know this, but apparently you do.

"It was in my deb season, too, and I wasn't about to kiss my future good-bye. An older girlfriend, from a fine family of course, knew what to do. By the way, her daughters were at Miss Hutchison's when you were there. Anyway, I started having morning sickness immediately, so I knew right away what was wrong. I suspected that Vivien knew things I didn't, so I approached her. Cautiously. I was so relieved that I was right. How dreadful it would have been if I'd let my secret slip to the wrong person. It would have ruined me."

Geneva lit another cigarette for effect and paused while Channing absorbed the information.

"Vivien was quite sympathetic. I didn't ask how she knew what she knew. The doctor was just down in Hernando. Apparently, people run down to Mississippi to get married without a waiting period and to get rid of ... these situations ... without fuss."

Channing's stomach turned at Geneva's sardonic smile.

"We went to his house, a nondescript place in a middle class neighborhood. I wondered if his neighbors knew what he was doing in there. I imagined that girls were coming and going with some regularity. I wondered if they were as determined, but still frightened as I was. One of the bedrooms was turned into an operatory. Vivien waited in the living room with the cash I'd given her to pay him. I wished she was with me, maybe to hold my hand. But I was too proud to ask. I undressed and got on the operating table. The doctor went about his task in a methodical way. He said very little to me – just minimal instructions. It didn't take long. We left, and I spent the night with Viv as I'd told my parents, then I went home the next day and to bed for a couple of days complaining of cramps from my period. And then I got up, put it out of my mind, and returned to my life. It's imperative that one can do that."

Geneva went to Channing's room-sized closet and started sorting through dresses. Channing stomped after her and stood at the closet door.

"I'm sorry, Mother, but you put it out of your mind? You killed a baby! What a cold-hearted bitch you are. No wonder Daddy doesn't love you anymore."

"You're so naïve. Your father and I have a very cordial, well ordered marriage. Ah, this lavender dress will do just fine." Geneva handed the dress to Channing. "And never call your mother names. You have no right." She stepped back into the closet and started looking at the shoe racks.

"Not so fast, Mother. This doesn't add up right. I thought you met Dad later in college than when you'd have been a deb."

"That's true. I never said your father was involved in my situation. Take these shoes."

"Oh my God. And Dad accepted that you had ... well, a *past,* a pregnancy?"

"It wasn't any of your father's business, Chan. And it still isn't. Do you understand?" Geneva pushed past her daughter.

"I'm going to freshen up while you get dressed, Channing. We're very late, but I'll telephone. Do something with your hair, and take care of those dark circles under your eyes."

Channing threw the shoes into the far wall of the closet.

"You are such a piece of work!"

"We might as well settle the rest of this," said Geneva. "Tell me who the father is. If it's Rob, I need to call his mother and invite his parents over for cocktails and dinner so we can make plans. We need to get started on this. So, who is it?"

Geneva had never seen the transformation that slowly crept across Channing's face.

"Ask your cordial, well-ordered husband."

ABDUCTION

Agatha disliked her name. She thought it sounded like an old lady instead of a little girl. When she'd complain, Mama would smile, call her Aggie, and tell her that she'd grow into her name. It had first belonged to a great-grandmother, but what was the point in having a name you had to grow into? Mama claimed that Agatha's six-year-old body housed a grown-up soul anyway. Aggie thought she might like to be a little girl for a while longer.

Every day during that school year, Agatha walked the five blocks home from her half-day of kindergarten. A plate with her lunch would either be covered on the kitchen table or in the refrigerator. Mama, who worked the night shift at the hospital, would be asleep for a while. Step-dad would be in college classes on the GI bill, but in the mornings, it was his job to send her off to school since Mama was still at the hospital. He sort of did that, putting cold cereal and a glass of milk on the table. He didn't care what clothes she chose to wear. They seldom matched. Agatha knew how to get dressed by herself. She was six, after all, but the teacher worried about Aggie's home supervision when she observed the mismatched child arrive every day.

Step-dad and Aggie didn't have much to say to each other.

That afternoon was no different than any other. After her lunch, Agatha took her two favorite dolls out to the small lawn in front of the duplex where they occupied the bottom floor. She was responsible and knew to stay in her yard. The dolls were having a pretend walk through a deep, dark jungle where they barely escaped an enormous lion. Agatha didn't notice the car that pulled up to her curb until she heard the man's voice.

"Little girl, little girl. Can you help me?"

Agatha returned from the fantasy jungle where she and her dolls were playing. She took a look at the green car with the man leaning across the front seat toward the open passenger window. She left the dolls, now safe, and walked to the sidewalk next to the car.

"Yes sir?"

"You must be a very big girl to play outside by yourself."

"I am."

"You're polite, too. Are your parents inside so I can tell them how impressed I am?"

"Mama's there."

"Well, I won't bother her just now," said the dark-haired man. "I think such a polite girl could help me."

"How?"

"I have some friends who live around here – Mr. and Mrs. Bailey. I was invited to their house today, but, for the life of me, I can't remember where they live. Do you know the Bailey family?"

"No sir, I don't."

"Well, do you know where they live?"

"I said I don't know them."

He leaned farther across the front seat and pushed open the passenger door. "I wonder if you got in and we drove around, that you'd recognize their house. Come on. Let's drive around the neighborhood. It would be a big help."

"I don't know them, so I don't know where they live."

Agatha stomped back up the little slope to the dolls in her yard. Dumbest grown-up she'd ever met. She paid no attention when he drove off.

In the late afternoon, Mama got up, and they played a game before Mama started dinner. Step-dad got home from college, but Mama wouldn't let him spread his books on the kitchen table because dinner would be ready soon. He patted Agatha on the head, but said nothing.

After dinner, Agatha and Mama talked and giggled as Aggie took her bath and got into bed. Mama read part of a book they were working on, then gave Aggie a big hug and kiss. It was just another nice, ordinary day.

Everything changed the next afternoon when Agatha came home from school. Mama was awake. She was still in her nurse's uniform and greeted Aggie at the door when she entered. She pulled Aggie to her and held her tight. When Aggie was less suffocated by Mama's midsection and could see around her, she saw the two men in suits sitting at the kitchen table.

"Aggie, these gentlemen are from the police department. They want to talk with you." Mama's voice was tight. It told too much.

"Am I in trouble?"

"No, not at all, Agatha. My name is Detective Barrow, and this is my partner, Detective Gentry. Why don't you come sit with us? Your mother has brought out some snacks."

Agatha was uncertain, but she wouldn't be bought off by a plate of cheese and crackers. There was the special cheese that Mama never put out. Did they think she'd be bought off by this – whatever was going on?

"We understand that a stranger wanted you to take a drive with him yesterday."

Agatha frowned at him and then at her mother. She gave in and put the special cheese on a cracker. She crunched into it. Her mouth was full when she answered.

"That stupid man? He was just silly, that's all. How did you know?"

"You must not have noticed the men working on the roof of the apartment building across the street. They saw what was going on and thought it didn't look right, so they called us. As it turned out, we think he was the same man who approached another girl just a few blocks away. She got in the car, but, fortunately, got scared and jumped out and ran. She wasn't hurt much. Now she's safe."

"What grade is she in? Why did she get in the car anyway? He was just dumb," said Agatha.

"You might not know her. She's in the first grade at your school."

Agatha smiled. "A first-grader got in? Then I guess she's dumb, too." Agatha felt quite superior.

Detective Gentry spoke. "He's a bad man, Agatha. We need to find him and stop him from hurting more children than he already has. So, we need to ask you some questions, okay?"

The cheese no longer tasted good. "What does that mean – bad man?"

"Sugar, why didn't you tell me what happened?"

"Nothin' to tell. I was playing with my dollies. He was just dumb. He wanted me to get in the car and help him find the house of people I don't even know. That's crazy."

"My sensible child," said Mama. "Tell the detectives what they need to know."

Agatha didn't know anything about cars. It was green, and she didn't think it looked new like Mr. Daugherty's spanking new car down the street. Mama had wondered how the Daughertys could afford it.

Agatha said there was a big roll of what looked like movie theater tickets on the front seat. She didn't know how old the man was – just grown-up and maybe old like her step-dad. Mama broke in and told the detectives the age of her husband. The bad man had very dark hair that was combed straight back, and he had light-colored eyes. The eyes were funny looking. How? She didn't know how to say. Like an animal in one of her books.

"Was I wrong not to find the house?"

"No. There was no house to find. That's just what he said hoping you'd get in the car. You did exactly right. You're a smart girl." The detectives stood, and they both smiled at her.

"Will he come back? Is Aggie in danger?" asked Mama.

"No, ma'am. This neighborhood didn't work for him, so he'll try someplace else. All the same, it wouldn't hurt to keep her close for a while. Maybe have someone watch her while you're getting some rest. Or keep her inside till you get up. I understand your situation," said Detective Barrow. "We're working hard to find him. Not all little girls are as smart and lucky as your Agatha."

The policemen left, and Mama hovered over her as Agatha had her after-school lunch.

"Why didn't you tell me?"

"Nothin' to tell."

Gosh, Agatha thought. *Sure didn't seem like anything to get excited about.*

Mama changed clothes and had Aggie bring her favorite doll into the bedroom while she did. When Aggie wanted to play outside, Mama suggested that they color pictures at the kitchen table instead. Mama was looking so tired, but she got out a big coloring book and crayons. They both worked on pictures of princesses and castles.

"Mama, why would a grown-up who doesn't know me want me or that other girl to take a drive with him? Doesn't he have children of his own?"

"Baby, it's hard to explain, but you deserve an answer." Mama put down her crayon and cupped Aggie's face in her hands. "I love you so much. I wish I could be with you every minute to protect you. There are bad men in the world who look like anybody else and pretend to be nice like anybody else. But they're not. They might take children away from their families, and they might hurt them. I don't know why. They're just evil. But you're smart. You used your head. You would never get in a car with a stranger. If someone tried to take hold of you, you'd yell loud and kick and run home or to another adult. I know you would."

"That makes me scared."

"I don't want you to be afraid. Most people are good and kind. I believe you can tell the difference and use your good sense. You have more than an average share of good sense. I'm here to take care of you forever and so is your dad."

"My Daddy lives in Memphis far away." Aggie said coldly. She withdrew her face from Mama's hands and started coloring hard.

"You know what I mean, Agatha. Just give him a chance. Our pictures are pretty, don't you think? Let's put them on the refrigerator and see what we want for dinner."

"He might be good for you, but not me. I'm little, but I know he doesn't like me, and I don't like him either. I want my own Daddy. You said I have good sense. Remember?"

"Aggie, I'm too tired to explain that again. Please, let's take care of one thing at a time."

After dinner and clean up, Mama talked quietly to the stepfather while Agatha bathed. Mama wondered if he couldn't come home earlier from school to keep an eye on Agatha while mom got some sleep. He didn't seem to think that would work. Mama tucked Aggie into bed and cuddled next to her. They fell asleep holding each other. Later in the evening, step-dad had to wake Mama so she could get ready for work.

Agatha didn't tell her school friends about the visit from the police. They probably wouldn't believe it anyway. When she left school at noon, Mama was waiting in front of the school.

"Surprise!" Mama said. "I thought I'd come walk you home. I haven't done that in a long time."

Agatha knew the real reason. It made her look carefully at all the cars as they walked home. Was he watching her? At home, Mama said that she had to sleep for a bit, but made Agatha promise, cross her heart, that she'd stay in the apartment. She should eat her lunch, then play inside until Mama woke up. From now on, Mama explained, Tina, who lived with her parents two doors down, would come over as soon as she got out of school. Agatha would stay in the house until Tina arrived, and then the two could go outside.

"But you said I'm smart and responsible," protested Agatha. "Why does she need to stay with me like a baby?"

"You're *very* smart, but this is for me as much as you. I'll feel better if someone is with you. We may not do this forever, but, for now, this will be best. I've already put in for a day shift. A little less money, but we'll make this work."

And that's the way it went for a while. Tina wasn't so bad. She was good at making up pretend stories with the dolls, and it was fun to have someone to play with in the afternoons. Their new routine settled in, and Mama didn't look so tired. No strange cars pulled up to the curb to lure away little children.

Four weeks later, it was Agatha's birthday, an important one. She was seven, and that's how old you have to be to go to full-day first grade. Agatha was thrilled. It would be wonderful to be a first grader. The tradition in her class was that the birthday child brought cupcakes for the whole class, and they'd have a party. There wasn't exactly open competition, but the children noticed whose mother brought the prettiest and tastiest treats. As Agatha carefully carried the large box of cupcakes to school, she knew that these would be the best of the whole year. If Agatha knew fractions, she'd know that one-third of the cupcakes were frosted in pale green, another third in creamy yellow, and the rest in sky blue. Each group was topped in matching, sparkly sugar crystals. They glowed like rainbows and magic dust. She'd be very popular.

The party always started about thirty minutes before dismissal. The teacher kept paper plates and napkins in a special cupboard so the birthday child's family didn't have to provide them. Agatha was so excited that she almost dropped the box as she entered the school. The children thought the cupcakes were exceptional. Her girlfriends gave her birthday hugs. When everyone was served, Agatha sat at her group table to begin her blue cupcake. But the classroom door opened. It was Mama. She smiled at Agatha and was greeted by the teacher. The two whispered, then the teacher came to Agatha and told her she'd need to go with her mother.

"But my party!"

"I'm sorry. I'll put up cupcakes for you to have tomorrow. Your mother needs you to go with her now."

"But it's my very own birthday party," Agatha mumbled to herself as she went to her mother, and they stepped into the hall. One of the policemen was waiting there.

"Hi, Agatha," said Detective Barrow. "Remember me? I'm sorry we're breaking up your party, but we need you for something important. We think we've arrested the man who tried to take you. My partner is picking up the other girl and her mom. We need to take you to the police station so you can take a look and tell us if it's the right man."

Agatha felt a chill and looked to her mother for help. "I don't want to see him. I don't want him to see me."

"Detective Barrow explained it to me, honey. He won't be able to see you at all. It's okay. You'll see."

At the police station, they walked through a big office with a lot of desks, people, and noise. Telephones were ringing. People were talking all at once. No one paid any attention to them. They walked down a hall at the far side of the room where the din slowly faded. Mama never let go of Agatha's hand.

"Agatha, when you're ready we're going through this door to another room," said Detective Barrow. "The room is very dark. There are chairs that you and the other girl will sit in. I'll sit right behind you. A ways in front of you is a small stage with a glass front. The man we arrested will walk out onto the stage. There are extremely bright lights on the stage. Some of the lights are shining right on him so you can see him easily, but so bright that he can't see past them to whoever might be in the audience. He absolutely can *not* see us. He can't hear anything from our room either. I've tried out being on that stage just to check, and I'm certain that he can't see or hear anything outside the place he's standing. You'll take a good look at him, and tell me if he's the man who tried to get you in the car. You'll tell me if this guy is or isn't the one in the green car. No pressure. You'll just say whatever is true for you. Do you understand? Do you have any questions?'

"What if I don't know?"

"Then you'll just tell me that. I don't expect any particular answer from you. Just look at him and tell me what you think. Are you ready?"

Agatha looked to her mother.

"It's okay. Just take a look and see if you recognize him. That's all," said Mama. "I'll be right here waiting for you."

Taking Agatha's hand, Detective Barrow led her into the dark room. The first grader was already there with the other detective sitting behind her. Agatha sat on the first row next to the first grader. That girl didn't seem afraid, but didn't look at Agatha. More lights snapped on at the stage. It was brighter than the sun. A man walked out to the middle of the stage. He wore dark slacks and a white shirt like most grown-up men did. He had very dark hair that was combed straight back. He looked straight ahead. He had pale eyes, so pale that they almost disappeared.

He turned to his right, paused; turned to face the opposite direction, paused; then turned back to the front.

The girl next to Agatha blurted. "That's him. I know. It's the man who took me."

She started sniffling. She must be scared after all.

"Take your time," one of the detectives said to Agatha.

The man's eyes moved, seemingly scanning the room, then they rested on Agatha.

“Remember, he can’t see you, and he can’t hear us,” said the detective. He reached forward and patted her shoulder.

Agatha felt his stare all the way into her soul. He knew she was there, and she knew he was evil. If they put him in jail, he’d get out some time. He knew where she lived, and he knew it would be her fault that he went to jail.

“Agatha, what do you think?”

“I want to go home.”

“I understand. This feels hard, but we’re almost done. What do you think? Is it him?”

The man’s ghost eyes didn’t blink or stray from hers.

“I don’t know. Maybe. I don’t think so. No, that’s not him. I want Mama.”

Agatha bolted to the door, and the man watched her leave.

HEAR NO EVIL

The past is never as important as when that's all you have. As when the future is only measured in hours or minutes. The last time the past was this important was when I was sixteen, and my period was late. What I'd done in that most recent past was an overwhelming concern. That turned out much better than this will.

Sometimes I pretend I'm unconscious so nurses and daughters will leave me alone, and I can listen. They're like a flock of chickens pecking on each other instead of the corn. I'm the corn.

The hospice nurse told them that the last sense retained by a dying person is the sense of hearing. She told them outright that I can hear them, but they've forgotten. They're just waiting – each in her own way. I'm the lump in the bed that's keeping them from getting back to their lives. Give me a little more time, chickadees.

The hospice nurse entered the room and smiled at the three daughters before going to Mrs. Pettigrew's bed. She inspected Mom's arms and legs, again smoothed the sheets, took Mom's pulse, and lightly touched her face.

"Everything's holding steady with your mother right now," said Jean. "I don't think her passing is imminent. In the meantime, it's so reassuring to see you ladies here, together for your mother. This time of passage sometimes brings out the worst in families. Be grateful you're not facing that. I'll be back later. Is there anything I can do for the three of you?"

"We're fine, thank you," said Adellaide. She was the oldest and always felt obliged to speak for the trio. They all plastered on plastic smiles that would expedite the nurse's departure.

"Well, if nothing's getting ready to happen here, I think I'll go outside for a breath of air," said middle child Marigold.

"It's not like the second act intermission, for Pete's sake. We're here to spend Mom's remaining time with her. It's a privilege to be here," said Glorianna.

"You smoking again?" Adellaide asked Marigold.

"What difference does it make to you, Addy?" she snapped.

"You never could just do what was good for you. And you never could sit still either. Your teachers always complained about that," said Adellaide.

Marigold smirked. "Not doing what's good for me? I'm not the one who had an abortion. Gee, was getting knocked up good for *you*? Was having the baby in your uterus scraped out good for you? Get off my back."

Girls, stop fussing! I can't send you to your rooms right now, so Adellaide, leave your sister alone and let her take a walk to go smoke or whatever she wants to do. I'll try not to die till she comes back. You two have bickered all your lives. I don't think you made each other nearly as miserable as you made ***me****. I don't want to die listening to you arguing.*

Glorianna stood. "Just shut up. Both of you. I can't stand it." She walked to Mom's bedside. "Can't you finally show some respect? Marigold, go outside and cool off. Addy, get hold of yourself."

Marigold left, probably appreciating a quiet exit strategy. She didn't like fighting with her older sister, but she never could back down either.

"Glory, why didn't you let us know sooner how bad off Mom was? Keeping her all to yourself?" Adellaide moved on to her next victim.

Glory didn't turn to look at her sister. "I've been taking care of her for a long time. I guess you might have called more often or actually come to visit to see how she was doing."

"I live a thousand miles away. I send money every month to help with her care. The phone works both ways, young lady."

"You exhaust me." Glorianna sighed. "Maybe we both did the best we could. Maybe not. For the last week I've only been out of this room to briefly run home to shower, change clothes, and run back. I'm too tired to put up with your bellyaching."

"Kid, now that we're all here, you can actually stand down for a bit. Or are you still working on your merit badge for being Mommy's little angel?'

"What is wrong with you, Addy? You never did know anything about me."

For Christ's sake. Children, shut the hell up. I'm trying to die here – or maybe trying ***not*** *to die. I forget. But if you want to give a thought to who you don't know, just take a look at the lump in this bed. Even after you were adults, you never gave a thought to who I was. Who I* ***really*** *was.*

I wasn't just car pool and classroom snacks. Not just the nicely dressed lady who showed up for your college sorority mother's club, and not just the woman who did battle with your father to get every frill and fandangle you girls said you'd simply die without if you didn't have it for your weddings. Did you know I organized volunteers for the library, the high school, and the homeless shelter? Recruited, organized and trained them. It wasn't just "Mom stuff." I was an organizer, a problem solver, a creator of opportunities, a keeper of rosters and work schedules, and, by the way, the winner of a few awards for my work. No. You girls went on with your lives and frequently dumped grandchildren on me whether or not it fit my schedule. ***My*** *schedule.*

And while you're wondering who I was as a woman, did you know that I cheated on your father? I wasn't a sleep-around, but there was a sweet man I spent time with infrequently for several years. One day in church, my conscience finally got to me. I stopped seeing him, but never stopped missing him. You'll want to know if your father was aware of my dalliance, but I don't know. I hope not. He didn't deserve what I did. He never gave any indication that he knew. He was happy as a clam in our family, and that shamed me. You're probably not going to put any of this in my obituary. Damn. I should have written it myself ahead of time. I didn't know that time was so short.

"I'm hungry," said Adellaide.

"So am I," said Glorianna.

"Me, too," said Marigold, sitting across the room to prevent Addy from noticing the cigarette odor. "So someone needs to go to the cafeteria to bring back food, and it's not me. I was just out of the room, and I don't want to leave again."

"It's certainly not me," said Glorianna, "so it's up to you, Addy."

"It's always up to me, isn't it? All right, I'll go for hamburgers and fries. I'm not taking specialty orders. I will put whatever I want on the burgers, and you'll eat what I bring you. Got it?"

The other sisters rolled their eyes in unison as they always did in response to one of Addy's pronouncements.

The burgers were lukewarm by the time Adellaide returned. Marigold fetched soft drinks from the soda machine. The sisters spread out their picnic on whatever surfaces were available. They ate silently for a while.

"Eugene cheated on you with me, Addy," announced Marigold between bites.

"What?"

"You heard me. The end of the summer just before your senior year. You went to Destin with your girlfriends for two whole weeks at the beach," said Marigold. "You should have known that he couldn't be left unattended for that long. We went out constantly. He was a good kisser. Everyone knew except you."

"Yep, I knew," said Glorianna chewing on a French fry.

I knew. Didn't approve, but I knew.

"And no one told me?"

Adellaide's sisters laughed at her shock and dismay.

"Guess not," giggled Marigold.

"You just thought you knew everything," said Glorianna.

Adellaide slammed down the remains of her burger on the paper towel and a squish of ketchup blasted out. "What the hell else don't I know?"

Glorianna winked at Marigold and grinned.

"Well, a lot of times when a boy called for you, I'd imitate your voice, say something stupid or rude, and hang up."

"You little brat! But, in retrospect, it explains a lot." Adellaide wasn't happy, but she hadn't thrown anything yet.

"Marigold, you're up," said Glorianna.

Adellaide thought her sisters' laughter was getting out of hand.

Marigold wiped laughter tears from her eyes and began. "When you graduated, and I entered high school, I got tired pretty quickly of hearing teachers carry on about what a perfect student you'd been. So I started telling them that after graduation you became a dope head and ran off to a commune. It was a terrible tragedy for the family. They were much nicer to me after that."

"Oh my God," moaned Adellaide. "But that does explain some odd reactions at our first class reunion. You two are crazy!"

"Me next," chirped Glorianna.

"Will this ever end?" Adellaide asked in a pained voice.

"Maybe not," said Glorianna. "Occasionally, I stole one of your padded bras and took it with me to pajama parties. We all tried it on under our pajama tops to see what we'd look like when we got breasts. They were all amazed at how much padding you used. They might have told their brothers."

When Marigold laughed really hard, she snorted, and she was snorting now. She and Glory laughed so hard that Addy couldn't help herself and joined in.

"I'm going to wet myself!" Marigold screeched as she sprinted for the bathroom.

This is what my girls used to sound like. They would close themselves up in their room and rolled on the floor, laughing so hard that I had to do another load of their urine-soaked laundry. They never told me what was so funny. I didn't need to know. It made me smile, and I loved them so much for their devotion to each other. Maybe they will have that again when I'm gone. I wonder if they can see me smile right now or if it's all inside me.

Marigold returned, and the sisters mostly settled down.

"Why did the two of you pick on me so much?" asked Adellaide.

"Kiddo, you were such an easy target," said Marigold.

"You still are," grinned Glorianna. "Look in your purse."

Addy looked from one sister to the other and reached for her purse. She opened it slowly. Then, she stifled a scream.

In a stage whisper, she said, "A dildo? Really? A huge dildo? Y'all are insane!"

Then, the three erupted again in hysterical laughter that was only silenced when the nurse entered the room. She went to their mother and respectfully looked her over.

"Girls, there's now mottling on Mrs. Pettigrew's legs and arms. It's a sign that her organs are shutting down. It means that it won't be very long now. Please let me know when you need me," said Jean.

Now somber, the girls went to their mother's bed. One stroked her face. The others each took a hand and kissed it. They said a prayer aloud. They cried, and they waited.

I can go now. My baby girls will be just fine.

THE PINCH

The birth was not widely a joyous one. Just another little Irish girl born in The Pinch, an area in Memphis next to the Wolf River lagoon, so named for the pinched look of the underfed residents. Mary Elizabeth saw the birth's blessing, however.

"Katie, Molly, come see your new little sister," she called as soon as the midwife allowed. "What a precious blessing she is to push the sad shadows from our hearts." It was exactly five weeks and one day since her husband's funeral mass. Michael James was buried in consecrated ground at Calvary Cemetery, but there was no money for a marker. No matter. Few outside The Pinch cared for the death of a poor Irishman anyway.

"She can carry her Da's name since she'll never know him. It will honor him sure. We'll be calling her Mary Michael."

Two-year-old, freckled Molly climbed up on the bed, and poked a finger at her sister's tiny hand. Ten-year-old Kate scowled.

"I'll be the only one without an M. Ain't that bad luck?"

"No, no, little worrier. I'll call you *Miss* Kate. Now there's an M for you, lovey. How will that suit you? Now, both of you, give your Ma a kiss, and go out with Mrs. Lyden. Me and the babe need some rest."

Kate had greeted newborns before. It had been five for sure. The Manley's first-born was Coleen, followed quickly by Kate who never knew her older sister. Coleen died before Kate reached her first birthday. Only Fiona survived of the babies who followed one after the other –one being born, another dying. It was the way of The Pinch. As Kate grew older, her awareness of each little tragedy grew clearer, and she grew more superstitious. Mostly the Manley babies died before turning three. There was pneumonia or tuberculosis or measles or some other disease too ferocious for a little one to fight. Fiona was the exception.

Kate was two when Fiona was born. She didn't remember the birth, but distinctly recalled Fiona's first birthday, and the special cake that Ma made. Other babies came and went, but Fiona and Kate thrived, and were best friends. Kate called her younger sister Fee, and they were inseparable. They did little chores for Ma and Da, but mostly they played up and down the block with the neighborhood children. Sometimes they'd go in Uncle Patrick's market, and he'd give them a pinch of cheese or a pickle that they'd take to their secret hidey place where they'd eat, and spill their hearts to each other. They giggled when someone walked by, and couldn't see them.

Fee was everyone's best friend. She was adored, and Kate was never jealous because she knew, more than anyone, just how special her sister was. Of all the redheaded children in the family, Fiona's coppery hair shone the brightest. Her ruddy cheeks were like summer apples. She ran and skipped instead of walking. She moved so lightly that she nearly took flight, but her blue eyes were deep, and had the look of an old soul. The air around her seemed to shimmer. She laughed and giggled, and was Ma's little helper, particularly with the new babies. Though he loved all his children, Fee was the light in Michael James' eyes. She was the air that filled his lungs. A sprite who gave him hope. Fiona ran to him when he came home from his job. They played games, and she danced and twirled in circles when he sang. When the other babies died, it was Fiona who sat in Da's lap, and kissed his tears. Mary Elizabeth and Michael were certain that she was an angel, and a great blessing to their family. They quite nearly worshipped the celestial being who lived in their tenement apartment.

In 1878, Yellow Fever made a return visit to Memphis. Because the city had experienced a small epidemic in 1873, the first 1878 death attributed to the fever sent thunderbolts of terror throughout the citizenry. Those who could afford it fled the city. Some refugees were refused admission to other towns for fear that they carried the incurable fever.

Collin Hearn entered one of the only pubs still open in The Pinch.

"Connell, I need me a pint over here," he called out. He stood next to the table where his friend, Michael James, sat. Collin waved a large sheet of paper above his head.

"Look at this, boyos. This is what the *Avalanche* calls a newspaper today. Two pages – and most of that is a list of the dead. Looks nearly like two hundred to me. Is there no way to fight this plague? Gather 'round, and I'll read what this reporter writes."

"*We are doomed.*

It is hard as we write in this dark, dismal night of death, not to realize the full meaning of that brief sentence. It is hard for any man of the few left in this city of sorrows not to take the sentence to himself with a painfully personal application as the sentence of death. Scarcely any are left but those who are crowding down personal care in the noble purpose of others' good. Seventy dead today and at least one hundred and seventy-five new cases. God help us!"

A few men walked out without word, leaving nearly full pints on tables. There was nothing to say. Most still felt the anguish of lost family and friends. Collin took his pint, and sat with Michael.

"The trolley's no running anymore, so I walked south out of The Pinch. Everything's closed. Everyone's gone. Do you still have work?"

"I do," said Michael, "but I don't know for much longer. Who's left to order work from a tinsmith?" He took a deep swig, and wiped his mouth on his well-worn sleeve. "I have a family. What the feckin' hell am I to do to keep them well and fed? How are you faring, Collin?"

"We're all in the same fix, I'm tellin' you." Collin lowered his voice. "Here's sumethin' I want you to know. You can tell your good uncle, but no one else. The supply would dry up if all knew. Go see the doc, and get carbolic acid from him. Have Mary Elizabeth mix it with water, and scrub the floors. All the floors. It's said to kill the plague. Do it quick before others ask the doc for it. My family's still well, thank Jesus. I'm goin' home, and you need to do the same. It's hot as blazes, but they say to close your windows at night like there's sumethin' wrong with the night air. That's all I know. Go home, Michael."

The poor Irish, Italian, German, Jews, and Blacks of The Pinch couldn't flee like the wealthy did. There was nowhere to go, and nothing to do to protect themselves. No one knew what caused the deadly disease, and no one could cure it. The victims died painfully.

Mary Elizabeth gave birth to Molly that year. She instinctively kept the baby's basket in a closet as if to hide her from the phantom that walked the city's streets randomly stealing lives from the unsuspecting. Mary Elizabeth went to church every day, lit candles for the children she'd lost, and prayed for the ones still living. On her way, she passed one burning pile of linens after another where families cleansed by flame any item touched by their departed fever victims. The flames, the smoke, the stench of death confirmed that they surely lived in hell.

When she could, Mary Elizabeth shared a spare cabbage or potato with neighbors more desperate than her family. She was grateful that Michael's uncle owned the grocery store downstairs from their three-room apartment. Although food deliveries to the store were nearly nonexistent now, Uncle Patrick shared what he could, even when grief-stricken at the loss of two of his own children. Another neighbor child weighed on Mary Elizabeth's heart as well. The little Jewish boy in the building next door was near death from the fever. The Manleys and Cohens were good friends, and Mary Elizabeth's heart ached for the parents' sorrow, but even more so for the child's soul. Without baptism, she believed he couldn't enter heaven – at least not *her* heaven. Mary Elizabeth struggled with her conscience. It was not her way to question another's faith, but she also felt an obligation to the boy who had played with her children. So one afternoon, she tucked a vial of holy water in her apron pocket before visiting the neighbors. When she was alone with the boy, she secretly baptized him, and said prayers over him. *Helping him into heaven was a more important gift than cabbage soup*, she thought. Each family did what it could for its neighbors.

The Manley family wasn't spared from the ravages of Yellow Fever, and it wasn't baby Molly who was stricken, but their blessed Fiona who fell ill. She told Da not to worry, touched his cheek, and tried to smile. Every day he rushed to her bedside when he came home from work – until there was no longer work for a tinsmith. Mary Elizabeth hoped to take in laundry and ironing to offset the loss of Michael's pay, but few who could afford those luxuries were still in town. While Fee's health failed, Kate, now solemn and distant, went every day to the hidey place behind the building to cry where no one could see her. Fee was already six, three years beyond the crucial three-years-old curse. Kate thought her sister would be her best friend forever. They would celebrate each other's weddings to handsome lads with good jobs. They'd have healthy babies, and live next door to each other, and always keep each other's secrets. But now, if Fiona could die, Kate was in danger, too. Not so much from the fever, but from the vengeful demon that stole the Manley children.

"Did the doctor say sumthin' good today?" Michael asked his wife nearly every day.

"He's no comin' every day now, love. He says that we're to pray."

"Pray? Pray to who or what? There's no a god that would let this perfect child get the fever! The doctor's desertin' her, just leavin' her to die sure. Don't you talk to me like I'm a slow-witted child. I might no have a job, but I'm no a feckin' ijit!"

"Michael, your language!"

His boots pounded the wooden floor as he stormed out of the apartment.

When he wasn't at the pub with the other out-of-work men, Michael James sat next to Fiona's bed, and wept. He didn't notice that Kate was missing for most of the afternoons. He forgot that baby Molly was hidden away. He didn't see that Mary Elizabeth was holding the family together by a string thin as a spider's silk. She tended Fiona, did her best to locate and console Kate, and held Michael close in the night as he cried. She saw her living children as blessings from the Almighty. Michael James saw them fading away, one by one, before his eyes, stolen by wicked faeries.

Fee lasted longer than most with the fever, but her skin finally jaundiced, and she began vomiting blood and black stomach bile, a sign that the end was close. Although she wouldn't tell Michael, Mary Elizabeth prayed then that God would take Fiona quickly. But even the saints suffered, and so did Fiona. When Fee's breath finally stopped, Michael threw himself, sobbing, across the foot of her bed.

Mary Elizabeth pulled him to her, and stuffed back her own cries until she could calm him. "Michael me love, she was an angel loaned to us by our Savior. She wasn't meant to be here forever. Fee was a gift that God needed to take back to heaven. She'll sit on the lap of our Lord now."

"Don't be talkin' to me of heaven! There is no heaven, and no God, and I will curse that false God till the end of me days. Stay away from me, woman. I can't stand us without her."

Funeral bells rang solemnly for Fiona, and she was buried quickly in the mass grave for fever victims at Calvary Cemetery. Michael James was nowhere to be found.

The epidemic slowly ended when winter's first frost came to town, killing the disease-bearing mosquitoes. The residents, reeling from the devastation of the epidemic, didn't notice the coincidence. The fever came, and then it went without telling its secrets. It would be years before the connection between mosquitoes and the fever would be discovered.

When the wealthy residents returned to Memphis, Mary Elizabeth got work doing laundry and ironing. Kate was nine now, and old enough to be a good worker alongside her Ma. Between the two of them and Uncle Patrick's generosity, they kept food on the table and a roof overhead. Mary Elizabeth praised God for the blessings of her two beautiful daughters and the gift of work.

Michael never again looked for work. He spent most of his time at the pub. Where else he went, Mary Elizabeth didn't know. He rarely joined her in their marital bed, so she was surprised and thrilled to learn months later that she was once again pregnant.

Shortly after her discovery, Michael began spending more time at home. Mary Elizabeth hoped that he had spiritually re-joined the family, and she was cheerful and loving to him. He ignored the impending birth of another child. Little Molly toddled close to him, and raised her arms to be picked up, but he was weak and couldn't lift her anymore. Kate observed him with skepticism, and kept her distance.

Kate heated water on the stove to add to the tub where Mary Elizabeth scrubbed a fine lady's sheets. "Ma, what's wrong with Da? He's no right. I can see him, but I feel he's not really here."

"You're a wise girl, little Katie. Part of him's not yet here because he's slow makin' his way back from the loss of Fiona. We'll be patient with him."

"It's more than that. I can carry a clothesbasket of laundry for ten blocks, and he can't even lift Molly. She so wants Da to pick her up and love her. He's sick, ain't he? He's going to die now, ain't he?"

"We can't be thinkin' that, daughter. We'll take good care of him."

Kate ignored the sound of boiling water behind her. "You think I'm a little girl, Ma, but I know better than what you say." Her face flushed, and tears welled in her eyes. "He's going to die like everyone else. Does the Almighty hate our family or does He just hate you?"

Mary Elizabeth resisted the urge to slap her.

"They all die," said Kate, "and look at you – you with another baby in your belly. How can you keep bringing them to life only to see them snatched away? You birth them, then you bury them."

"You watch your tongue. Family is everything. I trust the Lord to protect me and mine because He always has. Me folks and me, which was only a baby, came to this country in what they called coffin ships."

"I don't want to hear this," said Kate, but Mary Elizabeth grabbed her arm.

"Yes, you *will* hear this. You must. Just the only difference between those ships and the ones bringing Negroes as slaves was that the Irish weren't in chains. Our people were crowded, nearly twice the number of poor souls as should be in the ship. Hardly any food or water, but there was sure the filth and the typhus and dysentery. There were narrow wooden slats stacked three high that went as bunks. When sickness took over one in an upper bunk, putrid waste dripped down on those below. When the ships reached these shores, dozens and dozens and dozens were already dead. If me Da knew how bad it would be, he'd kept us in Ireland where, if we starved, we'd at least starve on Irish soil, where we'd rest under its sod. But he took us on the ship, and he and Ma died. I don't remember them at all. A family that boarded with us in Liverpool took me in. Saved me life.

"Your Da and his family came on one of those ships, too. He was four so he remembers the hunger and the sick and dying. His little sister was there, and they were with their parents. All four of them survived the crossing – the whole family together. What a blessing."

"I never heard this," said Kate softly.

"There wasn't no need," said Mary Elizabeth still standing defiantly close to Kate.

"Mrs. Casey, the good woman who took me, raised me till I was twelve when she let me go into service at one of the fancy houses over on Adams. And you know who I met? A lovely, sweet lass old enough to show me what to do, but young enough to be me great pal. It was your Aunt Bridget."

"Da's sister?"

"What other Aunt Bridget do you have? Oh, we were fast friends, still are. Slept in the same bed in our quarters at the big house. When time went by, she introduced me to your Da. He was a good lookin' fellow. He was full of plans and ambition, and was already an apprentice tinsmith. In time, he courted me, and we started puttin' aside money from our wages to help us get started. I was always a hard worker, so I made good wages. The day we married and walked into our own room at Uncle Patrick's was the happiest day of me life. I finally had a family of me own, and soon we'd be makin' a bigger family, praise God. Katie girl, the Lord's plan for us ain't for us to know. I tell you, family is everything, and babies are glories. You'll grow up, have babes of your own. Then you'll see. You'll understand."

"I don't think I will."

"You won't understand?"

"No, I don't think I'll be growin' up." Kate poured the hot water into the tub, and took Molly outside. It was one of those days when no one knew Michael's whereabouts.

"Play with me; play with me," Molly insisted, but Kate paid her no mind.

It became easier to locate Michael as he grew weaker, and stayed in the apartment, then in bed. The doctor called it liver failure.

Michael James died one afternoon while Mary Elizabeth and the girls knelt in prayer at his bedside. When he exhaled his last ragged breath, Kate leaned to her Ma, and hissed, "I told you so."

Five weeks later, the last daughter, Mary Michael, was born. Two weeks after that, the four Manley women walked north on Second Street to St. Brigid's for the infant's christening. Ma carried Mary Michael, who seemed pleased with the outing. Kate held Molly's hand, and studied her sisters. She looked irreverently at the symbol of her Ma's faith, the towering spire of St. Brigid's. She knew that soon the malignant hand of her mother's God would reach down, and snatch another one of the Manley children. She pondered which one of her sisters must be taken to ensure her own life. She should say a prayer when they reach the church.

RUNAWAY

Mom's head tilted toward the sound from the living room. She peeked around the door from the kitchen, and saw five-year-old Priscilla tip-toeing, nearly to the front door.

"Priscilla, where are you going?"

"Away. I'm running away."

"I see." Mom walked into the sun-drenched living room, and sat on the sofa. "You weren't going to tell me? That makes me sad."

"Sorry."

"So, where are you going?"

"Mimi's. She loves me. She's not mean to me."

"She certainly does love you, but Daddy and I love you, too. Why do you think I'm mean today?"

"You made me eat that ucky junk for lunch."

"I see. Those are called vegetables, and, toasted up like that, they're crunchy and really good. I think you actually liked the few bites you took."

"Maybe."

"Is that the only reason you're leaving?"

Priscilla finally sat on a living room chair, but just barely so her feet would touch the floor. She was wearing her angry face.

"You made me stay in my room by myself when I wanted to go outside and play. I heard the other kids outside."

"Do you remember why I had you stay in your room for a while?"

"No."

"Pris, yes you *do* remember," Mom's sweet face looked firm. "I asked you to pick up your toys and put them in your toy box. When you stomped your pretty, little feet, and refused, I said that you should stay in your room until you picked up your things. Do you remember that now?"

"Maybe. But I'm still going to Mimi's."

"Okay, but it's a long way from Memphis down to Jackson, Mississippi. How do you plan to get there?"

"I'll walk."

"Oh, my. That's a very long walk. It could take weeks, out there all alone, nothing to eat or drink. No bed to sleep in. You know it takes us more than three hours to drive down there, and we're driving at sixty miles an hour. I'm pretty sure you don't walk that fast."

"Well, then I'll call Uncle Fat. *He* loves me. He'll take me there."

"He's pretty busy with the harvest right now, baby. I'm not sure he can get away to drive up here, then down there, then back to his farm. But anyway, don't you think you should pack some things before you go?"

Priscilla stomped off to her bedroom without a word. She pulled out her little red cardboard overnight bag, opened it on the bed, and surveyed the room's contents. Mom followed, and sat on Priscilla's bed. She pressed her hand against the kicking baby that seemingly couldn't wait to be born.

Priscilla put her favorite teddy bear in the bag. He filled most of it. She added the bag containing her jacks and ball, and turned to her mother.

"That's all."

"Oh, no clothes?"

Priscilla gave her mother an impatient look, went to her closet, and grabbed her Sunday dress and patent leather shoes. She tried stuffing them into the red bag, but had little luck. That's when she spotted her little baby doll clad only in a diaper. She picked it up. Her face flushed red, and she threw the doll across the room.

"Why do I have to have a baby brother or sister?"

"Sweet girl, you don't *have* to, but you certainly *will* have one, and we're so happy. It will be a very good thing for all of us."

"No it won't. Sheila has a baby brother, and she hates him."

"You're going to be a very important person to this little baby. As the baby gets older, you're the one it will look at to know what's what in the world. He or she will want to be just like you because you're so smart and precious."

"It can't play with my toys. They're mine!"

"Of course they are. And it will be a long time before the two of you have any interest in the same kind of toys."

"I don't want it in my bed."

"And it won't be. This is your bed. For a while, the baby will be in a bassinette in Daddy's and my room. That will make it easier for me to care for the little one."

"It will stay in there?"

"For a while, Pris, but you know we only have two bedrooms. There will be a time when we need to rearrange this room for the two of you. We'll fix it up nice so that one side is yours – the big girl side – and the other side will look like a baby's."

"I don't want it in here."

"I understand. In a little house like this, we all have to make some changes. Daddy is working very hard so that one day we can have a bigger house, and then you and the little one will have your own rooms. It's going to take a little while to get there, though."

There was a long pause while Priscilla folded and re-folded her Sunday dress that was sticking out of the overnight bag.

She whispered, "What if you like the baby more than you like me?"

Mom wrapped her arms around the child, and held her close.

"I could never love another child more than I love you. You are my first-born, and my very heart. I will love this baby dearly, but differently. You love Daddy and me, but you don't really love one of us more than the other, do you?"

"I guess not."

Mom kissed Priscilla's forehead and cheeks. "Tell you what. Daddy and I haven't decided on a name for the baby. Will you help me?"

"How?"

"Let's get paper and pencil, and go to the table. We can make a big list of names for a little boy, and one for a girl. Then you and Daddy and I can choose one of each. Would you help me name the baby?"

"I guess I can. I know lots of names."

"Then let's go do that; then we can call Mimi later, and tell her what's on our list. It's so good to have a big girl like you."

"Can we have cookies, too?"

"You bet we can, Pris."

THE SUITCASE

She paused on the veranda of the old house. Her face was blank and ageless. The dress had fit her decades ago when it was stylish, but now hung loosely on her tiny frame. Her hand caressed a porch column as if touching a lover.

"Miss Guidry, the rest of your luggage is in the car. May I take that suitcase for you?" The social worker was fond of Evangeline Guidry, and tried to make the move easier.

"No, thank you. Are you certain that I must go?"

"Yes, ma'am. You'll be more comfortable where you're going to live now."

"Are you quite certain, Bernice?"

"Ab-so-lutely! Everything's going to be fine. I'll walk you to the car."

"Why are those people standing next to my garden?"

"Don't pay any mind to them," said Bernice. "They won't hurt anything. I believe they're just happy to see you. *I* always am. My car is right over there. Let's keep walking."

Evangeline settled onto the front seat with the last suitcase on her lap.

"Miss Guidry, that will fit in the back seat. Shall I take it?"

"Thank you, no. Are you sure you know the way?"

"Absolutely. Everything's under control. I've lived in Memphis all my life."

The clump of neighbors had remained silent while gawking at Evangeline, but erupted in gossipy chatter as soon as the car drove away.

"I thought we wouldn't see her until they carried out her dead carcass, just like with the old lady," said one.

"You know, her mother was bat-shit crazy," said another. "She hid out in that house years ago. Made that daughter of hers stay in there to take care of her."

"It was all a damn shame," said a man who'd stopped at the group, but moved on, shaking his head.

"Why didn't the daughter just take control, and move her mother and herself out of this place before it started falling down on them?" asked a woman.

"I think Miss Guidry was completely under the sway of her mother, and they both loved the old place so much that they couldn't bear the thought of leaving. It was crumbling around them, but they just didn't see it. Or maybe they were both crazy, and we should have done something," said a kind neighbor.

"But, look at it," insisted a bystander. "I've seen raccoons going in and out like they owned the place. Dogs, too. I haven't seen the rats, but you know they've gotta be there."

"Don't you know that the house was condemned months ago? It just took authorities this long to get Miss Guidry out," said yet another.

The group stood quietly, staring just like observing a beached, rotting whale. All that was left was the arrival of the wrecking ball.

Bernice and Evangeline pulled under the portico of a two-story, brick building. It shared a campus with a multi-story retirement complex, and a one-story nursing home. It was

St. Anthony's home for indigent women. The sign only read, "Welcome to St. Anthony's."

"Excuse me, Bernice. Isn't this a mistake?" asked Evangeline. "This isn't a house."

"There are darling, little apartments inside. You'll like it. You'll see."

Bernice opened the door for Evangeline, and they entered the lobby. The administrator, Mrs. Ballew, welcomed Evangeline warmly, and began the grand tour. Evangeline, chin trembling, repeatedly looked in desperation to Bernice for explanation and escape.

"And here is your lovely room," said Mrs. Ballew with enthusiasm that ratcheted up her voice nearly two octaves.

Evangeline remembered the butler's pantry that was this size in her real, but abandoned home. She said nothing.

"I'll help you unpack," said Bernice. "We can make this room real homey, don't you think? Here, let me take that suitcase you're carrying."

"No! Oh, forgive my sharp tone. There was no excuse for it. But I'll take care of this one myself, thank you."

It doesn't take long to die of heartbreak. It only took Evangeline a month. She was found, seated in the rocking chair, hands primly folded in her lap like the lady she was. A visitor might have thought she was only resting except for the impossible crook of her neck.

When all was done for Evangeline's earthly remains, Bernice was summoned to empty the room.

"Bernice, here's this old suitcase sitting on the table by the rocker," said Mrs. Ballew. "I don't think she ever unpacked it."

Bernice closed the box she'd just packed, and went to deal with the suitcase, wiping her dusty hands on her slacks. She opened it.

"Dear, sweet Jesus. Look here, Mrs. Ballew. It's flowers – what's left of them. They must have come from her garden. This most likely is nearly all of her garden. It was the only part of the house that was ever tended. And then, this was all she had left."

GRACE'S STORY

Told to me as a gift for the purpose of this writing by my long-time friend and writer, Grace Estes Henderson.

It was long-time maid and companion Magnolia who discovered that Mrs. Thurgood had not simply overslept. The elderly lady had passed away gently in her sleep.

"No, Miss Penney, I never thought you were meant to leave me so soon. We were gonna get real good and old together. You know I'd always be coming to take care of you."

Magnolia sat on the side of the bed. She took a comb to Miss Penney's hair and cried for twenty minutes. Finally, she wiped her eyes, blew her nose, and made telephone calls – first to the doctor, and then to Miss Penney's only child, Mrs. Adella Benoit, down in New Orleans.

Mrs. Benoit arrived that day at a late summer sunset. Magnolia had stayed at the house all day, tidying up the already tidy home and waiting for Mrs. Benoit.

"It's good to see you, Magnolia. You certainly have stayed with Mother for a very long time. Thank you."

"The spare room's all ready for you, and I can whip up a supper for you in thirty minutes," said Magnolia. "I'm so relieved you're here."

"Thanks, Magnolia, but I won't be staying here. I've checked in to that little motel, and I'm on my way to the catfish restaurant next to it. I just wanted to stop by."

Adella paused and looked around. "I haven't been here in quite a while, but it never changes, does it?

"Anyway, I'd appreciate your help for the next few days. I'll pay a nice severance to you when we're done. You must be more than ready to retire. I'll go to the funeral home tomorrow, then come back here. Will you meet me here about lunch time?"

"That'll be fine, ma'am. Well, there's nothing for me to do here tonight, so I'll head out. Doesn't seem right not to hear Miss Penney tell me bye.

"Begging your pardon, Mrs. Benoit, the funeral director will be wanting to know what you want Miss Penney to be buried in. I took the liberty of gathering some things out that Miss Penney always looked pretty in. I laid them out in the spare room if you want to look."

"That was quite thoughtful. I'm sure they're fine, so lets just take them to the car."

Adella Benoit was decisive in making funeral arrangements the next day. Suggestions from the small-town funeral director and Brother Blaylock, Mrs. Thurgood's pastor who arrived unannounced, were politely disregarded.

At the house, Adella was not surprised that Magnolia was already there and looking for anything to keep her busy.

"The funeral will be tomorrow, Magnolia."

"So fast? I thought there would be more time before putting Miss Penney away."

"Well, there's no one else to come. My husband's tied up with business, and I'm sure the whole town knows by now. Anyway, while we're at the funeral I'd like you to prepare for a reception here after we go to the cemetery. You'll have a better idea than I of how many people might show up. Charge what you need at the grocery, and I'll take care of the bill before I leave town."

"Mrs. Benoit, I'd hoped to go to Miss Penney's services myself – to say good-bye and all."

Adella's eyes widened. "I never thought ... well, of course. You get a couple of your friends to do the reception. You can tell them what to do." Adella walked around the living room, looking down one hall and then another. "I guess there's nothing more to do here until after the funeral. I have to go to the attorney the next day. So, the day after that, you and I can meet here to decide about the house."

Adella turned on her heel and left. Magnolia stood in place shaking her head.

Magnolia carefully timed her arrival at the church the following day. It was still the 1950s, and she knew not to attract too much attention. She didn't arrive early. That would be bold. She took her time so that others would be milling about, greeting each other and Adella who stood in the vicinity of her mother's open coffin. Arriving friends whispered about what a fine lady Miss Penney had been. All of that was true. Magnolia quietly entered the church and slipped into the back pew. Despite the haste of the funeral announcement, the church overflowed with beautiful floral tributes. Magnolia smiled, knowing how much Miss Penney loved the beauty and scent of flowers.

Brother Blaylock recognized Magnolia and went to her.

"Magnolia, I'm pleased to see you again, but I wish it wasn't on such a sad day. You and Mrs. Thurgood were together for a very long time. I suspect this is very difficult for you – losing more a friend than employer."

"Yes, sir. I hadn't counted on this so soon. We never know God's plan, do we?"

"She looks lovely," said Brother Blaylock. "I wouldn't be surprised if you helped

Mrs. Benoit select her dress. Have you been down front to see Mrs. Thurgood?"

"No, I haven't, pastor. I didn't know if it would be proper."

"I say it is, and I'll walk with you."

Magnolia returned to her seat, struggling to hold back sobs. A number of Miss Penney's friends recognized Magnolia and stopped by her pew to greet her. Adella took note.

Magnolia had hired two women she knew to manage the reception, which had turned out more mourners than had been expected. Magnolia stepped in to help the other two clean up when Adella handed Magnolia an envelope of cash.

"If you would, Magnolia, pay these women what we owe them when they've finished cleaning up. I'm exhausted. I'm going back to the motel to lie down for a while. Tomorrow, you know, I have the appointment with the attorney, so I see no reason for you and me to be here at all. I'll just see you day after tomorrow – mid-morning. We'll get through this as quickly as possible, and you won't be troubled by this much longer."

Magnolia was already at Attorney Alwind's dusty office when Adella arrived.

"Magnolia, I had no idea that you'd be here." Adella pursed her lips.

"Mr. Alwind called and told me to come. I didn't expect to be needed."

Despite Adella's clearly being in a snit, Mr. Alwind asked them to be seated and began reading Mrs. Thurgood's will.

"That good lady didn't have much, but she had me draw up this when she was still clear-headed," he said.

Mrs. Thurgood left Adella $9,000. To Magnolia, she bequeathed $3,000. Adella's lips pressed more tightly into a barely visible line. Adella received the house and all its contents to disperse of or retain as she wished. Attorney Alwind completed their business after a haphazard search to locate a pen for signatures. Adella wasted no time in leaving.

"I'll see you in the morning, Magnolia."

"Yes, ma'am."

Wasn't it just like Miss Penney to take care of me like that no matter what anybody thinks? thought Magnolia.

As had become recent habit, Magnolia was puttering around the familiar house when Adella arrived. Nothing was said of the bequest to Magnolia. Adella walked through every room, studying the contents. She met Magnolia in the sunlit kitchen over which Magnolia had presided for years.

"This won't be hard," said Adella. "I don't want the house or anything in it. None of this furniture would suit my décor. I want you to take whatever you want from the place, and have Goodwill pick up everything else. The only thing I was curious about was Mother's jewelry. She used to be so organized, but as she got more daft, I wouldn't be surprised if she gave it all away. Oh well. It's not in her bedroom and wasn't in her lock box. I'm not going to waste my time on it."

Magnolia said, "Whatever you say, Mrs. Benoit, but have you given the kitchen cabinets and refrigerator a good look?"

Adella rolled her eyes. "Fine." She brusquely opened and closed all the cabinets and drawers.

She opened the refrigerator door. "You should take these leftovers from the reception. They're still good. Throw away whatever you don't want."

She obediently opened the freezer door. "Yes, packages of frozen food, nothing I have any need for. Do what you want with all this."

"Yes, ma'am."

"My suitcase is already in the car. I'm leaving now to get home before dark. I've put an envelope for you on the telephone table that should more than adequately compensate you – particularly in light of Mother's bequest to you." Adella couldn't resist the jab. "I've also left my address and telephone number. Let me know when the house is empty, and I'll put it on the market. Someone would surely buy it. Anyway, thank you for your help these past few days. We'll be in touch when I can sell the house."

Almost as if she'd never been there, Adella was out the door. Magnolia stood at the living room's picture window to watch Adella's car disappear down the street.

Walking back to the kitchen, Magnolia muttered to herself. "I encouraged her, Miss Penney. She just didn't show any interest."

Magnolia removed neatly wrapped packages from the freezer and lined them up on the kitchen table in order of the alphabet letters neatly printed on them.

Magnolia lightly touched each and chuckled. "A is for amethysts. B is for broaches. C is for choker, the pearl one. D is for diamonds. E for emeralds. That took care of it all, didn't it, Miss Penney? I might just buy this house."

HOSPICE

The hospital required that a patient be approximately ten days from death before admission to the palliative care unit. They had their ways of assessing and just plain guessing. That unit was the place to die with love and peace. No needles, no bodily intrusions, no "treatments." Only comfort, pain relief, and human tenderness. Every two weeks, a harpist set up in the corridor and played beautiful music. On alternate weeks, a string quartet provided a calm backdrop. Once a week, the plump woman brought her therapy dog to visit each patient. He was a Golden Retriever, a spiritually gifted dog who looked much like his mistress. The nursing staff had more love than any ordinary person could conjure up. The unit was a place where anyone would hope to get an advance reservation for their last days.

Miss Mamie was evaluated eleven days ago, declined, then accepted three days ago. They should have taken her sooner. For her daughter, Nora, moving from regular hospital – no matter how caring the staff – to this place was like stepping into an alternate universe. It was the VIP suite for dying.

The nurse talked to Nora's mother. "Miss Mamie, my name is Amy. We don't know how long you'll be with us, but we will make you as comfortable as possible and will be completely with you throughout this journey. Your daughter, Nora, is here also and will be here most of the time. Is all of that okay with you?"

Nora appreciated, but with some surprise, Amy's straightforward presentation to her mom. Of course, Miss Mamie knew she was dying. Hearing the words, however, were painful – at least to the daughter. Nora was startled to see Miss Mamie blink her eyes and give an impression of a nod. She had understood.

"Thank you, ma'am. I'm going to get some pain medication for you now. You'll be as alert as you want to be, but we want you to be comfortable. You'll be our guide."

Mother made the same slight acknowledgements.

"Mama, I'm here," said Nora. "Stan and the grandkids will be here in a while, but for the time being, it's just us girls. The nurse, Amy, is so lovely. She's going to take good care of you. I love you, Mama."

Miss Mamie scrunched her eyebrows. Nora took it as a good sign. She pushed the plump chair close to the bed. It was some sort of vinyl – easier to disinfect – but it would do. She'd brought a cozy throw and pillow from home along with toothpaste, toothbrush and extra undies. The signs indicated that time was running out. She wouldn't need much.

Mom hadn't eaten in days. Nora thought it was deliberate – that it was all Mama could do to take hold of her dying. Mama was always a take-charge lady. Now she slept more than she was awake. She hadn't spoken in several days, either.

Nora curled up in the mostly comfortable chair. She held her mother's hand. Mom seemed to relax. Nora propped her feet on the underpinnings of the bed and dozed. She'd spent sixteen hours a day at the hospital with Mom for the last two weeks, but wouldn't admit her exhaustion. She felt the nurse enter and jerked awake, groggy and confused.

"Nora, it's just me. You were getting a bit of a doze that you surely needed. Nothing significant is going on yet," said Amy. "Her blood pressure has lowered some. Her breathing has slowed. We'd expect those things, but nothing's going to happen very soon.

"I don't think you've eaten lately," Amy continued. "Come with me. I'm going to take a break. Let's go to the coffee room, and see what goodies are there."

Nora obeyed and stuck her feet into the loafers that had wandered underneath her chair.

Amy produced fresh, hot coffee and chocolate fried pies that she'd had shipped in from northeast Arkansas.

"This must be heaven," Nora whispered after her first bite. "I don't think I've ever tasted anything so good."

"Sure is close to paradise, for sure," said Amy. "I moved to Memphis from Jonesboro, but I couldn't stay away from these for too long. Having them shipped in every month is my one, great indulgence, my guilty pleasure." For a while, they only sipped the chicory blend and licked their chocolate-coated lips.

"I don't want to speak out of turn, but I hope you know that you're a good daughter, Nora. I see a lot here, and I feel that someone needs to tell you that. You know you're doing it right, don't you?"

"Maybe yes, maybe no. We've had our challenges, our ups and downs. I guess she and I are both difficult. How do I make it right at this late date? *She* can't make it right either. Seems like all I can do is forgive her for all the wrongness. And then there's my wrongness. How do I get absolution for that? About a year ago, she apologized to me for something I'd never imagined that she remembered. But she did. It was really big for me at the time. No, not 'at the time.' It was really big, but it's a thing you hide away in some dusty part of your brain's attic. It hurt like hell back then. And she remembered, and she was sorry. That was a huge deal for me. I was so touched, and I couldn't even tell her how important it was. I just said – "Gee, that was a long time ago." Did I just brush her off with that response? Did I diminish the importance of what she did? That should have opened a conversation, but neither of us went there. And now, here we are with limited time. She's dying, and we have so much unfinished business. Why isn't there a schedule, an alarm that goes off and says 'finish your stuff. The clock's running'? Why does life make you wait until it's too late?"

Nora ignored the tears slipping down her cheeks. She took another sip of the no longer hot coffee. She thought she should get this blend at home.

"I can't believe I just dumped all that on you. I'm so embarrassed," said Nora

"Absolutely no problem. Our mission in this unit encompasses the entire family, and I'm grateful that you shared with me. May I offer a thought?"

"Sure."

"A lot of data indicates that the sense of hearing is the last one to go. Miss Mamie can hear you. I know you tell her that you're present and love her. What else do you need to say? Ask her forgiveness, if you need. Give her yours. Say whatever you need to say in order to lovingly clear the air between you. She'll know. It will ease her journey."

"I'll try. I need to get back to Mom. I've been gone too long. Thanks for all this – your wisdom and the treats, too. I need to think on what you've said."

Mom looked little different. Her right arm was bent, that hand grazing her temple and saluting her right eye as if she was blocking the light.

"Mama, I'm back. It's Nora. I'm just going to sit here with you for a while. I love you dearly." She didn't expect or receive acknowledgment.

Back in the chair, wrapped in the throw, Nora looked around the room and stared into the shadows aligning themselves in the corner. Sleep deprivation does screwy things.

The scene was the corner bus stop where little Nora and Mom frequently waited. That was their only transportation back then. Nora was a third-grader and shivered in a coat that was insufficient for the frigid day. Mom turned her own back to the January wind, opened her coat and pulled Nora against her body before wrapping the coat around the child. Nora would always remember how warm Mama's body had been, how good she smelled, and the relief of being swaddled. She was still standing on the corner wrapped in her mother's love when Stan touched her shoulder.

His work usually kept him late, but he'd left promptly at 5 p.m. to get to the hospital as quickly as traffic allowed. Nora again jerked awake.

"Hey, baby, it's just me. How's Miss Mamie? Any change?"

"She's pretty much the same. Her body's slowing down a little."

Nora looked to her husband for comfort. Stan looked all floppy like a marionette whose strings had been cut.

He said, "I called both kids. Daphne said she'd come over after she feeds her family. Junior – well, I don't think he'll be here soon. He doesn't know how to handle ... this ... his grandmother dying."

"Wonder where he got that," Nora spat angrily.

"Look. I'm here. I don't know what else you want me to do. There's no user manual for this."

"Jesus, Stan, it doesn't require a manual. It comes naturally for most people. Except you. It's just not in your nature at all. I don't know why I've ever expected comfort from you. Look, I'm sorry. I'm just too tired to be patient with you right now. My mother's dying, and I need more than you can give. Just never mind. Why don't you go down and get me something hot to eat? I can depend on you at least for that, can't I? No burgers. Get me some vegetables."

Stan gratefully fled the room.

Nora grimaced. "Mama, I can hear you loud and clear. I know – you told me so. You'd say it again, if you could."

Forty-two years ago, Mama picked at the lace neckline of Nora's wedding gown.

"My dearest child, you do not have to go through with this if your truest heart doesn't believe it's right. I will walk into that church right now and deliver the most obscure speech about why there will be no wedding today. I will cancel the reception, return all the gifts, write all the notes. I will do everything that's needed to keep you from making this terrible mistake. Your eyes don't lie. You don't want this."

"You're imagining things, Mama. I love Stan, and we'll have a good life."

Nora's tone was flat. Miss Mamie couldn't break through the wall. The son who came too soon after the wedding answered Mamie's questions. They called him premature, but he weighed nearly eight pounds.

Nora spoke to her unresponsive mother. "Yes, Mama. I could have made other choices back then. But what would we have done? What would our family have said? Where would you have hidden me away, and what place would there have been for my son? You were right about Stan, okay? You were right. But, please. He's not a bad man. He's been a good provider and a faithful husband. As for me ... not so much, I guess. Despite his faults, maybe he's the better person."

Nora felt every reprimand that Mama would have expressed if only she could. Nora left the room, walked to the end of the hall and stared out the window. *Is it possible that Mama was never more difficult than she is now that she's dying and can't speak? Couldn't she just stay out of my head?* Nora wondered.

Stan arrived at the room shortly after Nora had given up and returned. He offered a plate-sized Styrofoam container.

"I don't think Mama needs these smells," said Nora. "I'm taking this meal to the coffee room. You stay here until Daphne arrives or I come back. I won't be long."

"You want me to stay *here*? I don't know what to do."

"Stan, you don't have to *do* anything. Keep an eye on Mama. If you need a nurse, call for a nurse. I'll be across the hall if you need me."

Stan handed over the carton with meat, two overcooked vegetables and a soggy roll. It smelled better than it was going to taste. He awkwardly paced the room, hoping that no one would discover his discomfort. "Please, God, don't let Miss Mamie die while I'm alone with her," he prayed aloud.

Nora returned to her mother's room with onion and bacon grease on her breath.

"Go home," she told Stan. "I know you're miserable, and that doesn't help me at all. Maybe our kids will be here for their grandma. Maybe not. Maybe we've been lousy parents. I'm okay to be alone. Go on. It's easier that way."

"I really am sorry, but I love you, baby." Stan kissed the top of her head.

'I know you do. I'm just really stressed. Go home." Nora didn't care about Stan or the kids. She didn't care about much right now.

How is it that the beginning and end are all the same? You start out with mommy, try to pull away for years as you grow up, spend decades with a husband and children, and, at the end, it's just you and mommy again?

Her cell phone vibrated. She stepped into the hall to answer.

"Daphne. Are you on your way?"

"I don't think I can, Mom. Sorry. John is late coming home from work, and all the kids are hyper. I think someone gave them candy earlier. On top of that, the baby feels feverish. I'm not going to be able to get to the hospital. Is it important that I'm there tonight?"

"Only if you ever want to see your grandmother alive," Nora stage-whispered from the hall. "Daphne, do whatever you think is right." Nora hung up.

The nurse and Nora walked into the room together.

"Amy, how's she doing?"

The nurse checked Miss Mamie's vitals. She used a swab to clean Miss Mamie's tongue, and teeth. She tenderly wiped her face with a warm cloth and put balm on her lips.

"Miss Mamie, can you hear me?" No response. "That's fine. We just want to make sure you're comfortable. You're not alone, Miss Mamie." Amy smiled at Nora. "Nothing out of the ordinary. We seem to be moving slowly. Get yourself a little rest."

The death watch didn't allow Nora any rest. She saw the slight rise and fall of her mother's chest. Oddly, this vigil churned up a gut-full of anger.

"Mama, you were mostly right about Stan, but you missed the mark about me. Why did you make me be the mother? Daddy had been dead six months, and I was closing in on my sixteenth birthday. You were barely functional. I know you lost your husband. *I* lost my father. Didn't that count for something? We should have grieved together."

Maybe it wasn't fair to talk this way to someone who couldn't respond, but long-held hurts were unstoppable.

"You were a grown woman. I know you were in mourning, but I can't credit you with that excuse. I came home from school, and you were in bed, which wasn't unusual. I tried to wake you to see what I should do about dinner. But you wouldn't wake up. I called your name louder and louder. Rubbed your face. Shook you. And then I knew. I dialed the operator and, in near hysteria, said that I needed an ambulance. 'Please hurry,' I said. 'She may already be dead.' Of course you weren't. They pumped the pills out of your stomach and kept you in the hospital for two days.

"While you were there, I got my girlfriend's mother to take me to get my driver's license. Your doctor told me that you shouldn't be left alone for a couple of weeks. So I drove downtown to get you when you were discharged. I got money from your purse to buy groceries. I called the school and said I'd be absent because of a medical emergency. I asked Joelle to bring me my class assignments. And for two weeks, I stayed home from school and watched you. I missed stuff at school, but that was just kid stuff, wasn't it? There was a contest I'd entered, and it was announced that I'd won, but I wasn't there. Instead, I took care of you.

"I want to let all that go, Mother. I really do. But why did I have to do the grown-up things? Why weren't *you* the one to help me mourn my Daddy? Why couldn't we have leaned on each other? I was just a kid, for God's sake. You took to your bed, and I had to tend you every year on the anniversary of his death. Didn't matter if I was sick or it was college finals or what was going on in my lie. I had to be there for you. Of course, you were barely there for me when my babies were born, but you liked them better – and me – as the kids got older. And now and then, you were a perfect mother. And now you're leaving me permanently and with such confusion."

Nora rose abruptly and left the room. She hurried to the other end of the hall where the elevators were. Amy watched from the nurse's station, but didn't interfere. Nora's pursed lips made deeper wrinkles around her mouth. Her head pounded. Getting on the elevator, she jabbed 'lobby.' *Let her handle this one herself,* she thought. *I'm tired of being her mother.* She got to the front door before she remembered that she didn't have her purse. Neither did she have the will to leave her mother to die alone. The lobby Starbucks was closing, but Nora pulled a crumpled five-dollar bill from her jeans pocket and persuaded the baristas to make one more latte.

Nora returned to Miss Mamie's room, but made no apologies.

"I'm back, Mama. It will just be you and me for a while. Just like the old days. We grew up together after Daddy was gone, didn't we? He was the real adult in the house. Things would have been so different between you and me if he had lived."

The latte soothed Nora. The crisp, white sheets barely bulged over Mama's shrunken body. Nora walked down the hall to the restroom rather than use the one in Mama's room. Returning, the sound grew in volume as she neared Mama's room. Amy was outside the open door, obviously waiting. She began saying things that Nora didn't understand and didn't want to hear. Nora interrupted.

"That noise. Is it my mother?"

"Yes."

Nora pushed past the nurse. The loud, shaky rattle seemed too big to come from that tiny woman. It shook the room. Nora thought the curtains swayed in response. Nora stood at bedside. She hadn't expected anything like this.

"What's happening?" she asked as Amy came to her.

"This kind of breathing is not unusual at this point. There's also a mottling on her arms and legs that takes place as organs start shutting down. Miss Mamie is displaying that, as well." Amy put her arm around Nora's shoulders. "It won't be long now. Why don't I call your husband?"

"Yes, please." Nora was barely able to whisper. She took Miss Mamie's hand and held it to her own face. The hand was chilly. She kissed her mother's forehead.

"Mama, I forgive you everything. Please forgive me. We struggled, you and I. We committed other sins against each other, but here we are. Just the two of us like it has been most of the time. Daphne and I struggle, too. I don't know if she'll be with me when I reach this point. I hope she will. But, most of all, I'm glad to be here with you. I love you more than you know. Daddy's waiting for you on the other side, you know. I'll be fine. It's all right for you to go to him now."

Amy had re-entered the room noiselessly. She put a stethoscope to Miss Mamie's chest and listened hard. "She's gone."

Nora didn't try to stop her tears. "Hail Mary, full of grace . . ."

THE WALK

Viola was proud to be ten. Now there were two digits to her age like all *the teenagers and grown-ups. Only babies had a single digit like one or seven or nine. Two digits meant she was nearly grown. On her birthday, Mama had baked a cake, decorated it, and made a big 10 in the center. Mama knew, too, just how important it was.*

Mama and Viola lived alone. Daddy was dead, and Vi couldn't remember him. Because they were on their own, Mama worked hard to support them. She was a medical secretary to a group of doctors in the medical center. She worked five and a half days a week, and took two buses each way, making a transfer at Union for the longer leg of her journey. Every day, she hoped the second bus would be on time so she wouldn't have to stand in the hot or cold or wet weather. Mama looked tired a lot of the time. Partly because of expense, Mama had stopped hiring after-school sitters when Viola was eight. Vi was a good girl, and very responsible, but still, she spent a lot of time on her own. Mama trusted her. Viola was to take out the trash, wash the dishes she used during the day, and telephone her mother before and after she went outside to play. Those were the rules, and Viola obeyed them.

"Viola, sugar, you're such a grown-up, and I'm so proud of you. I know you're by yourself a lot, but I know I can depend on you to make good decisions and do the right thing. It's not always easy to make proper choices, but

I'm sure I can trust you. I couldn't go to work every day without knowing you're dependable and safe. I love you, little violet."

Mama's work schedule didn't change in the summer just because school was out, and Viola was alone full-time. If Viola was through watching television, playing with dolls, and reading books, she made the quick call to tell Mama she was going outside. Quickly so that she didn't interrupt Mama's work.

Vi easily entertained herself. She flitted like an urban sprite through her neighborhood, and adjacent ones. She wandered through pricier areas observing how people lived in the big, two-story houses. She wanted to live like that some day. She slipped into alleys that were oddly clean and well-ordered, so she could peek through back fences to see their yards, and perhaps the well-heeled children at play. Up on Belvedere, just off Union, there was a grand house with a high, terraced front lawn that had two or three flat places before drop-offs to the next tier. Viola regularly walked blocks to get there and up the steep driveway to lie down on the top grassy ledge, and roll all the way down to the sidewalk, laughing all the way. No one ever shooed her away. She never considered herself a trespasser. How could it be wrong?

Closer to home, there was a big, but less grand, house with an unfamiliar tile roof that appeared to come from a foreign land. Viola thought it to be very exotic with the red roof and arched window frames. Best of all, in their smallish, front yard was a giant evergreen tree with branches growing so low that they caressed the manicured lawn. When she carefully stepped inside the prickly greenery, it was open like a towering tent. She could sit on a low limb, and pretend many fantasies or climb a couple of branches for other make believes. If she heard a noise in the yard or street, she'd freeze, scrunch into a ball, and hold her breath until she was certain no one was coming to run her off. She thought she might even become invisible on those occasions.

As she slipped through alleys, into fluffy trees, down terraced lawns, and darted in and out of big house properties, Vi never knew that homeowners might be watching her through their stately windows, and smiling at the little waif.

There were few children around the Crump Stadium apartments, but there was a boy, Jimmy, who lived in one of the small houses on the other half of the block. Friends of his from another block came to see him, and sometimes they'd let Viola play cowboys and Indians with them. On other days, the boys would point their index fingers at her, yell "bang, bang," and run away laughing. When those boys weren't around, sometimes she and Jimmy would sneak into Crump Stadium where all local football games were played. They explore all the areas that would get them in trouble if anyone caught them. *Innocent fun*, they thought.

One afternoon when time slipped by, Viola and Jimmy were still in the big stadium and near the gate closest to the apartments when Vi heard, then saw her mother stalking the streets and calling her name. Mom looked hot and really mad. Viola ducked out of sight until Mama went around the corner. For the first time, Viola awkwardly climbed the stadium's tall, iron gate, terrified that she'd fall, more terrified that her mother would see her. Unscathed, she looked both ways, and ran across the street to enter their complex from that side which allowed her to scamper through rear courtyards to the stairs leading up to their apartment's back door. She could still hear her mother. Out of breath, she ran out onto their front balcony and answered Mama's call.

"Here I am, Mama. I'm home!"

Mama was at the corner, and turned at the sound of Viola's voice. She looked at Vi, her face hard, and not amused. Vi's stomach sank. She accepted her fate, and went inside to sit on a living room chair. She waited and listened to Mama plod up the stairs. Mama opened the door.

"I'm sorry," said Vi. "I was wrong. I was too far away to be home on time. I didn't mean to be late."

It was a good apology, but it didn't work. Mama got really angry when Viola wasn't where she was supposed to be. Mama never touched her in anger, but, on the receiving end of her mother's words and tone, Viola always shriveled in shame and tears. She'd do almost anything to keep Mama from being disappointed in her. Mama carried more than enough burdens in making a living, and raising a child by herself. Viola mustn't do anything to add to those difficulties. Vi understood this without being told. Being a good girl was *her* responsibility.

"When I get home, and you're not here, when I have no idea where you are, I get frantic." Tears welled in Mama's eyes and in Viola's. "I have to go to work. I have no choice, so I need you to help. When you're not here, I think you've been hurt or kidnapped or who knows what. You absolutely must be more responsible than this. Go to your room until I can bear to look at you again."

Viola cried until dinner, and thought her mother was crying, too.

In a rare privilege after turning ten, Viola was allowed to walk to the Crosstown Theater to see a movie. It was fourteen blocks – a long way, but not too much for a ten-year-old. In that mid-summer week, Mama had a spare quarter and renewed confidence in her daughter. She fixed toast and jelly for breakfast, and solemnly handed over the quarter to Viola.

"It's what they're calling a rock and roll movie – *Rock Around the Clock*. It's for kids, and I think you'll love it. You've been totally responsible lately, so I believe you can do this. Don't you? Eat lunch early, and then start for the movie theater. It's a long walk, so you'll need to get on your way about noon. It will be such fun, baby. You'll easily be here when I get home, and you can tell me all about it. Maybe sing the songs for me, right? Be a good girl, and be careful. You know how."

Mama gave her a big hug and kiss, and left to catch her first bus toward work. Mama always smelled good when they hugged.

Viola was excited about her upcoming adventure, but watched her morning television shows, then ate a lunch of three, raw hot dogs wrapped in bread. She liked them that way. She put on her good Bermuda shorts and a clean, white blouse, slipped the quarter into her pocket, and set out for the movie feeling quite grown up.

She'd wandered all over that part of town. How could this possibly be any different?

Her posture was perfect, head held high. She nodded greetings to people who passed. She occasionally broke into a skip. The day was glorious. At first it was fun to look at all the tall and short office buildings, restaurants, shops of all kinds, and people going in and out of them. But then, despite the heat, an ice cube of fear grew in her belly. The buildings and shopping centers looked alike. She couldn't recall the number of blocks she'd walked. She was grateful that it was a straight walk with no turns, but she'd never walked this far in this direction. She felt lost. There was nothing familiar in the blocks ahead or behind her. Could she have passed it? She frequently touched the quarter in her pocket to make sure it was still there. Even when she crossed streets at traffic lights, she became fearful of the cars and trucks rushing by. Maybe a person should be eleven before taking this walk.

Just when she wanted to sit on the curb and cry, Viola saw the movie theater ahead of her. She ran the final block, and set down her quarter at the ticket booth. The pimply teenager barely looked at her, and shoved a ticket and two nickels back to her. The air-conditioned lobby smelled of popcorn and dispelled her previous fears. The movie was already in progress, but that was okay. She spent a nickel on an Almond Joy candy bar, and entered the spacious auditorium, dark except for flashes of light from the movie screen. As her eyes adjusted to the darkness, she was pleased to see that only a handful of people were there. Good. She located a seat that was nowhere near any other moviegoer. She didn't want to hear them chew their popcorn or even breathe. Vi wanted to be alone with the movie and her imagination.

She smiled at the teenagers dancing on-screen, and began the precise consumption of the candy bar.

The movie was over too quickly, and left her unsatisfied. Viola went to the lobby to decide what to do. She didn't remember how long the walk took, so she didn't know if she might stay a while longer to see the movie from the beginning and still get home on time. She looked at the movie posters in glass cases on the lobby walls. She marveled at the enormous concession stand with surely every candy in the world. She wondered which she would choose on her next trip. The longer she enjoyed the sights and smells and cool air of the theater, the more convinced she became that she could stay. Vi spent her last nickel on a big, dill pickle, and located her seat before the movie began again. She was already totally immersed in the film when the man sat next to her. Viola was startled and looked at him in the light of the movie. He stared straight ahead and ignored her. Why would he choose to sit there with so many empty seats available? Stupid man. The intrusion made her uncomfortable, irritated.

When she couldn't sit still any longer, Vi rose and stomped up the aisle to a seat distant from the stranger. There was no other movement in the theater, and she relaxed again into her privacy bubble. But only minutes later, he sat next to her again. Before she could jump up to find another seat, he put his hand on her left thigh. She gasped. He said, "shhhhh." The large hand was hot and damp. His fingers, puffy like sausages, draped over her knee. Nothing in her ten years told her why this was happening or what she should do. Vi couldn't breathe. When he squeezed her leg, she whimpered and fled the auditorium. She burst through the swinging door to the lobby and sprinted for the outside door, nearly crashing into the pimply teenager as he stepped out of the ticket booth. No one noticed her distress.

She ran for her life, though she didn't quite know why. The first three blocks flew by in a schmear of blurred colors worthy of the storybook tigers chasing each other round and round the tree until they became a puddle of butter. The painful catch in her side forced her to halt. She backed up against the brick front of a building, rubbed her side and discovered her tears. Viola looked back toward the theater. Was he back there following her? Was he hiding in some doorway so she couldn't see him? Had she waited for green lights at the intersections or had she bolted blindly into traffic? She didn't know any of those things.

A man stepped out of the building. "Are you all right, little girl? Are you lost?"

"I'm fine."

Another stranger to get away from. She started walking quickly toward home. *Mama will understand. She'll explain all this and hold me tight and keep me safe. I wasn't big enough to do this. Like the man at the building said, I'm just a little girl.*

Vi walked more calmly. Her blouse stuck to her skin with sweat. She covered a block and a half before the sound behind her made her turn quickly, tripping over her own feet, and falling to the sidewalk on a knee and hand. Tiny pieces of grit stuck in both scrapes. She tried to brush them off, but only smeared the bloody areas. Her knee was sore and caused her to walk awkwardly. She wiped her drippy nose on her bare arm. It was a long way home.

The realization hit her as sharply as the sidewalk slammed her knee.

It's my fault. If I hadn't stayed to see the movie again, the man wouldn't have sat next to me. If I hadn't wasted time this morning, I would have been at the movie on time in the first place. Mama told me to leave early, but I didn't. I disobeyed her. And all of those things are why the man touched me. I know I'm late getting home, too, and I'll be in big trouble. The man could probably tell that I'm a girl who makes mistakes and disobeys. Someone like me wouldn't tell on him for touching me. And I won't tell on him, because it's all my fault, and I'd just be in bigger trouble for being the kind of girl he'd touch. That's what happens to bad girls. Bad things happen to them. I'll never tell. No, I'll never tell. This only happens to bad girls.

And so, it begins. One woman after another who just won't tell.

THE CALL

Dorcas was just getting ready for bed when her cell phone chirped. Pulling up her jeans enough to avoid tripping, she retrieved her phone, looked at caller ID, and froze. She shot a hard look at her husband, and held out the phone for Tony to see. Despite his frown, she answered.

"Yes?"

"Where are you? I don't even know how long I've been waiting, and you're still not here. You're late. Why do you always keep me waiting like this? You never could keep up with the time."

"Mother, where are you?"

"You know exactly where I am. I'm on the porch of the old folks' home where you dumped me. Just stuck me away like I stick away your presents that I never like. You never had good taste."

"Who is this really?"

"Good grief, child. Don't you know your own mother's voice? I'm ashamed of you. Now come get me for my visit."

"There is no visit."

"Listen at you! Always a bad daughter. Almost never came home for holidays during college, then ran off, and got married without even telling me."

"Mother, I always tried. I always tried to make you proud."

"Well, you didn't. You were a great disappointment to your father and me. Thank heaven I only had one child to break my heart."

Dorcas looked helplessly at Tony. He took away the phone, and smoothed her hair.

"She'll call back, Tony. You know she will."

"We need to go to sleep, baby. It's too late for all this."

The cell phone continued to ring throughout the night. At seven o'clock, Dorcas answered.

"Well, sun's up, and you should be, too. What time are you coming? I'm still waitin.'"

"My eyes aren't even open. I can't deal with you yet."

"Deal with me? *Deal* with me? Shame on you for talking like that to your loving mother."

Tony knew the tears that would come, and fetched her medication.

"I want your phone," he said. "I'm going to put an end to this."

"No! No, you can't do that. You can't shut her off." Dorcas shoved the cell phone under her pillows.

"Okay, for now. I'll leave it alone for now, but this has to stop."

The sun was setting when Dorcas woke up, and groggily checked her phone. Four more missed calls. Tony walked into the room munching on some snack. It must be past dinnertime.

"She called four more times while I slept. See?" Dorcas handed the phone to Tony. He looked at the calls missed list.

"I see."

"You don't understand. You had normal parents, and don't believe that this woman continues to torment me. She's relentless."

"She's not, sweetheart."

"That does it. That just *does* it. You have to stop patronizing me. I'm getting dressed and we're going to see her. We're going to the home right now."

"Baby, that's not a good idea."

"I don't care what you think. I need to face her."

They parked in front of the porch, and empty row of white rocking chairs where mother and her friends used to sit. Tony put his hand on Dorcas' arm as she reached for the door handle.

"Baby, please don't. No matter how many times we do this, she'll never be there again. Try to remember. She died. We buried her. We grieved. Let it be over."

Dorcas slammed out of the car, and went to the porch, walking back and forth in front of the empty rockers.

The facility's administrator approached Tony. "I saw you drive in. I thought she'd be past this by now."

"Thank you," said Tony.

"Is she still going to the doctor?"

"Yes, and taking medication. But, you know, the phone really *does* ring."

THE BUS STATION

She raced up the back stairs to their second story apartment. It was Friday, and Talent Roundup Day on the Mickey Mouse Club. She hurried home from school every day to see this favorite television show, but Fridays was the best. Even so, she jerked to a stop on the landing with the back door to their apartment. The door was open. No one should be there. Mama was at work. The girl couldn't move, didn't know what to do. And then, through the screen door, she saw Mama breeze into the kitchen.

"Baby, why are you just standing there? Come on in."

"Are you sure? Is there a criminal with a gun in there making you act like everything's okay, so I'll come in, and be captured, too?"

"Good gosh, Zuzu. Get in here. Where did you get that imagination? Never mind. I know where it came from." Ex-husbands get that way for more complicated reasons.

Mama laughed, and didn't look afraid, so Zuzu went in the apartment.

"I have a surprise for you," said Mama. "My sister called, and Phoebe wants you to come over for the weekend."

"My cousin Phoebe?"

"Yes, baby. That's the one. Now, you should change clothes, just clean school clothes. I'll brush your hair then. I've already packed a little bag for you."

"Why are you home?"

"Sissy called, and wanted you to come over this afternoon so you'd be there the whole weekend. I don't know what they have planned. I got permission to run home and get you on your way."

"You're not going with me?"

"No, not this time."

"What will you do all by yourself?"

"I'll probably just miss you a bit. I'll be just fine."

"Then you're going to drive me."

"Zuzu, we need to get started. No, I'm not driving you. I'll explain when we get in the car. Get moving. We're in a hurry."

Zuzu saw the little, red bag on her bed, so it must be true. She decided to leave on her skirt and just put on a clean blouse. She was in the fifth grade. She could make fashion choices like that. Mama came into her room as she was fingering the last button. Mama took a hairbrush and clip from the bag.

"Let's make a nice, neat pony tail." She brushed Zuzu's hair gently.

"Will I ever have pretty, brown hair like you?"

"You have beautiful hair, baby. It's distinctive. People notice you."

"Yeah. *'I'd rather be dead than red in the head.'* I don't like getting noticed like that."

"You look beautiful. Let's go. Here are four quarters to put in your purse."

Once in the old car that Mama called The Rocket, Zuzu asked, "If you're not driving me, but we're already in the car, how will I get to Arkansas? Is Uncle Walter picking me up?"

"You do ask a lot of questions, child. Uncle Walter's not coming over here. You're going to have an adventure, Zuzu. I can't take off long enough to drive you over and get back to work, so you're going to ride the bus."

"These buses go across the bridge?"

"Oh, not city buses. You'll ride a Greyhound bus. It's simple. I'll get you settled at the bus station; you'll board the bus, and Uncle Walter and Phoebe will be waiting for you when you get off."

"How do I know when to get off?"

"You'll hear the bus driver. He'll say 'Marked Tree.' That's where you'll get off."

"I don't know," Zuzu whispered.

Zuzu fell silent trying to decide what she thought about everything Mama just told her. When they walked into the downtown bus station, Zuzu knew that the feeling in her stomach was fear. The room was bigger than even the cafetorium at school. There were doors and counters on both sides of the room. On the left was a section of little doors, maybe four levels tall. It reminded her of their cubbies in kindergarten except these had doors with painted numbers on them, and they looked metal. At the far end were big windows and glass doors. But most of the room was filled with wooden pews like in church except without the cushions. Mama held Zuzu's bag in one hand, and Zuzu's hand in the other. They went to a counter where Mama bought a ticket and traded the overnight bag for a different ticket. Zuzu couldn't stop looking around.

"Put these in your purse, and pay attention, baby. Let me tell you what will happen."

They walked out the glass doors to what looked like a bus parking lot. It smelled like a great, big service station. She wanted to hold her nose. A few spaces away, she saw people getting on a big bus.

"Zuzu, there will be an announcement over the loudspeaker inside. A man's voice will call out the name of the town you're going to – Marked

Tree. Then, he'll say what lane the bus is in. See those big numbers? It will be one of these."

Back inside, Mama settled her onto a bench close to the doors.

"This is hard. It hurts my butt," said the child.

"Well, you won't be here long. Now, listen. I can't wait with you, but you're very responsible, and this will be easy. You just sit right here. Listen for the announcement, and go to your bus where you'll give your ticket to the driver. Uncle Walter will be waiting when you get there. And don't let go of your purse. I need to leave now. Can you do all that?"

"I don't want to go. I don't want to do this."

"But you're such a big girl, and Phoebe's looking forward to seeing you. Y'all will have such fun. You can surely do this, don't you think?"

"I guess so. I *am* very mature."

Mama kissed her twice, and hugged her. "I love you, little Zuzu." Then, she walked quickly across the big room, and out the front door. Zuzu fiddled with the handle on her pocketbook, and wished she was home watching Talent Roundup Day. It was the best day of the week.

"Don't stare at me."

"Excuse me?"

The old lady sitting catty-corner from her on the facing bench was speaking to her. Zuzu hadn't noticed her, but the lady would have been hard to miss. Her hair and skin were all so pale that she appeared ghost-like. But the brightly flowered blouse, and coordinated red stretch pants that strained around her abundant thighs would certainly have caught your attention. Now Zuzu stared.

"I told you not to stare at me."

"I don't mean to. I'm sorry."

"Was that your mother?"

"Yes ma'am."

"Why did she call you a zoo?"

"It's Zuzu. It's my nickname."

"Well, that's crazy."

"Sort of. Mama said that Daddy's mother insisted that I be named a certain thing from her family. Mama said it was awful, but that Daddy would do anything his mother told him to. She said he'd drop dead if his mother told him to. He did drop dead, but Mama said it was from shame. I never understood that."

"You have a lot to say, don't you, little girl?"

Zuzu's head snapped to the left. There was an announcement on the loudspeaker. She squinted hard as if it would help her understand, but it didn't work. The words were a mumble-jumble. She looked to the old lady questioning.

"I don't know what he said either. I can never understand. My son always gets me when it's my time to board the bus. Where are you going?"

"Marked Tree. It's in Arkansas."

"I don't think he said that."

"Where's your son?"

"Somewhere over there, maybe at the lunchroom. He'll stay over there as long as he can before putting me on the bus. He's sending me to my daughter's for a while. He wants to get shed of me."

Lunchroom. That was the only part that stuck, and it sounded good. Mama rushed her out so fast that she didn't get her after-school snack. And she had money clanging in her purse. This wasn't so bad. Zuzu started making the circuit around the big room looking for the place that had snacks. She crossed from her seat to the wall to her right, and started down the outside aisle. Sometimes there were packages or grocery sacks of belongings or smelly foods, so she looked down a lot while still looking for a door to a food place. A colorful poster on the wall caught her attention. It must be someplace you could go on a bus. It was a beautiful, white church with big, double doors and a tall spire. There was a park in front of it with sidewalks and grass and trees and happy-looking people. In big letters at the bottom of the poster, it read NEW ORLEANS. Maybe she'd get on a different bus, and go there, and go into the church, and become a nun, and live a life of poverty and devotion. Well, maybe just devotion.

She stubbed her toe on something, and stumbled.

"Watch where you're going, brat."

"I'm sorry."

He had a beard with maybe food bits in it, and he smelled bad. His eyes looked red and crazy. He might be a demon sworn to kill would-be nuns. Zuzu moved away quickly, and quietly. Did she hear him growl? It was the first time since she'd entered the bus station that she'd been truly scared. She didn't see any signs of a lunchroom either.

"Clarence, come back here. Oh, shush, baby, baby."

The mother looked like Zuzu's high school baby-sitter, but there were three children she was trying to corral by herself. One was in her arms and crying; another was holding onto the bench and enjoying the delight of taking steps while his mom tried to keep a hand on him. Clarence, who was probably closing in on three, was trying to escape. So much for a toddler to explore. Zuzu scooped him up.

"It's all right, missus. I've got him."

The young mother had tears in her bleary eyes, and looked as if she'd collapse if someone said 'boo.'

"I've got him," said Zuzu again. She liked little kids a lot. "I can sit with you for a while. Do you have a toy or a book I can help him play with?"

"No, I just have diapers and bottles for the two little ones. I didn't think it would be this hard. Ain't never had to do this before."

The loudspeaker man made another unintelligible announcement. Zuzu frowned again, and looked to the young mother.

"Where are you going?" the young woman asked.

"Marked Tree. My rich grandparents have a plantation over there. They have a mansion and lots of servants. When I get there, I'll be sort of like a princess, but I don't mind helping you while I'm here – before I become a princess."

"I don't think he said Marked Tree. Is it in Mississippi? That's where we're going."

"No ma'am. I'm going to Arkansas to the plantation. I thought I'd be gone by now."

Zuzu grappled with wriggling Clarence. His face and hands were dirty, but Zuzu knew better than to ask for wipes. His mother fished into a diaper bag for a bottle of formula, and calmed the baby with it. The middle child found his mom's purse, and started digging in it for playthings.

"You're a good little girl to help me, and I thank you," said the frazzled mom. "You listen up close. Don't you never get with a boy in that way. You know what I mean. Don't never start havin' babies like this from thinkin' you gotta let him have his way or he'll leave you. He'll leave you anyways. My man married me when I first got knocked up. I had to drop out of school and everything. Never got to go to no proms or nothin'. And now he's gone to the Army overseas, and I'm goin' to his parents. They say they'll help us since I've birthed their grandbabies – one after the other whether I wanted to or not. I only pray that he comes home alive, and not in a pine box. I think he went into the Army to be free of us. If he dies, his folks will likely kick us out. It's a bad end for some fun in the back seat. You're a pretty girl with all that pretty, red hair, and boys are gonna come a sniffin' after you. Listen to this lesson."

"You really think my hair is pretty?"

Another mumble-jumble announcement blared across the big room that the worn-out mom seemed to understand.

"That's us." She started reaching for children, and their immediate bags.

"I can help. My bus isn't here yet."

Zuzu picked up Clarence who still wanted to run away, and she grabbed the diaper bag. Mom had the other two, but looked as if she was moments from going up in smoke. Zuzu followed her out the big doors to a proper bus and watched them loaded in. *How would that mom, just a girl, manage?* Zuzu watched the bus back out of its slot, and drive out into the city She wished she'd gotten on board to help with the kids, and go on to a new life. She'd help raise that girl's children, and open a prestigious school where she'd have all the children reading by age four. They'd enter college by fifteen, and she'd receive many, many awards for her amazing work. Her picture would be on the cover of all the magazines. The smell of gasoline fumes brought her back to reality. She looked around. Where was her bus? When would she leave for her Arkansas family? No other buses slid into their parking spaces. Zuzu went back inside. She first stopped at the place her mother had originally placed her. The ghostly old lady was gone. For the first time, she noticed an enormous clock, but she hadn't seen it before so the time told her nothing about how long she'd been there. Thinking about school dismissal though, it looked late. And she was hungrier than before.

There it was. Down there, very far, on the left. "Diner." That meant food. Careful not to trip on any of the other characters, Zuzu entered the diner, and shook her purse to hear her money jingle. She sat on a stool at the counter. It was a lot like the drugstore counter around the corner from the library where she walked on Saturdays when her mother worked half-days. She read at a high school level, so the menu was a snap.

"May I help you?"

"I think I'll just have French fries. That's all." It would cost a quarter.

The French fries were hot, freshly made, and special good. Zuzu dumped a plateful of ketchup on the saucer to amply coat her snack. She alerted to another announcement.

"Sir, what towns did he say? Did he say Marked Tree, Arkansas?"

"Nope. No Arkansas towns. How long have you been waiting? Where are your parents?"

"My parents are in Europe in hiding. I shouldn't say, but they're royalty. You won't tell, will you? I'm supposed to go into hiding with a humble family in a small Arkansas town. It will keep the assassins from finding me. Did the announcement say Marked Tree, Arkansas?"

"No. You need to finish up, and move on, little girl."

It had been such a long time at the bus station. Zuzu was embarrassed at his reaction. Did she not look like the daughter of royalty? Of course she did, but he was a problem. He might tip off the assassins. She scarfed down all of the fries, and left the diner. She finally admitted to herself that something was terribly wrong.

There was still the nice, pink-faced man at the window where Mama bought the tickets for Zuzu and her little red bag.

"Sir, do you remember me? My mother bought a ticket earlier for me to go to Marked Tree, Arkansas."

"Yes, pretty girl. I love redheads. Why are you still here?"

"Oh, gosh. I can't understand the announcements. When is my bus going to leave?"

"Little lady, your bus left more than an hour ago. There's not another one until the morning."

Zuzu choked. "Gone? But I'm supposed to go to Marked Tree. How can I get there?"

"I'm sorry. I can't help you. I can only give you a telephone call. Shouldn't you call someone?"

Call someone. Go tomorrow morning. Zuzu ran out of ideas. She was only in the fifth grade.

"What's the big street out there?" she asked the man at the window.

"That's Union."

"Where's Madison Avenue? That's where my mother works."

"It's a block over that way." He pointed toward the back of the bus station.

I'm an orphan now, she thought. *No one is here to help me. I must be a brave explorer, and find my way out of this dangerous melodrama.* Her imagination made her brave for a little while.

As the sun stole toward her back, Zuzu walked one block east, then south, then tuned east again on Madison. She knew that Mama's insurance company was just the other side of the big hospital on Madison. She kept walking. Her feet began to hurt, and her confidence was slipping away faster than a water slide. Zuzu passed the big hospital. Then, she went by the doctors' clinics. She was finally at the insurance agency where Mama was a secretary. The child gratefully entered the building, and recognized Thelma, the front-office receptionist. Zuzu wanted to throw her arms around the woman, but didn't.

"Hey, Zuzu. What are you doing here?"

"I need to see my mother."

"But she's been gone all afternoon. She had the day off."

"That can't be. She left me at the bus station. She was going back to work. I was supposed to go to Arkansas."

"Darlin', I'm so sorry," said Thelma.

Zuzu took a breath instead of crying. She was tired. Her feet hurt. She was hungry. And her mother was gone somewhere.

She looked up at Thelma. "What do I do now? Somebody needs to come get me."

GREENER PASTURES

Lisette sat at the kitchen table trying to concentrate on spelling words despite multiple distractions pulling at her like so much silly putty. The pot and skillet on the stove sent up tantalizing scents and bubbly sounds. The big pot's lid tap-danced metallically from the escaping steam. Lisette was ready for supper, but supper wasn't ready for her. And then there was Nana on the telephone in the living room. Her tone was uncharacteristically firm, even angry. And here came the boarder. Nana, Lisette's gramaw, rented out room and board to help make ends meet beyond her meager pension. The boarder was pleasant, but odd. Not so much, however, that she'd attract much attention in a small, Southern town where eccentricities were not out of the ordinary.

"Time for homework, is it? May I help? The sooner we get this done, the sooner we can eat whatever smells so good in here. How 'bout I help, huh?"

Miss Teensie *was* probably teensie at some point in her life, but it had been a long time ago. Right now, she bore a striking resemblance to a sweet potato – all lumpy and bumpy in the body, but with skinny arms and legs sticking out, and a pointy head of faded red hair. Lisette was intrigued with the oddly put together appearance, but admired Miss Teensie's many attributes. The elder woman had beautiful, twinkling blue eyes, and a smile that bespoke of her kindness and intrinsic joy. Lisette liked her a lot.

The girl took a pass on Miss Teensie's offer. She had to memorize the spelling words, and she was still eavesdropping on Nana's conversation.

"Thanks, Miss Teensie, but I just need to learn these words. It's an in-my-head thing. Maybe after supper you can test me. That okay?"

"Maybe so. I'll go sit on the porch for now. A new family moved in down the street today. I'll see what I can see. And what's wrong with your grandmother? She hasn't sounded like that since the yard boy mowed down the hydrangeas."

Lisette shrugged. "I'm getting back to my school book now."

But not so much. Lisette stared at the seventh grade speller, but she strained to hear Nana. "No you won't. You're just too late" was all Lisette could make out before Nana slammed down the phone. Nana stomped into the kitchen, wiping her hands absently on her apron as if eradicating her anger.

"Supper's going to ruin if I had to stay on that phone any longer."

"Nana, who was that? Are you all right?"

"I'm fine. We're all fine." She picked up a wooden spoon and started evaluating the contents of the bubbly pot and the skillet of corn bread. "You have ten minutes till supper. If you're not done, you'll have to finish homework later. Put your books away for now and set the table, please."

Lisette gathered plates and flatware, but kept an eye on Nana. This surprising display of anger made Lisette's stomach knot up.

Nana and Lisette were mostly quiet during supper. Miss Teensie didn't notice, and her chatter bubbled like one of the pots on the stove had. She described the new family down the street, the mom and dad, children, furniture, and even the family dog. The mom and dad appeared all right, but she thought their furniture was too fancy for their little town. Nana and Lisette made polite smiles and acknowledgments, and enjoyed the hearty meal of steamed cabbage with onions and sweet potatoes in the pot, too. Country cornbread would sop up the good juices from the rest of the meal. No matter how tight the budget, they always had the house to live in, and homey food on the table.

Miss Teensie politely thanked Nana, who she called Mrs. Potterfield, for the meal as she always did, and exited the front door for her evening constitutional. Lisette helped clear the table, and dried dishes while Nana washed. Silence stood between them. With the table wiped clean, and the dishes put away, Lisette could stand it no longer.

"Nana, I know something's wrong. On the phone you said 'it's too late.' Do we have a bill we can't pay? We in trouble?"

"No, child, we're not in trouble, and you're not to worry about such things. We have our bills covered. Don't you worry about that. It's a grown-up thing that won't ever concern you if I can help it. What's left of your homework?"

"I'm not grown up, Nana, but I'm close, and I can be trusted. You should tell me what made you so mad. You've never been mad like that."

"You're certainly growing up very fast, and you're smart as a whip. I'll be sure taking you into my confidence if it comes to that. What test do you have tomorrow – spelling or arithmetic? Let's turn on the fan, and I'll put the questions to you."

Lisette knew she'd been brushed off, but went along with Nana. She breezed through the spelling words. It wouldn't have been so with arithmetic. Nana produced chocolate-covered almonds she'd hidden from Miss Teensie. They sneaked out to the back porch to enjoy their contraband. Lisette's questions disappeared with several pieces of the candy. Nana was the foundation of her life, the core she could always depend on. If Nana didn't want to talk about whatever it was, then that was probably just fine.

The next day, Lisette walked home from school as usual with friends who lived along the way. Girls and boys drifted off as their homes were reached until there was only Lisette and her best friend, Frieda, who lived on the same block. It was Friday, and they plotted going to the nearby movie theater that night to meet up with other friends and maybe some boys. While sitting on Freida's front steps, Lisette saw Miss Teensie on the sidewalk in front of her house, pacing and wringing her hands.

"Oh good grief! Something's wrong," said Lisette. "I need to see about Miss Teensie." She shouted, "See you at 6:30?" as she ran down the block.

"Hey, Miss Teensie, what's wrong? Let's go into the house, okay?"

"No, oh no. It's wrong in there. Bad ju-ju. Can't go there."

"All right then. Let's go up here to one of those wonderful rocking chairs on the porch. It's a good place to relax. C'mon, Miss Teensie."

Though distressed, Teensie allowed herself to be escorted. Lisette led her in spite of a background soundtrack of tense, angry voices from inside. Teensie was settled, swatting at the late fall air with the lace fan she always kept nearby. Lisette soundlessly slipped into the house.

There were two women: Nana, plumply ample, a solid woman both of body and character. She wore cotton slacks that probably had a stretch waistband topped by a flowered overblouse. Shortly cropped hair, mostly gray and regularly permed. Perfect skin, perfect heart. Face deeply flushed in current anger, something Lisette had never seen.

The other woman was Nana's antithesis: Young, beautiful, even glamorous, slender, stylishly dressed in a black, tailored suit, exposing a burgundy blouse – probably silk. She didn't wear much jewelry, but it looked really expensive She had the same auburn hair that Lisette bore. She didn't look like anyone in their little town of Beederville. In the midst of their shouts, they saw Lisette.

"Oh, sweet Mary and Joseph, you're my baby! I know you are." The pretty woman's hands went to her face, and she looked like she would faint. She stepped toward Lisette.

The girl looked from the stranger to Nana.

To the stranger, Nana said, "Never you mind, you tramp. Just stop right there. Keep away from my girl. Lisette, go to your room and stay there. This isn't for you."

"I won't go. I think this *is* for me." She approached the beautiful woman. "Who are you? Why are you here? Nana, what's going on?"

Nana viciously turned on the stranger. "Don't you answer the girl. This shouldn't be happening. You've given up your right. Lisette, I told you to get to your room. And you – you whore – get out of my home! Now. Go."

The younger woman smiled tentatively at Lisette. She turned to Nana. "I'll go for now, but this isn't over. You know it's not. I'll be back." And she left without slamming the door. Lisette heard Miss Teensie gasp.

"Nana, what's going on? Who the heck *is* that woman, and why are you so mad?"

"She doesn't matter to you. It's too late. Too late to stir that pot. I won't talk about this, and you won't ask again." Nana stormed off to the kitchen, and looked around the room, lost, trying to recall why she was in there.

Lisette followed. "I *will* talk about it, and you need to explain You've never been this way, so it must be important. What do you mean it's too late, and she doesn't matter to me?" She grabbed the back of one of the kitchen chairs. "Oh, my God. Oh, my God! I get it. She's my mother! That's what this is. That woman is my mother, isn't she? And you don't want me to talk to her?"

"You need to forget that she ever darkened our door. She's no better than a cat that drops a litter of kittens twice a year and then leaves them. She's unfit and unwelcome."

"Then I'm right." Lisette pulled out the chair she'd been leaning on and sat down hard. "You have to let me talk to her. I *will* talk to her. I must. No matter what you do. God, she's my mother! You never told me why she left me here, why she didn't want me. I need to know what I did wrong to make her go. I have a right."

"Baby, there's not a thing you did wrong or that you've ever done wrong. You were two years old and precious. How can a two-year-old do wrong? All right, we'll talk about it some other time, but not now. My heart's a'flutter. I need to lie down."

"You're avoiding me. Stop. I can't get all stirred up, then have you walk off. Talk to me, Nana!"

"I really must lie down. I can't breathe right."

"I won't feel sorry for you. I think you're faking, and you're keeping me from my mother, and I'll get the truth from *her*. You're just hateful, hateful!"

Lisette stormed out the front door and turned sharply toward Frieda's. Teensie almost fainted. Lisette didn't notice a blue car driving in the opposite direction that pulled over to the curb. She tried not to bang loudly on Frieda's front door, but Mrs. Bowen answered immediately and saw her distress. Mrs. Bowen called Frieda into the living room. Mr. Bowen lowered his newspaper while his wife fetched kleenex as Lisette began pouring out the strange story.

"She must be my mother, don't you think? But Nana refused to talk to me about her. I don't know what to do."

"For starters, I'll call your grandmother and tell her that you're spending the night here," said Mrs. Bowen. "It will be good for you both to take this break, then you can talk tomorrow when you're both calm. I'll go with you if you like."

Lisette relaxed. Frieda's mom was just nearly as dear as Nana had always been until today. As Mrs. Bowen's telephone conversation with Nana wrapped up, the doorbell rang.

Mr. Bowen opened the door and saw the auburn-haired stranger.

"I'm sorry to disturb, sir. My name is Dulcy Potterfield, and I believe my daughter is here."

Mr. Bowen looked behind him for some unspoken direction from his wife. He saw Frieda and Lisette holding hands. Mrs. Bowen nodded reluctantly. The pretty lady entered and smiled at Lisette, waiting for permission to sit. Lisette thought she might drown in the silence that flooded the room.

Finally, Mr. Bowen took charge. "Have a seat. Lisette is our daughter's best friend and like another daughter to us. She's told us about the dust-up down at Mrs. Potterfield's a little while ago. We've known Mrs. Potterfield for a long time. She's a fine woman, and we don't want to meddle in her business, but there's questions about who you are and why you're here. This might be a good time for you to explain yourself."

"May I get you some water or sweet tea?" Mrs. Bowen was ever the attentive hostess. If Beelzebub himself came in her house, she'd likely offer him a bucket of ice.

"I'm fine, thank you. Or I soon hope I *will* be fine."

Lisette found her voice. "Are you my mother or maybe you know her?"

"I *am* your mother, sugar. It's been so long. I'm sure you can't remember me."

"So, why has it been so long? Where have you been? If you're my mother, how could you give me away?"

"I guess there ought to be easy answers, but there aren't. I'm afraid to tell you I'm sorry, because it's too simple. It's true, but I know it's not an excuse, and it doesn't solve anything or earn me forgiveness."

"Tell me why. Get to the point," Lisette insisted.

"I was very young. Only sixteen. I hung out with the wrong people, and I was making really bad decisions. Then, I was pregnant and horrified that I'd have to tell my mom – your Nana." The woman coughed and cleared her throat. She wouldn't make eye contact. "Ma'am, maybe I could have that water after all?"

Mrs. Bowen fetched the water, but Lisette didn't wait.

"Okay, you were a teenager, and you got knocked up. Then what?"

Dulcy sipped from the plastic glass before going on. "See, I'd been running away off and on since I was fourteen. Mom didn't know what to do with me. So when I got pregnant, I did what I always did. I ran away again. After a while, my belly got so big. I was more scared than ever and worn out from sleeping in cars or strangers' living rooms. So I came home. Mom took care of me till I had you. I loved you so much."

"Can't prove it by me. If you loved me so much, why did you run out on me?"

Dulcy looked to Mr. and Mrs. Bowen. "I'm so ashamed of my behavior back then. I guess I still wanted to be a kid, to party with my friends. It was hard to be tied down all day and night taking care of a baby when my friends were having a good time. Mom was always strict, but after I had you, she didn't want me to do anything but take care of you and stay in the house. Sometimes she'd nag me about going back to school. I might have sneaked out a time or two. I was too young and too rebellious."

"Did she kick you out?" Lisette was even less sympathetic now.

The woman studied her daughter's face. "I guess it was kind of mutual. She made demands. I didn't want to comply, so I agreed to go. She told me not to come back, and for a long time, I've been afraid to contact you."

"Who's my father?"

"That's not important. I'm here now."

"It *is* important. I don't know what to think about any of this, but I'd like to have a daddy, too."

"I don't actually know." She nearly whispered.

"You don't know? How couldn't you know? That's sick." Lisette recoiled.

"Like I said, there were bad decisions. I had a lot of boyfriends. But it doesn't matter because I had you – such a wonderful, beautiful baby."

Mr. Bowen rose from his chair. "I think that's plenty for now, Miss Potterfield. I think Lisette's heard more than enough for today."

"No, sir, please. Not yet." Lisette moved to the end of the coffee table close to her mother and perched. "It's been ten years. Why are you here now?"

"I can take care of you now. I want to take you home with me. I'm doing quite well now, and I want to raise you."

"You just show up and want to take me home with you? I'm not a stray dog. I don't even know you, and you can't do that anyway. I belong to Nana."

"Sugar, you *do* belong to me – legally. Your grandmother never got legal custody."

Mr. Bowen spoke again: "That's enough, young lady. I'll ask you to leave our home. This is not the way to proceed. You might still have legal rights, but you abandoned this child ten years ago. Do you even have a decent job and place to live? A place to raise a child? How would you support Lisette?"

Dulcy stood up, but didn't go to the door. "Sweet baby, I want you to come with me because you want to, not because of who has legal this or that. I have a good life in Memphis. I'm in sales. Pharmaceuticals. It pays well. I can give you everything you want, and we don't have to bother Nana with lawyers."

Lisette didn't notice herself being drawn into the web.

"You could come with me right now. We'd have the weekend, and you could skip school Monday. You don't need to go back to Mom's to get anything. We'll get everything you need in Memphis. We'll call your Nana when we get home. I don't want to worry her needlessly. I have a big, beautiful house and a housekeeper who's a great cook. We'll go clothes shopping tomorrow. We'll cruise the mall. In Memphis there are movie theaters, restaurants, art galleries, a huge zoo, an amusement park. Everything you could ever want to do. And there are excellent, private schools. I suspect you're very smart. It would be no problem to get you admitted. Won't you come with me just for three days? Then you can decide what to do. I love you, Lisette, and I want to be with you and give you every wonderful thing. I want to make it up to you for all the time I wasn't there for you. Please let me."

Lisette and Frieda exchanged concerned looks.

"She can come visit on weekends and holidays. We'll take Frieda shopping, too." Dulcy winked at Frieda.

The question boiled down to this: A life of routines as she'd always experienced, or a new, exciting life. Beederville was predictable, and here was the chance to become a new person in a new world. It was like a movie at the downtown theater. A magical queen wanted to scoop her away into her rightful role as a princess in a magnificent castle. Would it be a mistake *not* to go?

"Lisette, we don't know enough to let you go running away with this woman tonight," said Mr. Bowen. "Let's get her telephone number, talk this over tomorrow with your grandmother, and make decisions later on."

"I'm going," said Lisette. "I'm going to Memphis with my mother."

"We'll call my mother when we get home, but it's fine if you want to call her when we leave. She shouldn't worry, and there's nothing she can do to stop us, anyway." Dulcy was matter of fact. She held out her arms, and Lisette awkwardly allowed herself to be embraced. And then they were gone. The Bowens were dismayed. The three immediately walked down the block to Mrs. Potterfield's.

The latest songs on the radio almost made the trip to Memphis feel normal. Lisette couldn't help thinking this was a crazy adventure. She'd never, ever done anything crazy. She stared a lot at her mother, convincing herself that this was real and the right decision. It was then that Dulcy pushed back her hair, and Lisette noticed the tattoo on her neck.

Once in the outskirts of Memphis, they turned off the highway onto a long road then into a circular driveway that took them under the porte-cochère where they left the car. It was a word Lisette learned that night. The bronze-skinned housekeeper in a black dress met them in the foyer and seemed excited to meet the girl. She took Lisette to her room – large and beautiful in pastels and antiques – and directed her to all the amenities that were in place for her. Clearly, she'd been expected. The housekeeper's name was Verity. She was kind, but not a cuddly person. Her dark eyes failed to give away any unnecessary emotions or perhaps secrets. Verity explained that Miss Dulcy was making business calls and would see Lisette in the morning. She showed the girl the adjoining marble bathroom and the operation of the bedroom's large television. It was the home of a princess for sure.

"I'll be right back with a tray," said Verity. "You need something to eat, and you can watch television. We'll see you in the morning."

On Saturday morning, Verity woke Lisette with a breakfast tray of pancakes, rasberries and cream, and hot cocoa that had a minty flavor. Verity pulled out clothes from the closet and a chest of drawers.

"Me and your mama bought a few things hopin' you'd be here," she said. "Your mama wants you downstairs in an hour. We sure are happy you're here to fill up this big house."

Dulcy and Lisette went to stores too fancy for the girl's comfort. The clerks, however, were deferential to her mother, and it made the girl feel special by association. Dulcy was very picky about selections for her daughter, and they moved to other stores. They bought casual slacks and shirts, sweaters, everyday dresses, and dressy clothes. Everything from underwear and shoes outward. Lisette was dazzled. Dulcy ordered that the packages be delivered to the house.

"We don't need to think about school clothes because if you stay, and I *so* hope you will, your private school will have uniforms. That's so the scholarship girls won't be uncomfortable if their clothes aren't as nice as the wealthier girls. You certainly won't be a scholarship girl though."

Late afternoon, they returned to what Lisette decided was a mansion. The packages had arrived, and Verity had unpacked them and put everything in place.

"I have to do a little work, baby. Rest a bit and let Verity choose some dinner clothes for you. I'll take you someplace super special." Dulcy gave her a kiss on the cheek and walked into her office while scrolling through text messages. Lisette watched, but Verity guided her upstairs.

"Your mama has business. She works real hard. You'll rest now, and I'll pick your best new dress for dinner. I ain't had no little girl to fuss over in a blue moon."

"Why's she working on Saturday night?"

"She just has lots of work. That's nothin' for you to worry your pretty head about. She makes us a good life, right? Now, let me get you a pretty dress to wear."

The restaurant wasn't like anything Lisette had even imagined. She didn't know how to act or what to do, but Dulcy did her best to put the girl at ease. She suggested a meal that Lisette would enjoy, and discreetly showed her which forks to use.

"Don't fret about all this," said Dulcy. "It won't be long until it's all second nature. This is the life you should be living."

It must be a dream. Her mother was like a movie star and sophisticated and, best of all, she was completely focused on Lisette. Dulcy wanted to know everything about her daughter's life for as far back as the girl could remember. There was no asking about Nana, though.

On Sunday, they went to the new amusement park just outside the city. They stayed until all the colored lights came on and the fireworks exploded in the sky like Lisette thought her heart might.

On Monday, Dulcy enrolled Lisette in an exclusive girls' school. Lisette called Nana and told her that she was staying with her mother. Nana cried. She tried to change Lisette's mind. "It won't be what you think," said Nana. But Lisette was firm – and only twelve. She loved this new life.

In the next three weeks, Lisette made friends at school and was even invited to a party at the end of the month. Some of the girls were too snooty for words, but more than that welcomed her. She was invited home after school one day with one of her new friends. The girl's house wasn't quite as grand as Lisette's new home, and it made her smile.

Lisette's mother usually picked her up after school. They'd have a snack and chat when they got home. Lisette had settled in to this good life. Most nights they had a good, family dinner in the dining room, sometimes with food she didn't recognize. On nights when Dulcy was working, it was just Lisette and Verity at the table. On those nights, Lisette helped clear the table and wash up the dishes just like she had with Nana. She wondered what Nana and Miss Teensie had eaten for dinner.

She didn't know anything about jobs in the city, but was curious that Dulcy didn't go to work every day like people did in Nana's little town. Dulcy would shut herself up in the home office to make phone calls, or go out for a few hours at odd times. Lisette didn't understand, but she was too busy being rich to think about such trivia. That changed two weeks later.

It was late one night when loud voices from downstairs woke Lisette. She followed her curiosity downstairs and slipped into the shadows on the side of the staircase opposite the closed drawing room doors that didn't muffle the noise. She didn't know why she should hide, but she did. The voices belonged to men, and they sounded angry. Dulcy's voice rose sharply above theirs and silenced the men. Her voice was strong, authoritative. "*Wow,*" Lisette thought. "*She must be the boss. She made them be quiet. My mom rocks!*"

It wasn't anything Lisette heard. She just sensed the presence and turned to see Verity standing behind her, stone-faced. Verity lifted a dusky index finger to her lips. The drawing room doors opened and Lisette took one quick look before ducking farther into the dark. Three rough-looking men headed to the front door, making apologetic sounds and giving submissive nods to Dulcy. One man's jacket pushed back exposing the butt of the gun stuck in his waistband. He made a half bow. This was a different kind of movie. One that confused and scared Lisette. Dulcy tucked a thick envelope under her arm and went down the hall toward her office on the opposite side of the stairs. Lisette held her breath. She heard the door close.

"You got no call to be messin' in your mama's business," hissed Verity. "I won't be tellin' her about you snoopin' around, but that's just *this* time. Don't you never do this again. You stay to your own business, and you'll be just fine. I won't be tellin' you again. Now git up to your room. I'll bring your breakfast up in the mornin' and then take you to school. You don't need to see your mama till after school. You'd be forgettin' all this by then. Understand me?"

Lisette nodded.

"Now git."

Lisette ran up the stairs, two at a time. She slept little that night. Ate little breakfast the next morning. Verity was distant, but stayed in the room like a warden throughout breakfast. Verity neither smiled nor spoke on the drive to school. Lisette didn't know where to put her fear, but knew that she couldn't talk about this with her new friends – or with anyone. She stayed at the school's lobby window until Verity and the car disappeared. Then, she waited ten more minutes to be sure she was gone. What was she really waiting for? Would the man with the gun come to get her? She gave up her post when the bell rang and she fled for imagined safety in homeroom.

Verity waited in the school's driveway at the end of the day.

"I'll be takin' you home," she said.

Lisette tried to do her homework at the desk in her room until she gave it up at dinner time. She encountered Verity on her way downstairs.

"Your mama's out on business. I'll bring you up a tray. Go back to your room."

The next morning was a replay of the day before. Verity sat with the car's motor running while she watched Lisette enter the school. A teacher tried to shoo Lisette on to homeroom when the bell rang, but Lisette claimed a stomach ache.

Continuing to look out the window for Verity's departure, she said, "I'll go in just a minute, ma'am. I promise."

And go she would.

Nana's house was dark and locked for the night when Lisette knocked loudly on the door. The porch light flicked on. Nana opened the door. Miss Teensie was halfway across the living room behind her, grasping her housecoat tightly to her abundant body. Nana exclaimed and pulled Lisette into the house and into her arms. Lisette wore her school uniform and looked exhausted.

Nana's questions erupted without pause. "What happened? Are you all right? How did you get here?"

"I hitched. It wasn't very hard to get rides except when it got dark. Then, I had to walk for a while. Things aren't always like they seem, are they, Nana? Dulcy won't come after me. She'll be glad I'm gone. If you'll have me, forgive me, I want to be back here in my real home – forever."

MOTHER KNOWS BEST

The house looked different now. Miranda didn't get to this part of town very often, but she pulled to the curb and put the car in park. Being there, wrapped in memories, alternately made her smile, then broke her heart.

Over there, the bare patch of dirt beneath the big oak tree, that's the spot that always turned into gumbo mud after a storm. That's where she'd made the perfect mud pie and decorated it with sugar sprinkles that she pilfered from the kitchen. It looked so pretty when she offered it to her little sister that Penelope had eaten half of it before realizing that it wasn't right. She threw up violently. Miranda still smiled at the fun of it.

When Penelope took off screaming to the front door to snitch to their mom, Miranda ran like crazy to the back door and up to the stuffy attic where she hid for the rest of the afternoon to escape punishment. She'd let them get really frantic about her disappearance before reappearing. That should be enough to avoid a spanking.

Looking through boxes and trunks in her hideaway, Miranda remembered that Aunt Mooney had promised to teach her to crochet whenever Miranda got some yarn. And there it was. Just a super-old crocheted bedspread. Who'd care? So to while away the afternoon, Miranda unraveled the piece, not knowing until far too late that her deceased great-grandmother had made it for her parents' wedding gift. It was an antique, a family heirloom. It wasn't Miranda's best day.

The house-sized evergreen at the back of the yard was where she hid to read away warm days, lost in the fantasy of someone else's life. She quickly dismissed the recurrence of hiding in so many of her memories.

There used to be a gravel road veering off from the driveway and leading to the back of the workshop and storage shed. Back there was where she and Buck, her high school steady, would park and neck. Naturally, Penelope caught them one evening at an inopportune moment and ran in horror to the house.

The girls were never close. Miranda used to torment Penelope by telling her that she'd been adopted – left on the front porch in a shoebox. More likely, Miranda thought *she* was probably the one who'd been adopted. She never quite fit into the family. Maybe it had been her aspirations followed by multiple college degrees and then followed by fancy corporate titles. On the other hand, it might just have been her ego. In another version of imagined heredity, it might have been their mother who was adopted. Mom had always wanted them to be the kind of family that played board games on Thursday nights and expounded on their blessings at the Thanksgiving table. But they weren't. They were more like a pile of crayons that had been dumped out of the box, none of the colors matching, only connected by the paper wrappers bearing the word Crayola.

After dad died ten years ago, mom sealed off the downstairs into a separate apartment and added the necessary functions on the second floor to make her own residence. A steep wooden staircase and small porch now led to mom's new front door. Miranda could see two pots of droopy mums on the little porch.

That second floor window all the way to the right had been her parents' bedroom. That's where her father died. Miranda often wondered if he knew that last night as he fell asleep that he'd never wake up again.

Today, she had been summoned to the house by her mother, so she climbed the outside staircase.

The door opened just as Miranda reached for it.

"Hi, sis. You're late."

"Looks like you were late, too." Miranda stared at Penelope's swollen belly announcing itself beneath the long, muumuu dress. "My God, Pen, is that number six or ten?"

"I love being pregnant and having babies. You should try it some time. It might melt that ice sickle that's stuck up your ... "

"Oh, praise the Lord and Porter Wagoner! No wonder I don't have you both here at the same time. Come on in, Miranda. I need to get a beer."

Mom's fuzzy house shoes scuffed down the hall toward the sound of Wheel of Fortune. The daughters followed, pretending they weren't racing.

Mom popped the top off a longneck and sat on the couch. Penelope engulfed her mother, arms around her, head resting on what little of Mom's shoulder was available.

"We're here now, Mommy. You can tell us the bad news. It's cancer, isn't it?"

"Child, for someone so dedicated to giving life, you've always been the most gloomy person I've ever known. And, back away. You're smothering me."

Miranda turned down the sound of the game show. "Then what do you want to share with both of us, Mother?"

"I'm getting married."

"What?" Penelope bolted upright.

"You're what?" Miranda pushed a chair closer to the couch.

"Getting married. Don't you two still speak English?"

"But, Mother dear, you're over sixty now. Why would you do this?" asked Miranda.

"I'm not saying that I'm gonna rob a damn bank. I'm getting married. It's legal. I'm over twenty-one. Way over as you've so rudely pointed out."

Miranda was the practical one. "Maybe you could tell us something about this man. Who is he? How long have you known him? That sort of thing."

"Daughters, you act like I'm asking your permission. I'm not."

"But still, Mother, we have your best interests at heart and ... well, you've not always made the best decisions." Miranda wasn't even embarrassed about bringing up the past.

"Well, whoever's sitting in this room and hasn't made a mistake or two – just raise your hand. Right. I don't see any hands going up."

"Mother, remember the gas station attendant who you let move in here? Six months later, you came home from work and he was gone. So was your diamond engagement ring. Then there was that would-be country singer who gladly allowed you to back his tour. Unfortunately, the tour didn't end back here. Oh, Mom, remember the supposed real estate investor?" Miranda took no pleasure in her recitation.

"I don't have to listen to this." Mom went to the kitchen. "I think I'd like popcorn. Wouldn't you girls like some? You always did when you were little."

"Mother, I don't mean to be harsh. We only want to be comforted that you're making a good decision. Aren't we, Pen? Can't you say something?"

"Mama, what about Daddy? Don't you still love him? Is this the way to honor his memory?"

"Daughter, I honored that sweet man while he was alive. And I nursed him day and night for two years as his life faded away. In his last three months, I slept on the floor next to his bed to be near when he needed me. He was so fragile that it hurt him if I climbed in bed next to him. I mourned him for a year after he passed. Some days I couldn't even get out of bed. But I decided not to crawl down in that grave with him. It's been a long time now."

Mom threw the popcorn bag with a vengeance into the microwave.

"I don't think I feel right about it," said Penelope.

"I'm just this close to tellin' you both that I don't give a damn what you think, but I want everyone to get along when we get hitched."

"Let's try a different approach," said Miranda, taking charge of the chaos as she usually did. She walked into the kitchen and retrieved bowls from a cabinet. "Let's sit down with our popcorn and hear all about your suitor. We haven't even heard his name."

"Ennis. It's Ennis Mathis."

Miranda distributed popcorn into the bowls. "No salt for you, Pen. I can see your ankles swelling from way over here. Ennis, that's good, Mom. Where did you meet him?"

"At the senior center. Mondays are luncheons. Wednesday there's bingo. Fridays are tea dances."

Miranda said, "Sounds like fun. Which one of those did you meet at?"

"All. He sat next to me one Monday. There he was again on Wednesday, and we danced all afternoon on Friday. I wouldn't tell him, but I went out on Thursday and bought a new dress for Friday. And we've just been together ever since."

"Mom, you two don't ... you know ... do stuff?" Penelope looked away as soon as she posed the question.

"Christ on a crutch! Daughter, do you think you invented sex? Ennis and I are grown people. Don't even ask me such a thing."

"Can we stay on point?" *Having a serious conversation with the two of them is like herding cats*, thought Miranda. She looked at her watch, wanting deeply to leave.

"So, that's nice, Mom. How long ago was that?"

"Three months."

"What?"

"What!"

For once, the sisters were in unison.

"Oh, Mother, you couldn't possibly know him well enough to consider marriage."

"Miranda is right – for once. It's too soon. You're just infatuated."

"You girls don't know what you're talking about. Sometimes a person just knows. We're not teenagers, you know. We fit just fine. We're good friends, and we want a comfortable future together. We're gonna buy a fine house and sell this one. I want to look ahead, not back."

"Oh, Mother, you can't sell our home! Pen and I grew up here."

"I know where you grew up. And neither one of you lives here now. You rarely visit. It's not up to you."

"But Mother," Miranda nearly pleaded. "If you do marry this man, and it doesn't work, you should have this place to come back to."

"You don't want me to marry, but you'll plan my divorce or abandonment?"

"Pen, help me out here. Say something."

Penelope awkwardly emerged from the cushy couch and began pacing and rubbing her back.

"Oh, don't you dare," ordered Miranda.

"They're probably false contractions. I've had experience, you know." She took a deep breath and kept walking. "This should be a Miranda question, but what does he do, anyway?"

"He's retired."

"Oh great." Miranda returned the empty bowls to the kitchen and poured a glass of water for Penelope. "You need more fluids, sis. Mom, so does that mean he's on Social Security? Does he plan for the sale of this house to be a meal ticket? You'd probably get a decent price for the place as a rental for two apartments – not that I think you should. So, he's counting on the sale, right? And this *fine house* will be in a trailer park I suppose."

"No," said Mom. "He's retired, but he has interests."

"What does that mean?" asked Miranda.

Penelope paced.

"Interests. Investments."

"And he wants you to put your money – maybe the proceeds of this house – into his investments?" accused Miranda.

"Not at all."

Penelope leaned on the counter separating the living room from the kitchenette.

"We haven't even asked this, and we need to wrap up this conversation quickly according to my onset. Mommy, how old is Ennis?"

"He's eighty-five."

"What?" the girls said jointly.

"And he's rich. And he has no children.'"

The girls broke into twin-like smiles and simultaneously approached their mother, kissing her on the closest cheek.

"Good work," they said.

ANGELS WITH ONLY ONE WING

We are each of us angels with
only one wing, and we can only
fly by embracing one another.
- Luciano De Crescenzo

It was a superbly ordinary neighborhood. An unkempt, eight-unit apartment building was the inglorious centerpiece of the block. Drab duplexes stretched to the corner, and timeworn bungalows waited for nothing in particular toward the rarely traveled eastern intersection. The surrounding blocks were just as mundane. Sometimes boys in dungarees and white tee-shirts sat on a curb, smoking and telling dirty stories. Girls in short shorts and peasant blouses would stroll by and giggle at the boys' catcalls. The ice cream man quit going there when the boys threw rocks at the bell-ringing pushcart. It was not the neighborhood where families went for a Sunday drive.

Minette and her parents lived in the top, right apartment facing the narrow street. There was a porch-style balcony where Minette liked to sit cross-legged on the floor, watch the neighbors. Sometimes she smoked a filched cigarette. Her family hadn't lived there long. The old neighborhood had been brighter, greener, cleaner. Children played outside and visited each other's homes.

Mother clerked in a dress shop only a short bus ride away. She took later, more lucrative shifts these days because Minette was eleven and old enough to be at home alone. They needed the money. Dad worked on the railroad and was sometimes gone for several days at a time. It used to be that Mother would drive him to the station and keep the car until time to pick him up. It didn't make sense to Minette that the car now sat useless at the station while she and Mother rode the bus and struggled with packages and transit schedules. The vertical line between Mother's eyebrows grew increasingly similar to an exclamation point.

A boy and girl about her age lived with their folks in one of the bungalows. Minette played with them on occasion, but they were rough-talking and didn't really suit her.

Minette was happier during the school year when her days were mostly filled with activity and books. When class let out, she could sit on the school steps with her girlfriends to gossip and compare notes on the day. Those girls didn't live in her neighborhood. During holidays and the summer, she explored the neighborhood, walking blocks farther than she should have. She wanted to see how the rich people lived. Sometimes she boldly sneaked into their yards and hid in towering trees, pretending they were her playrooms and those, her houses. She only ventured out of her apartment when the boys weren't out. If they were, she just watched television. The Mickey Mouse Club was her favorite.

Spotting someone new after school one day was a welcome treat. An elderly woman sat on the front porch of the bungalow nearest the apartments. Had she been there unnoticed all this time? What was she doing there? Minette glanced at her covertly, but the woman was looking at something in her lap.

The school year was slogging by, and Minette was muddling through her studies with unimpressive grades. "If she'd only apply herself," the teacher said.

Mother switched shifts for Halloween and helped Minette create a funny costume. The girl went out alone, confined to their street – two blocks up, two blocks back on the opposite side. Before she was through, she wished she could join the boys one street over who were throwing eggs at houses. They were laughing loudly and sounding like they were having a lot more fun than she was, even though they'd surely get in trouble. Hardly anyone on her street had on lights and gave out candy. The old lady's house was dark. Minette had hoped to see the woman close up and say hello. One day after school, Minette had seen the woman glance at her when she walked home. Not tonight, though.

It was the next Monday when Minette walked home wearing a heavy sweater for the first time that year. She spotted the woman from several houses away. Minette walked past her apartment and stopped on the sidewalk directly in front of the stranger's bungalow, faced the little house and established a beachhead. She resolutely planted her feet and stood her ground until the woman eventually looked up.

"Hi. My name's Minette, and I live right over there, and I wanted to just say hi."

The woman was silent, but Minette wouldn't turn away.

"Thank you. Hello," the woman finally said.

There was a lilt to her speech that was unfamiliar to Minette.

"Okay then. Good to meet you. See ya."

When she left school the next day, Minette had something to look forward to. Maybe the old lady would be on the porch. Maybe they'd talk this time. Her curiosity and anticipation pushed at her quickening step. Success. The woman sat on her porch with a shawl wrapped around her shrunken shoulders. It was November, and a chill was settling in.

Minette stopped just in front of where the lady sat.

"Hi! It's me again. Minette. I'm glad you're there so I can say hi again."

The lady smiled.

"Guten tag. Good afternoon. You should not be at home now?"

"No one's there. Mother's at work. Dad's away on the railroad. I just came from school. See? Here's a book and my tablet."

"Then maybe you should come sit a bit if you will."

"Yes, ma'am!"

Minette tried to walk slowly to the porch so she wouldn't be clumsy. Sometimes on the playground she tripped over her own feet, and kids laughed. Mother said that it was just a growing phase. That her body would catch up with her feet. Only rude children laugh at other children. Mother always said the right thing.

Minette knew enough to wait for permission to enter the porch.

"Please. Come. Sit. My name is Weiss. Mrs. Hannah Weiss."

It was an unfamiliar name.

"Pleased to meet you."

Minette sat in a stiff chair and squirmed.

"Have a chocolate." Mrs. Weiss extended a small tin containing what looked like homemade candy. Minette took three, then saw Mrs. Weiss slightly shake her head. Okay. Too many. She hadn't known.

"Thank you, Mrs. Weiss." The first bite was heaven. "Have you lived here long?"

"Not so long. It's new that I'm here. I was in the north, but my son settled here, and moved me by his family. Not this block. He's in a fine neighborhood. He's a very important banker. This block is fine for an old lady. I don't need such a fancy-schmancy house like his wife must have."

Minette finished chewing and swallowed one of the amazing pieces of chocolate.

"My Mother and Dad and I have lived in that apartment down there for a year. Anyway, that's what I think it was. Nobody ever seems to be home, but me. Are you alone, too?'

"Sometimes yes; sometimes no. My son visits. Not so much his wife or children. Very busy people I imagine."

Minette had not previously noticed how small the woman was. Not much bigger than she was, and very slender with dark eyes that sparkled with knowledge and mystery. Her full mane of white hair was pulled back into a bun, but tendrils rebelliously escaped confinement. Although lines caressed her face, there was a blush of color in her complexion that defied her age. *She might be timeless.* Minette thought, *she was a new kind of beautiful.*

"This candy is so good. Did you make it?"

"Ja, sure. You make such?"

"No ma'am."

"Maybe not candy, but soup?"

"No, ma'am."

"Not by your age to cook anything?"

"We don't cook much at my house. We're all there at different times – and Daddy not much at all – so we just eat whatever."

"Cookies. At least you make the cookie?"

"No ma'am. Nothing."

Mrs. Weiss harrumphed.

"We shall talk of this again. You have schoolwork tonight?" "I do. I have to read a book chapter and do arithmetic. I have a worksheet."

"Then you should do the work and, if you will, tell me tomorrow what you have done. Will you do this?"

"Yes, Mrs. Weiss. I will. Will you wait outside for me tomorrow?'

"Ja. Yes, I will."

Minette bounded down the half block to the entry of her family's building, up the stairs, into the apartment and her bedroom where she spread the work on her bed. She could do this before Mother comes home. And she'd have much to tell Mrs. Weiss tomorrow.

Minette ran home the next day, and looked for her new friend as soon as she could see that far. They both smiled when she got there.

She likes me, Minette thought.

"Come, sit. Tell me what you did learn. "

Minette did so quickly. She described her book, *Anne of Green Gables*, and how she felt sympathetic to the main character who had no real family. While she talked, she tried not to stare at the plate of cookies on the small table between their chairs.

"Take the napkin. Have one."

They were still warm. Fresh from Mrs. Weiss's oven. Minette thought she'd never tasted a cookie so good or ever would again.

"Your chin." Mrs. Weiss made sign language brushes against her own chin. Minette started, stopped, then used the napkin to brush away errant crumbs.

"If you like, you might want to make, right?"

"These cookies? Me? Oh, yes. Do you think I could? People say I'm not so smart. You'd teach me, right?"

"Yes, but you must ask mutter, your mother to permit you coming into my home. It would be wrong not to have permission."

"She'll say yes. I know she'll say yes. I'll ask tonight. No one's taught me kitchen stuff. Can I have another?"

"Ja. But tell me more about your book."

"I think I like Anne because she doesn't fit in, but she really tries to."

"Not with full mouth, please."

Minette finished the bite.

Mrs. Weiss listened, nodded her head when appropriate, asked interesting questions. The book took a deep breath and became reality on the bungalow's front porch.

Minette wanted to make cookies. She wanted to see the inside of Mrs. Weiss's home. She wondered why the old lady was so alone, much like herself. So she'd have to explain it, or some version of it, to her mother who seemed already so strained by life itself. Mother might not want the child to befriend an unusual, old lady. Minette managed to spin an acceptable yarn to her mother, and gained permission for something that Mother probably hadn't listened to. No matter. She had permission, and she could honestly go.

Minette ran home the next day and right up onto Mrs. Weiss's porch.

"I have permission! We can cook."

The tiny lady nodded and rose.

They entered the house. A musty, sweet scent of age, wood, polishing oil, whispery perfume, and sorrow greeted Minette as would a gracious hostess. The room overflowed with massive pieces of dark wood furniture: Tables, china cabinets, bookcases, and a grandfather clock that must have counted cadence for thousands of days. At the end of the area was a dining room table surrounded by chairs with curved legs and with backs and seats padded with intricate, needlepoint cushions in dramatic colors, only slightly aged. At nearly the center of the room was a puffy sofa covered with indigo velvet. There were lamps with crayon-toned glass shades, and delicate bric-a-brac sheltered in the cabinets along with ancient-looking china.

Minette whispered, "I've never seen anything like this. So beautiful. Where did it all come from?"

"When we left, we could bring some things. Others left later and could take nothing. Then, they couldn't leave at all."

"Leave where?"

"Germany."

"Wow. When?"

"Not today. You think these cookies make themselves?"

The old kitchen gleamed with highly scrubbed counters and floors. Mrs. Weiss gathered bowls, utensils, and ingredients. She also produced paper and pencil for Minette.

"You will help make the cookies today, but you must also write how you do it. Then, you can make again."

They worked together effortlessly. Minette concentrated on her tasks, and Mrs. Weiss smiled in affirmation. They finally sat in the living room while the house filled with the scent of baking cookies. It made the girl hungry. Minette sank into the feather-filled sofa. She thought she could stay in this foreign room forever. Mrs. Weiss was pensive in a rocker. She fondled a wooden figurine from the side table and seemed very far away.

They each sampled a cookie when they took them from the oven and pronounced the outcome a success. Mrs. Weiss folded half the cookies into a cloth napkin and enclosed the instructions Minette had written.

"You're not to eat them all. You're to share with parents so they see what you have done here."

Mrs. Weiss went to her son's home for Thanksgiving. Minette's Dad was home for the feast day, and it felt like a family again. The day before Thanksgiving, Mother helped Minette make her spice cookies for their Thanksgiving dessert, and both parents bragged on her.

"Who taught you to do this," asked Dad.

"Just a nice lady down the street," said Minette. "I visit her sometimes."

Minette knocked on her friend's door nearly every day in December, spending more time in Mrs. Weiss's kitchen. While they cut vegetables, stirred pots, and sampled seasonings, they talked about both their upcoming sets of holidays. Mrs. Weiss spent a few days at her son's for Hanukkah, and Minette missed her. Minette went to Mrs. Weiss' house the afternoon of New Year's Eve to ask if the older woman was going to a party. Mrs. Weiss made the funny spitting noise that always tickled Minette.

"I should go to a party for just another day? It means nothing to me. I've seen more days and years than I remember. It's only one more, God willing."

Mother never went to Mrs. Weiss's home. When they met on the street going to or from the market catty-corner from their block, Mother nodded and smiled, and Mrs. Weiss did the same.

In January there was a warm spell so Mrs. Weiss and Minette took to the front porch to enjoy the air.

"Will you tell me now about leaving Germany?"

Mrs. Weiss stared off somewhere and nowhere. Her face darkened. The lines deepened.

"It was 1936. My husband, a good man, had his job taken from him. Jews were losing their homes, jobs, possessions. They were being treated badly. Very badly. Asa, my husband, said it would only get worse and we should go to his cousin in New York, America while we could. I didn't want to. I said, 'How bad could it get?' He insisted. Our children were teenagers. Rebekkah, my girl, was engaged. She was young, but he was a fine boy from a good family. It was a good match, a brocheh."

Minette tilted her head.

Mrs. Weiss read her mind. "It means a blessing. Rebekkah wouldn't come with us. She stayed with Avron and his family. We were able to send furniture then and get passage for Asa, me and our son, David. We were with the cousin a while before we opened a shop and got our own place above the shop. Asa died. David married and took the job here, so here we moved. And here I am."

"Rebekkah? Where does she live?"

"We never saw her again. All who stayed were gone."

"Gone? Where?"

"They took them to camps. Starved them. Tortured them. Murdered them. Everyone I knew. Only few lived to tell the stories."

"How could that happen? Who would do that? Who *could* do that?"

"Nazis. It was the Nazis. Soulless animals."

Mrs. Weiss's jaw clinched.

Minette got up and, for the first time, put her arms around Mrs. Weiss. The elderly woman also stood and wrapped Minette in her arms. They held each other and didn't speak.

"We're each other's family now, aren't we? Will you be my grandmother? How would I say that in your language?"

"Bubbie. I will be proud to be bubbie."

As she left, Minette paused at the porch gate.

"I love you, bubbie."

In February, there was an ice storm. Streets and sidewalks were covered with a dangerous glaze. Businesses and schools closed. Ice mounted on power lines and broke them. Minette's neighborhood was one of the many without electricity. As the temperature dropped into the teens, there were no lights. No heat. After most of the day fidgeting, Minette finally disobeyed her mother's order, bundled up and sneaked out to check on her bubbie – a term she never shared with her mother.

Minette walked, slipped and nearly crawled the short distance over ice to the Weiss house. Mrs. Weiss answered the door in a heavy coat and a wool headscarf. She brought in Minette and quickly fetched a blanket to wrap her in. She removed Minette's wet shoes. The gas stove still worked so Mrs. Weiss made them nutmeg-sprinkled hot cocoa. They sipped their warm drinks sitting closely on the velvet sofa with the blanket over their laps.

"I was so worried about you," said Minette.

"I've been cold before." Mrs. Weiss smiled. "A person can live with cold."

In less than an hour, Dad knocked on the door and announced that he needed to take Minette home.

"You're all right, aren't you?" He looked at Mrs. Weiss.

"Ja, sure, I'm good."

Minette stalled, silently defying her father, taking the mugs to the kitchen to rinse them and back to the living room to fold the blanket and place it in an aged cupboard with shiny, brass handles. She sat on the floor to put on her shoes that had been drying on the open oven door.

Minette frowned at her father.

He said, "Let's go, Minette."

To Mrs. Weiss she said, "I'll be back soon. Thank you for the cocoa."

Bubbie patted Minette's shoulder.

Dad nearly carried Minette the slippery way home. When they got there, he firmly told her, "You go down there too much. I don't like it."

Minette ignored him. In truth, she loved her bubbie much more than she now loved her father.

After the thaw, Minette and bubbie started doing delicate needlework. Minette stopped more than started and claimed she was too clumsy. Bubbie laughed at her.

"You think Rome was built in a day? Practice."

Flowers began blooming. The Weiss home was filled with wonderful aromas of both flowers and food. They made creamy potato soup and then blini stuffed with cheese and then fried. Mrs. Weiss always packaged half their fare for Minette's family. Being with bubbie was the best part of every day. When they didn't cook, Minette would take a reading assignment or library book to bubbie's and read aloud. They talked about the stories and frequently laughed. Minette's grades soared which made all the adults in her life proud. Dad might have been home a little more lately, but Minette scooted down to bubbie's every chance she got. Mrs. Weiss cautioned her to spend more time with her parents, but didn't really mean it. She wanted to be with Minette as much as the girl wanted to be with her.

The first day of summer vacation, Mom sent Minette with a grocery list to the market catty-corner from their block. They ran a tab there. Shopping completed, Minette stood at the corner traffic light shifting a full bag of groceries from one arm to the other. When she looked up, there was bubbie on the opposite corner also waiting for the light to change.

She's probably going to the store, Minette thought. *I could have gone with her.*

Mrs. Weiss broke into a big grin when she spotted Minette. She continued looking at the child as the light turned green, and she stepped into the street. She never noticed the car that was speeding through the red light.

Minette heard a nauseating thud and then bubbie wasn't there. She lay crumpled like a heap of laundry halfway down the block. Minette stood as still as Lot's wife transformed into a pillar of salt. She didn't realize how hard she was squeezing the grocery bag, but it was tearing, and ice cream dribbled down her leg.

Minette was motionless while people screamed and rushed to Mrs. Weiss and to the driver who tried to stagger away. People in the stores stepped out and shook their heads sadly. "That's old Mrs. Weiss, isn't it? Does she have any family?"

The police arrived first, followed closely by the ambulance. Minette watched the ambulance attendants carefully lift bubbie to a stretcher and completely cover her with a sheet. The ambulance left with no sirens. A tow truck arrived to impound the drunk's car. Police placed him in the back seat of a squad car, which also left. Everyone left.

All that remained of the accident was bubbie's abandoned shoe in the middle of the intersection. As the light changed again, Minette picked it up and took it home. In her room, she put it under her pillow. It was all she had left.

CAMP

Alma's family was more fractured than those of her school friends. Mom and Daddy were divorced, so he came and went. Mostly went. Aunts, uncles and cousins lived far enough away that they only made obligatory howdy-do's once or twice a year. Alma usually couldn't remember their names. She was an only child, so it was just the two of them: Mom and Alma.

It was in the third grade that Jimmy appeared in their world. He wasn't the first man who had liked Mom, but he was different. The others would make over Alma like they were crazy about her, and they'd bring her presents. Alma would tell Mom that she didn't like them. Even little girls could tell when people were faking. They were just trying to get to Mom through her. Mom would stop seeing them. Jimmy didn't try to kiss up to Alma. He paid just the right amount of attention to her. It felt right. And he didn't run away.

He became a special friend of Mom's, and he was at their apartment for dinner two or three nights a week. Mom's smile was beautiful when Jimmy was there, even more beautiful than she usually was. When they sat on the sofa to watch television, Jimmy put his arm around Mom. She'd snuggle against him. Sometimes they said things quietly to each other that Alma couldn't hear. A glow wrapped them in a magic love bubble that bound them together. Alma was glad for her mother's happiness, yet she wished that the love bubble was big enough to include her.

I guess the bubble is just for grown-ups, though, Alma resigned herself.

Sometimes when Jimmy caught Alma staring at them, he'd laugh and say something funny like "Did I grow another head?" And he'd take both his hands to feel around his head and neck. They'd all laugh. Jimmy never hugged Alma, but he petted Alma's head and looked her directly in the eyes when she talked to him. He asked her questions about school, but not the stupid ones that adults usually did. One night he brought over a pretty area rug for their sparsely furnished living room. It looked much prettier then. He started giving Alma a weekly allowance and kidded her, calling her the banker and asking if she'd make him a loan. Alma didn't know much about kidding so she didn't know if he really wanted his money back. She'd mumble and blush, and he'd tell her not to worry yet about keeping her wealth.

Fourth grade was coming to an end when Mom told Alma that she'd be going to summer camp that year – for two whole weeks.

"Camp? Isn't that in the woods?" moaned Alma. "I've never been in the country. I won't know what to do, and I won't know anyone there. No, I don't want to go away."

"Alma, this will be a great experience. You will swim and canoe and do crafts. You'll probably roast marshmallows over a fire. Not all girls get to do this. I surely couldn't afford to send you to camp. This is a gift from Jimmy."

"Jimmy? Why?"

"He cares very much for you, and you don't have any summer activities. At camp, you'll have fun and make friends and learn things."

"I've never been away from home that long," Alma said almost inaudibly.

"You'll be fine, baby. There's a parents' day on that middle weekend, and Jimmy and I will drive up. A lot of the other girls your age will be just as shy. It will give you all something in common."

Early on a Monday, Mom and Jimmy delivered Alma and her trunk to the Trailways bus waiting with purring engine in front of the YMCA. Older girls greeted each other as if they were old friends. The girls Alma's age gave each other uncomfortable smiles and found whatever vacant seats were available. Alma pressed her hands against a window as the bus pulled away. She watched Mom and Jimmy as long as she could see them and tried not to cry. It was a long drive, always farther and farther away from everything she knew.

Alma was a city girl, so arrival at camp was a shock, but the woods sure smelled good. The counselor at the fourth-grade cabin was a sweet high school girl. She assigned their bunks and played a game that had them introduce themselves. After dinner in the big mess hall, they lined up outside. Music played over the loud speaker, and two of the counselors lowered the flag. There was nothing familiar about the first day.

The cabin had large, screened-in windows on every wall that welcomed pine-scented breezes. But there were also sounds. Trees creaking and swaying. A distant animal noise. Footsteps? Yes, those were footsteps outside their cabin. Was the flimsy screen door locked? Couldn't anyone bust through there? That night she heard some of her cabin mates cry themselves to sleep. They probably heard her, too. Alma learned to love their counselor that night when she helped Alma change her bed and keep her secret when, for the first time since kindergarten, Alma wet her bed.

Alma wrote a post card home every other day. The fourth grade girls bonded in their fear and then relaxed into the activities that they experienced as a group as tight as sisters. The girls in the baby cabin helped each other through the strangeness of camp, and the two weeks slipped by faster than they'd thought.

A slightly more grown up Alma looked out the windows with her friends as they each squealed at the sight of their parents as the bus pulled in front of the YMCA.

Mom had a car now, an old one, but it was hers. While Alma was away, she'd learned to drive, sort of, at least well enough to get her license. Alma knew that Jimmy was a part of all these changes.

"Mama, is Jimmy gonna be my Daddy?"

"Not yet, baby, but in the future that's what we plan."

"Why not now?"

"It's complicated. Wait till you're older. Now, help me drag your trunk to storage."

One winter night in the fifth grade, Alma woke up and walked the cold floor toward the bathroom. Mom's bedroom door was closed, but the living room lights were still on. She wandered in there, looking around. The television sign-off pattern was on, and, look. There were Jimmy's shoes. She laughed to herself. How silly to go home and forget his shoes. Alma visited the bathroom and went back to bed.

When Alma went to camp after the fifth grade, Mother reminded her again that this privilege was granted by Jimmy. Alma understood and made a gift for him in crafts class. She pounded out designs on the front of a leather wallet, using several attractive tools. She used the plastic "thread" and whipped together the wallet's front and back. It would be a good thank-you gift.

She wasn't among the babies this year at camp, but some of her friends from the year before were with her in the fifth grade cabin. They hoped they were ready for the canoe test when the big day arrived. Each team of three girls was required to paddle their canoe far out on the lake, fully dressed over their bathing suits, and turn over the canoe. The expectation was that they could remove their tennis shoes, tie the laces and sling them around their necks. Then, they were to latch onto the overturned canoe and flutter kick back to shore. The dock looked awfully far from the swamped canoe, but Alma and her pals were strong, and they made it without incident. On shore, they hugged, whooped, and jumped up and down together. They were the first team to complete the test. They knew they'd get certificates on campfire night. Alma was proud of herself and her friends. Not even an overturned canoe could take them down.

Most of the cabins went on an overnight camp-out with their counselors. Massive trees and a carpet of pine needles surrounded the clearing where they set up camp with small tents encircling a fire pit. As the sun gave way to the moon's ascent, counselors ignited the bonfire. The blue and yellow flames licked the sky and spit back sparks like lightning bugs. The girls broke off slender, green tree limbs and threaded hot dogs onto them to cook over the fire. The firelight cast a spotlight on the beautiful, young girls touching heads to whisper and to help each other remove hot dogs to buns. When they were nearly stuffed, the marshmallows appeared for roasting. The trick, of course, was to let the marshmallow burn just until it was dark brown and just before it collapsed into a gooey glop that fell to the fire with a sizzle. The bite just before it fell was the sweetest. They laughed at each other when liquid marshmallow dribbled down their chins. Alma had never had a better meal in her life. Never a better night either. She wanted to stay at camp forever.

After eating more than they could imagine, the girls and their counselors sat around the fire and sang. Alma and her cabin mates walked arm-in-arm to their tent at bedtime and huddled together whispering, giggling, and telling ghost stories Not even a few, aggressive ants dampened their spirits.

In the summer after the sixth grade, Mother and Alma moved. Alma felt all at odds. There was the new, larger apartment. She'd be in junior high in the fall, a big enough change by itself, but it would be at a new school in a new neighborhood, and none of her friends would be there. She wouldn't know what to do. She pushed all of it to the back of her mind when Jimmy once more sent her to camp where she knew everything. Here, she was a survivor, a success. And she didn't have to think about the fearful fall. Camp was the place where she'd grown up.

Girls piled onto the two Trailways buses parked in front of the downtown YMCA. Some of the same counselors were there. They were now approaching college graduation. A few of Alma's old friends were back, too. It was sad to think that none of them would be coming back. The girls would be too old for this camp. She'd been so afraid here, but now she belonged, at least one more time.

Alma took archery that year, but it was harder than she'd expected. There would be no certificate there. On the other hand, she passed her intermediate swimming test even though her required dive left much to be desired. The achievement earned Alma an assistant's position with the swimming instructor. She would help monitor the little fourth graders. She and her girlfriends talked about training bras and whether they'd started their periods. And, of course, boys.

One night they heard loud music from across the lake, and someone said it was a boys' camp. Alma's cabin sneaked down to the dock to wait for any arriving canoes, but none came. Good thing. They got in enough trouble, as it was, when their counselor caught them.

Only a few days remained of their last summer. During free swim, two counselors quietly gathered Alma and the other senior girls. The counselors took the girls on a mysterious, mile walk to a cliff farther down the lake's meandering shore. They arrived at the top of a bluff with a large earthen area where the grass had been beaten down by countless footsteps before them. There was a long, long rope tied to a lofty tree branch. The girls looked at each other and shrugged their shoulders.

The counselors laughed at them. "Rest easy, ladies. You are the chosen few for this super-special treat. This is how it goes."

Alma's favorite counselor grabbed the thick rope and walked it to the back of the open, dirt patch. She pulled the rope taut and, absurdly, took off running toward the edge of the cliff. She left the earth and flew above the lake so far below her. She looked like a bird, then – at the height of her flight – she let out a ferocious yell and let go of the rope. She dropped like a boulder and smashed into the lake, throwing up plumes of water. She must have gone deep. The girls ran to the bluff's edge just in time for the counselor to surface, grinning and whooping.

The counselor who was still dry said: "It's the greatest fun. Such a rush. We chose you girls for this. If you touch the lake's bottom, you can see into your deepest self, and you'll be a woman. Who's first?"

No one moved. And then Alma stepped up. "Me. I want to do it."

By that time, the first counselor had hiked up the hill. Dripping lake water, she hugged Alma and walked her to the rope. Alma's heart pounded. Her stomach didn't feel so good either.

"Hold tight. Run fast to the edge, and then you'll take off. When you've soared to the highest point, let go. You'll love it, Alma. Make sure you touch bottom. It's amazing."

The other girls watched with wide eyes. Alma yanked on the rope for reassurance, took a deep breath, and ran. She flew. It was astounding. But then the arc reversed itself. She was on her way back to land. She awkwardly touched down and initiated the laughter herself.

"That was just a trial run. I've got it now."

With great deliberation, Alma walked the rope to the back of the earthen patio. Without a thought or deep breath, she began her run. She soared off the cliff and, at the apex, she let go. She had flown like a bird. Who gets to do that? She doubled up into a bundle and pounded into the brown water in a once-in-a-lifetime cannonball. She let the momentum push her deep into the lake. The descent was spectacular. When she'd plunged to the lake floor, she found it hard to push up for a return to the surface. Her eyes were open. She'd never seen such sights. And there was a fish that didn't know what to think of Alma, either. Finally, her aching lungs forced her to begin swimming up and up toward the filtered light. She burst through the surface with a whoop.

Alma walked up the steep path to the cliff's top. Rivulets of water gliding down her body looked silver in the sun. She was tall, beautifully slender with budding breasts. She was proud. She had conquered nature. She was not the same girl who flew from the cliff. She appeared to her girlfriends as a goddess purified by the god Poseidon.

The Trailways bus was quieter than usual as it pulled out of camp headed toward Memphis. It was an ending. A chapter of her life was over, and the next page was turning. Her friends felt it, too. The ride home was solemn.

The girls hugged each other tearfully as they departed the bus in Memphis. They all promised to be best friends forever, but they knew they were lying.

Mother and Jimmy gathered up Alma and her luggage and went off to a special dinner. At the table, Jimmy took Mother's hand and announced their engagement.

Another change. But Alma no longer feared change. She'd flown off a cliff, looked a fish in the eye and conquered nature. She could do anything.

REVIVAL

Lunchtime. The one hundred seventy-three students at Warren County Consolidated High School were in the cafetorium. They'd gone through the cafeteria line or brought their lunches from home, and they'd settled at the long tables with their buddies for the forty-five minute lunch break. Jocks sat together. Cheerleaders and their pretty wanna-be friends were at a different table. "Nerds" were in one group because no one else understood them. Kids who didn't know where they belonged formed loose, shape-shifting groupings. Alvaline Turner never fit in anywhere, and she didn't care. As usual, she made her rounds of all the tables, eating chips at this table, part of someone's sandwich at that one, some fruit at another. She never bought or brought her own lunch, and no one ever denied her.

She was only in the eleventh grade, but she'd been the talk of the school since the ninth grade when her figure bloomed. The good girls wore skirts that brushed their mid-calves. They topped them with white, puffed-sleeve blouses. A few, from families that couldn't afford decent clothes, wore dungarees, loosely fit, with blouses or sweaters that barely acknowledged their femininity. On the other hand, Alvaline's dungarees clung to every curve and cleft of her beautifully rounded body. Her blouses and sweaters did the same. The female teachers clucked at her appearance and regularly requested that she be sent home to change, but the principal was a man, and her mode of dress was never officially questioned.

Alvaline's curly, copper-colored hair touched her shoulders and always looked as if she'd just climbed out of someone's bed. She gave wet dreams to all the boys in school. Everyone thought she put out. Some boys claimed to have personal knowledge, but no one could really prove it.

When the bell rang for fourth period, Alvaline walked out with the rest of the students, but sneaked out a side door. She ducked down and rushed through the gravel parking lot, keeping a low profile to avoid detection. She sprinted across the track field and only slowed when she entered the tree line. On the other side, she found the dirt, fire road and Carl Ed's blue pick-up. He was on the other side of the road, on the bank of the big, muddy stream. Not a river; not a creek; just – a stream. He was trying to pick out a new song on his beat-up guitar, repeatedly humming the same tune till he got it. Alvaline laughed at him, shoved the guitar aside, and straddled his lap. Carl Ed gave her a quick kiss and pushed her off.

"Can't you see I'm working here?"

"Yeah? Workin' on what? You gonna be a Johnny Cash or something?"

"I'm gonna be something for sure, but today I've been waiting for you to leave school."

"It's easiest to leave out at lunch. They see me, then they don't. Everybody thinks I'm some place else." Alvaline had a good laugh at that trick. "They usually don't tell Momma. Yeah, you be Johnny Cash. I'll be somethin' else, too. Maybe Miss America."

Carl Ed laughed.

"You know I'm the prettiest girl in school, probably the prettiest in Warren County, and I'm not through 'blooming'. Why couldn't I be Miss America?"

Carl Ed laughed again. "Yes, little girl, you're the prettiest in that little school, but I'm afraid you're not Miss America. No offense. Is your Mom at home?"

"No offense at you bein' so wrong. Anyway, I suspect that Momma's at the house. She traded for an early shift today at the Piggly Wiggly. This evening's the first night of that tent revival over at Beederville. She'll be getting all gussied up to go there and carry on with them snake handlers."

"I've got a blanket and a bottle in the back of the truck."

Alvaline giggled.

The sun was considering the horizon when Alvaline trailed into the little house she shared with her mother. Momma was already dressed up in her Sunday-go-to-meeting finery. Alvaline suppressed a laugh.

"Where have you been, child? School's been out for hours, and I suspect you weren't there anyway."

"I was at school today. Just ask. Don't you look just fine?" Alvaline's taunting grin was lost on her mother.

"Get out of those nasty clothes," said Momma. "Put on something decent. We're goin' to the revival."

"You can go. I'm really tired. I think I'll get some sleep."

"What you need is salvation. Don't you doubt for a minute, daughter, that I know the sort of things you do, and why you're so tired. I need you to go with me tonight. Your soul is in peril, and it's my obligation to help you get redemption."

"When precisely did you get so holy, Momma? Was it when you dropped out of school in eighth grade? Was it when you got knocked up with me? So where is my dear daddy anyway? Did you say he died? Or maybe you just didn't know which one he was. You're a piece of work – all middle-aged and fat and holy now that nobody wants you. Well, I got people who want me, so leave me the hell alone."

Alvaline was almost out the door when she felt the pull on her hair. Momma grabbed those plentiful curls, twisted her around and slapped her hard. Alvaline managed to remain upright, laughed and walked out the door, her face stinging more than she'd admit.

"Just as I am, Lord, just as I am."

It was a country choir, but the tones were rich, and the emotions full. Three singers and the director traveled with the evangelist. They filled out the choir of locals. The preacher was from Oklahoma and on tour through Tennessee, Mississippi, Alabama, and Georgia. He and those few singers depended on food and housing from the local church members in addition to the revenue-producing offerings they hoped for. He was fervent in his desire to bring lost lambs to Christ. Momma was baptized when she was twelve, but she felt the magnetic pull to this man. Maybe she should confess her sins again, and beg forgiveness, and another baptism from this godly man.

Alvaline walked to the tourist court two miles from her house. She saw Carl Ed's truck and heard his guitar, so she knocked. He opened hesitantly, and she saw another girl – younger than she was – beyond his shoulder.

"What are you thinkin' with that jail bait in there?" she screamed, and punched him in the face. He staggered backward. She had a mean right hook. Alvaline resisted the impulse to slug the girl, too, so she stormed off.

Momma sang every song. Waved her arms in the air. Put half of next month's rent in the collection basket, and made lots of eye contact with the traveling preacher. She wasn't nearly as ugly as her daughter thought.

Carl Ed found Alvaline throwing rocks and crying down by the stream. When she heard him, she turned and hurled a rock at his head. Fortunately, she missed.

"Whoa! Slow down. You got it wrong."

"Sure. There's a half-nekkid, under-age girl in your motel room, and *I'm* the one that's got it wrong. I ain't nearly as stupid as you think I am. I don't do much with school books, but I know about boys."

"For starters, I'm not a boy. And, if you hadn't noticed, you're under age yourself."

"That's differ'nt."

"She was there for a guitar lesson. That's how I make my living. You know that. I don't know why she took off her shirt. I was telling her to put it back on when you knocked. There was nothing to it. Come over here to me."

"Git away."

"How long do you plan to stay all bowed up like this?"

Alvaline picked up another rock, and cocked her arm. "I'll stay *all bowed up* as long as I please, and I'll let you know if I change my mind." She threw the rock so it whizzed just past his head.

Momma made sure she was last in the line to congratulate or otherwise speak to the evangelist. There were dramatic streaks of silver n his hair, and his eyes were iceberg blue. She continued to let the faithful line up in front of her. When she was finally the very last, she made certain that her eyes brimmed with tears as she looked up into his. She began to sob, and he cradled her in his arms. It was several hours later before she disclosed her concerns about her daughter.

Carl Ed didn't go far after dodging the rock. He liked a girl with spunk, and she wasn't as bowed up as she put on. The sunrise woke them in the bed of his truck. Carl Ed produced two warm beers and some stale saltines.

"You never told me," he said. "Where did you get such a crazy name like Alvaline?"

"It's not so crazy."

"Sure it is. What's the deal?"

"Okay. My mother didn't pay much mind to when I was gonna get born. It was her first – and thank somebody's lord – her only pregnancy. When she finally figured out that she was in serious labor, Daddy – or someone – put her in the car and started for the hospital. Problem was that I was in a big hurry to get born. Pretty soon there was no stoppin' me. Daddy – or whoever – pulled into a service station to help her deliver me. All the time she was pushin' me out, the only thing Momma could see out the window was a sign – Valvoline. Thank God, she couldn't see the whole word. The "V" was hidden. She might have named me Valvoline, and ruined my life."

Carl Ed rolled over, laughing more than he could control.

"You think that's so funny? What kind of name is Carl Ed? You Carl or you Ed? What are you?"

"I'm just a transient. You know what that means? I don't think you do. I'm not your ticket out of here. I'm nobody's salvation, Alvaline. I'm just passing through. This is nice for now."

"Go to hell!"

Momma smiled as innocently as she could, and gently kissed the lips of the travelin' preacher. He kissed her forehead, and rose to get dressed.

"Sister, I'm as concerned as you about your daughter. We must pray together, get down on our knees, and plead to our Lord in order to procure the girl's salvation. Leave me for now so I may pray about tonight's message. I'll see you after the meeting. It will be for your salvation and that of your daughter. Trust in me and the Lord, Sister."

Momma and Alvaline arrived at the front door about the same time.

"Why did you name me after a gas station sign?"

"Why are you stayin' out all night at your age?"

"I'll ask you the same thing, old woman."

It was a face off.

"I've been prayin' with the preacher for your soul."

"So that what they call it, Momma? That's not what I call it. That's not what I've been doin'."

"Hush your nasty mouth. I don't want to hear it."

"You never have, Momma. You looked the other way all my life, and did what you wanted never mind me. You never paid no mind to what I was doing. Did you think the wolves were gonna raise me? Why didn't you just give me away?"

Momma started a pot of coffee, and looked into the mostly empty refrigerator. Her head ached.

"I guess I did give you away. There just wasn't no one on the other side of the givin'."

"Listen, Momma, I like the attention I get at school, mostly from boys. I don't care if they think I'm a slut. Carl Ed's the only boy I've ever been with. I just tease the others for fun. If I act bad enough, maybe you'll notice me. If you think I'm no good like you, at least you'll be giving me a thought. But you never did."

Momma poured two cups of coffee and added milk and sugar. She found the container of cinnamon and put a pinch in each cup. It was a bit like Christmas.

"You ain't a tramp," said Momma. "Me neither. But I have to take the blame for letting you go wild. Will you go to the revival tonight and get saved?"

"Momma, that won't save neither one of us. This might be all there is for me and you."

DECISIONS

Annabel stood in the spare room, cluttered with boxes and assorted junk, and struggled for inspiration. She needed to transform the mess into a snuggly nursery. She absent-mindedly stroked her burgeoning baby bump. The monotone of CNN was white noise in the background – that is, until the key words blared clearly: *Camp Leatherneck, Helmand Province, Afghanistan; shooting; Afghan police trainees fire on Americans; two Marine instructors down, mortally wounded; walking wounded Marines rounding up the trainees; all names withheld pending family notifications.*

Annabel found herself in the living room, seated on the coffee table, fixated on the news. That's where Josh is. That's his assignment. He – and others from here – are instructors. CNN said that, *upon being handed a loaded weapon as part of the training exercise, an Afghan police trainee turned the weapon on the Marines, wounding several, killing two.*

Annabel was grateful to be on base at Twentynine Palms. All the affected spouses would be on or near the base, and they could support one another. She knew she had frightened sisters even in her apartment building. She knew that it wouldn't be Josh, but, just the same, she was immobile in front of the television for more than an hour when the knock came at the door. Thank God, it was Pamela, red-eyes brimming with tears.

"Come in here and stop that, Pammy. If you cry, I'll have to. It's too early to cry. Neither one of us is going to be a widow today."

The young women hugged, and Annabel brewed tea. The phone rang, and Annabel startled.

"They don't give bad news over the phone. They come to the door," said Pamela.

Josh's mother, who lived in Memphis, was the first to call. She tried not to sound terrified and hoped that Annabel had more information than the TV news. Unfortunately not. Spouses from around the base began calling each other, trading rumors, offering support, telling pretty lies. The CO's wife sent out a message inviting the spouses from that assignment to her home for coffee and mutual comfort. She was a good woman. Annabel and Pamela appreciated the invitation, but declined. They didn't want to be in a big group. There was no news forthcoming.

"We need to go to the commissary," announced Annabel.

"You want to buy groceries?"

"Yes. We'll need to take casseroles to a couple of homes tomorrow. We should get them ready now. It'll keep us busy."

Annabel was only twenty, but she'd been a Marine wife for two years and a good Baptist for a lifetime before that. Casseroles were always in order.

Later, when two dishes were in the oven, Pamela made sandwiches for them. The phone calls had stopped.

"I can't go home," said Pamela as darkness settled over the base. They heard taps being sounded as the base flag was lowered.

"What if ... well, what if your neighbors need to know where you are?" asked Annabel.

"I left a note on my door with your address. And really, everybody here knows everything anyway. They'll know I'm with you. Annie, the television and newspapers get these things faster than the Casualty Officers can make contact. No one's going to come looking for us yet."

"No one's looking for us, period. I feel it. Tomorrow we'll know the awful news, and we'll comfort our sisters. Breaks my achin' heart, but we'll stand tall for them," said Annabel.

The girls curled up together in Annabel's bed, but slept restlessly listening for the terrible knock at the door. They woke up earlier than they wanted and surfed all the news channels while they ate a skimpy breakfast. Annabel took her prenatal vitamins while tea brewed.

"For God's sake. Don't they know they're torturing us? You know they have the names now, and they know where the spouses are. Damn them to hell!" Pamela threw the remains of her breakfast in the trash.

"No one's going to make any announcements for a while," she continued. "They're not through tormenting us. I'm going home, clean up, and come back. Is that okay, Annie? Will you be all right? Will you be all right too, little baby?" She leaned down and whispered to the baby bump, gently stroking Annabel's belly.

"Go home, Pammy. It could well be tomorrow before we know anyway. But I sure want you back for hand-holding. Don't you suppose that the others are buddied up, too?"

"I know they are. You do worry about everyone, don't you? I'll be back soon, really soon."

Before getting in the shower, Annabel turned up the TV sound all the way so the television noise and rushing water would drown out any knock at the door. She was sure it wouldn't be her door, but she dearly wanted Pamela to return.

Smelling of peach-scented soap, Annabel dug through her snack stash. She'd not anticipated how hungry she'd stay during pregnancy, but she indulged every craving. Dried fruit sounded good right now. But she dropped the plastic bag when the knock sounded at the door. She froze, but quickly relaxed, telling herself, *Annie girl, you are such a dumbass. It's just Pamela coming back. I should really give her a key.*

So Annabel was smiling when she opened the door and saw the two Marines in dress blues. She screamed NO and tried to slam the door shut. The enlisted Marine shoved her leather pump between the door and the jamb before it closed. The corporal stepped back for the officer to lead them into the living room. Annabel backed away from them, trembling, wailing, occasionally articulating words – "No. Go away. Do not talk to me."

The two Marines gently guided her to the sofa. "Who shall I call to be with you, Mrs. Gardener?" With no response, the officer sent the corporal out of the unit. "Go knock on doors. Find out who her friends are. Get someone here."

Annabel cried so violently that the officer called for a base doctor. Pamela arrived, wept softly and held Annabel in her arms.

"I'll call her mother-in-law. I know she'll come quickly."

The officer handed Pamela an information sheet with guidelines and telephone numbers.

"When she can, we'll help with transport of the Lance Corporal to the burial location and with the other aspects of the funeral. Of course, the Corps will provide a military funeral with honors. There's assistance available for her."

"Thank you. I'll go over this when she's ready. I need to ask – where do you go next? My last name is Worthington. Am I your other stop?"

"No, ma'am. You're not on our list."

They left, and Pamela felt guilty relief. Her best friend was sinking into a nearly catatonic state of denial. She grieved for Annabel and Josh, but sent up praises that it wasn't Tony. She disliked herself for that, but maybe all Marine wives feel those conflicting emotions right now. *I'm sorry it's you. Thank God it's not me.* How hard that is.

Pamela bore the weight of sharing the news with Josh's mother who choked back a scream, but regained her composure, asking about Annabel, the baby and what Annie might need. Pamela stayed with Annabel until Paulette Gardener, Josh's mother, arrived the next day. Pamela, afraid to leave Annabel, had another friend gather up Paulette at the airport and bring her to the apartment. Pamela and Paulette exchanged information in whispered tones while Annabel existed only as a shadow. Paulette remembered Annabel's sparkly, turquoise eyes which now appeared deep indigo.

Paulette took over care for Annabel and tried to engage her in the decisions that had to be made to return Josh to Memphis for a proper, Marine funeral and burial. He deserved those honors and, no doubt, medals.

The base doctor was cautious in prescribing medication for Annabel due to the pregnancy. With the help of Pamela and on-base sisters, they packed up the young widow's possessions and sent them from California to Memphis. Once in Tennessee, Paulette made a comfortable room for Annabel. James, her husband, did his best to welcome Annabel and his forthcoming grandchild, but he buckled in his own grief. The sight of Annabel and her round, baby belly only prompted painful memories of his lost son, his only son.

There would be a time when Annabel would be grateful for all that Paulette was doing, but that time hadn't arrived.

Annabel didn't remember much of the funeral. There were flowers everywhere. Kind words were spoken. At the cemetery, someone handed her a folded flag that she pressed to her heart. There was a mournful tune from distant trumpets and a gunfire salute that was a disturbing reminder of Josh being gunned down.

There was no discussion about the permanence of Annabel's move into the Gardener's midtown home. She had no close family and was clearly in need of tending. So she stayed. Though Paulette loved her sweet daughter-in-law, she confessed only to herself that it was Josh's baby she desperately wanted in the home.

She took Annabel to the best OB/GYN in Memphis and cleared out a small junk room near Annabel's for conversion to a nursery. She tempted Annabel with splurge shopping at Babies R Us, but Annie declined. "Too soon," she would say. Paulette fretted over barely touched plates that she removed from Annabel at the end of meals. She heard Annabel pacing in her room at night.

For her part, Annabel was aware in some part of her consciousness that Paulette was extending extraordinary care and love to her. She was vaguely aware that she should be grateful. Problem was that she hadn't the energy to care. When she sat at the breakfast room table, looking out the bay window to a back yard splotched with garish floral colors, all she imagined were the piles of flowers encircling Josh's grave, and, standing on crushed funeral displays, the specters of foreign men with guns. When she could, she chose a chair facing away from the window.

Paulette ignored Annabel's ambivalence and marshaled her to obstetrician's appointments. In ordinary times, Annabel would have liked Dr. Gooding, a round, middle-aged woman who simultaneously exuded skill and sweetness.

"Oh, Annabel, I know you're still grieving, dear, but you need to start taking better care of yourself and that little one growing inside you," said the doctor. "What can I do to help you do that?"

"Yes, dear, it's not just you that you're hurting," said Paulette. "I know you want Josh's baby to be healthy, don't you?"

"The baby!" snapped Annabel. "The baby's father is a ghost, and I'm a walking dead person. Can't you tell? You two just don't understand."

There wasn't much to say after that. Paulette took Annabel home and continued to gently encourage healthy habits. Annabel continued to pace at night.

A week or so later, Annabel was in her refuge, the shower. No one bothered her there. No one tried to make her eat or sleep or buy baby stuff or take healthy walks. She liked the water as hot as possible. It was the only time she felt anything. She'd stepped away from the showerhead spray to slather herself with the expensive, aromatic soap that Paulette provided. Using her hands, she soaped her body, her belly, arms, legs and breasts with the heavenly lather. That's when she felt it. In her left breast. She pressed on it, kneaded it, felt it from all angles. Shit.

She imagined the lump as the pit of a peach. That's what it felt like. It didn't frighten her or sicken her. It only assured Annabel that she was, in fact, a dead woman.

It took another two weeks for Annabel to get around to telling Paulette about the lump. She wasn't sure why she bothered except maybe to subtly torment Paulette with the possibility of losing the baby that Paulette so desired.

"How long have you known?" Paulette asked.

"I don't know. It's probably nothing."

"I'll take care of this," said the senior Mrs. Gardener.

A few telephone calls put Paulette in touch with the University of Tennessee Women's Health Clinic. On the phone she pressed the number for the critical nature of the problem and managed an appointment for Annabel only two days later.

Paulette and Annabel were assured that the lead apron over Annie's growing belly would protect the baby from the mammogram. No such problem with the subsequent sonogram. Annabel did what she was told and expressed no interest. The doctor, a breast specialist and surgeon, reviewed the results from the radiologist and told Paulette and Annabel that, for safety, a needle biopsy of the lump should be performed – quickly. They returned the next day. Annabel gazed at the ceiling as the needle withdrew cells from the peach pit.

Of course Paulette fretted during the days they waited for results. James, as usual, was unable to comfort anyone including himself. Annabel was oblivious. The call came. The breast doctor wanted them back for a conversation. Never a good sign. Patients don't go into the office for good news.

The office visit was the next day. Paulette choked and began crying at the word *malignant*. The doctor gently put forth the conundrum. If Annabel were not pregnant, surgery, chemo and radiation would be in quick order. Those things, however, would seriously, if not fatally, harm the baby.

"You're too far along to terminate the pregnancy," she said. "That makes for very difficult choices for you to make. I know what we need to do for your health. I'm also aware that you've lost your husband and that adds significance to this tiny child. That makes this horribly difficult. I'm afraid that you must decide which way we proceed. We protect your health or the baby's. That's the bottom line. I'm very sorry."

Paulette looked at Annabel with desperation. Annabel thought it odd that the baby took that cue to be so active inside her.

"I'll have to think about it," said Annie.

"Call me. Call your OB when you decide. We shouldn't wait long to determine our course of action," said the doctor.

Annabel felt Paulette's intrusive hovering for the rest of the day. Annabel escaped to her room as quickly as possible after leaving an untouched plate at dinner.

When Annabel had paced as long as her energy allowed, she went to bed and dreamed of Josh. He wore those old jeans that bared one knee and nearly part of his butt. And that was the raggedy tee-shirt she'd tried twice to throw away before he was deployed. Both times, he'd dug it out of the trash and triumphantly laughed at her. In the dream, he was in a room with glass block walls that permitted a rosy glow from somewhere unknown. Josh sat in a rosewood rocker and held a bundle, swaddled in a pink blanket. He smiled when he saw Annabel, rose and walked to her. He kissed her cheek tenderly, whispered in her ear, and handed her the bundle – a beautiful, tiny baby girl.

When Annie sat at the breakfast table the next morning and looked at the back yard, she saw only the colorful blooms of Paulette's plentiful rose bushes and hydrangeas. She accepted an ample breakfast and helped clean up the kitchen. Paulette saw the peace that had settled over Annabel and was relieved when the girl wanted to see the OB.

The conversation proved difficult.

Annabel told the obstetrician that she wouldn't have any cancer treatment.

"We're going to take care of this baby, then we'll see," she said.

"You're twenty-six weeks now, Annabel. Forty weeks is optimum for the baby, but we can do a cesarean section at thirty-seven weeks. The baby will be fine, and that's what I recommend. I'll contact the breast surgeon. We'll take the baby a little early and then get you into care."

Annabel was transformed with her new mission. She ate. She took walks for exercise. She tried to sleep. Paulette exulted. Annabel visited Twentynine Palms in California, her home. She didn't know if she'd be able to get there again.

Pamela sat with her at the Marine base coffee shop.

"Are you really okay with this? Should I go back with you? I can absolutely do that. I miss you, lady!"

"I'm better than I've ever been," said Annabel.

At thirty-two weeks, Annabel and Paulette sat in the OB's treatment room. After checking the baby's heartbeat and anticipated weight, the doctor pushed back the paper gown. Paulette held her breath when she saw the swollen, discolored breast.

"I want to move up the C-sec to thirty-four weeks. We can handle this for the baby and then we can move you forward as quickly as possible," said the doctor.

"Too soon," said Annabel. "We'll wait for thirty-seven weeks. That's the earliest I'm comfortable with."

Paulette saw Annabel shrink in the next weeks. Her natural color faded. Her energy dissipated. Annabel tired and weakened as the days dragged on. Despite her decline, she maintained the beautiful serenity that cloaked her.

Annie and Josh's mother showed up early for the delivery date. Annabel was thin. Dark circles accented her sunken eyes. Paulette and James kissed her as she was sent off to surgery. Annabel was relaxed as the screen was set up between her shoulders and her belly. She accepted the spinal anesthetic and noted the medical personnel working around her, and then the precious sound of her baby's cry. She could only smile and peer into the newly formed fog penetrating the room. She searched for Josh's approval. He stood in the dark corner and smiled at her. He mouthed, "I love you!"

Annabel's head was clear by the time Paulette and James stood next to her bed as she held the newborn.

"She's so very beautiful," said Paulette. "Do you have a name?"

"Yes. She's Esperanza. It means hope."

TARDY

"It's time to come in."

"Not yet."

"Graciella, I've been holding supper, and Pop's been real patient, but it would be wrong to make him hold off any longer. Come have your supper, baby."

"Sun's going down. She said she'd be here, and we'd be home by dark."

"Well then, she's just running late. Come on."

"Thanks, Gram, but you go eat. I'm not hungry. I'm just gonna sit here on the steps and wait for Mom."

"Gracie, I don't often boss you, but I'm not going to allow you to keep sitting out here right now. You *will* come in for supper. That's all there is to it."

The girl pouted, but stood up to go into her grandparents' home. She deliberately let the screen door slam as she followed Gram toward supper. Pop heard them, and put down his newspaper.

"It's about time, girls. I'm so hungry that my stomach thinks my throat's been cut." He always chuckled when he used that expression. Graciella always laughed, too, but more at his enjoyment than the worn-out joke.

"Gracie, I'll serve the plates. You set the bowls on the table," said Gram.

The child obeyed, but continued glancing down the hall toward the front door.

"You lookin' for mice, girl?" Pop thought that was funny, too.

"No, sir. I thought I heard a car door."

"It's the children next door slamming in and out of their house. They go in and out all day and night. They never have learned how to close a door proper," said Gram.

"Take this last bowl to the table, Gracie, and we'll be done."

Once seated, Pop said a short blessing. Graciella stopped pouting long enough to start working on her supper – stuffed peppers, broccoli, corn pudding, rolls, and pear salad. Gram put a meal like this on the table every night without even a blink of the eye. Graciella and Mom sure didn't eat like this, but Mom worked every day and Gram's work was in the house. Gracie enjoyed staying at Gram and Pop's. Besides the good food, there was a big yard, and other kids on the block to play with. She and Mom lived in an apartment where there were few children.

"Why did Mom go off anyway without taking me?"

Pop and Gram exchanged looks. Pop was the one to answer.

"You're a little girl, Graciella. Your Mom loves being with you and doing things with you, but sometimes a grown-up wants a grown-up weekend. It's okay for her to do that. You'll understand better when you get a little older."

"When I have little girls, I won't go off anywhere without them," said Gracie.

"Maybe so," Gram replied.

"I have school tomorrow."

"Everyone knows that, baby." Gram spoke again. "Start eating your supper before it gets cold."

"I heard a car stop!" Gracie jumped up and ran to the front porch. There was no car at the curb.

"I'll get her," Pop said. Gracie was still standing on the porch staring into the onslaught of evening gloom. There was a sweet smell in the air of fallen leaves that were decaying in a most genteel manner, throwing off a cloying perfume of creeping death.

"I think she's been in a wreck. She's probably in a hospital by now or in an ambulance on the way to the hospital. What if she's in a coma, and maybe she dies? What will I do, Pop? Will they make me go to Daddy? He doesn't want me. Maybe they'll send me to the orphanage."

She began crying and snuffling. Pop pulled the handkerchief from his hip pocket and handed it to her.

"Now blow, and come sit in this chair with me. Little girl, your Mom's fine. I'm sure of it. It's not right that she's worrying you like this. It's just plain thoughtless. But she's all right."

"You're just saying that so I'll stop crying until the police come to tell us about the accident."

"No, Gracie. I'm saying it because I know her. Gram and I raised that girl, and we never could teach her to be on time. I'm thinking we should have given her a better watch. What do you think about that? A great big grandfather clock we'd strap to her wrist. What a picture that would be."

Gracie laughed a little in spite of herself.

"My beautiful supper's gonna be stone cold if you two don't stop stargazing and come inside to the table," said Gram as she joined them on the porch.

"Let's not keep her waitin'. No need to worry Gram, too. C'mon." Pop took Graciella's hand, and they walked silently back to the kitchen. Gram took plates from the warming oven, and they started supper over again. Gram and Pop looked at each other in silent conversation. They did that a lot. It was another mystery that Gracie didn't understand. They always knew what the other was thinking.

"I guess your mother takes after you in being late," Gram said to Gracie. "When she was carrying you, we thought you'd never pop out. You were a stubborn little mess. But pop you finally did, so now you'll wait on her a bit."

"It's called the birth canal. Mom explained it all to me, and I don't think I popped. It's called a birth canal when something's coming out. When something's going in ... "

"Graciella Bloomfield!" It was Pop's stern voice. "That's nothing to talk about at the supper table – and sure not in mixed company."

"But I know things, and you don't know what I know. Mom has a boyfriend. I know she does. Did you know that? That's who she's with, isn't it?"

Gram frowned. "Gracie, pay attention to your supper. I want you to take three good bites before you say another word."

The child stuffed three big forksful of supper into her mouth until her cheeks puffed out like a chipmunk. She opened her eyes wide, staring at Gram, and making a deliberate show of chewing.

"Graciella, you may think you're big, but you're sure not acting like it," said Gram. "You stop showin' out right now or you'll go to your room. I mean it."

Gracie was almost ashamed of herself, but it didn't matter. The telephone rang.

"It's the police!" Gracie dribbled food down her chin, and nearly choked as she cried out, and gasped simultaneously.

"Be still." Pop went to the phone, spoke quietly and briefly, and returned to the table. "There's going to be a deacon's meeting before prayer meetin' Wednesday night. That's all. Nothing to worry about."

Supper progressed in silence. Pop got second helpings, and that made Gram smile. Gracie nibbled on this and that, but mostly stirred around the food with her fork. When directed, she helped Gram clear the table, and dump scraps in the trash. Pop went back to the living room where he lit his pipe, and returned to the newspaper.

Gram began the dishwashing. Gracie knew her job was to dry and put away things if she could reach the proper shelves.

Dishwashing usually encouraged important conversation among women. Tonight the sounds of running water, scrubbing, and dish clatter filled the room without conversation.

"It's pitch black outside." Graciella was just barely tall enough to stare out the kitchen window above the sink. "Can't see anything but fireflies, street lights, and lamplight from people's windows."

"You're right. Clouds must be hiding the moon and stars. I know you're worried, baby, and I'm sure sorry about that. But I am certain that your mother's totally fine. She's just terribly late. Very late and inconsiderate."

"I've decided that you're right, Gram." Her grandmother smiled before Gracie continued. "She's okay for sure. She's just run away without me. It's just too hard being my Mom all by herself and working and not having any fun, and I was bad the other day. I lied. Nobody wants a liar."

"Oh mercy, sweet child!" Tears filled Gram's eyes, and she hugged Gracie close to her with soapsuds sliding off her hands. "Your mother would never, ever go off and leave you. She loves you dearly, and you couldn't possibly tell a lie that would turn any of us against you. Lying is wrong, but it can be forgiven, and I'm sure she already forgave you. Everything will be fine. I promise. There's not much here to finish up. I'll do it, and you go watch some television with Pop."

Gram took Gracie's sweet face with both her hands, and tenderly kissed her forehead. "Go now."

Gracie tiptoed into the living room. She crouched, approaching Pop, then stood up tall above his newspaper. "Boo!" He startled briefly, then laughed. Graciella could always make Pop laugh. It gave her a warm spot in her chest. Pop put down the paper.

"You doing okay, girl?"

"Maybe."

"I already checked. There's nothing on TV for little girls right now. Want to play dominoes?"

"No sir. Since I'm nine now, am I too big to sit in your lap?"

"Let me think." Pop winked at her. 'Your legs might dangle, but I don't care if you don't." He held out his arms, and Gracie curled up on his lap. Her head was just at his left shoulder, and she could hear his heart beating.

"Why do you think Mom won't come to get me?"

"She'll come, Graciella. She's just very late. She should have called us. I'm disappointed in that, and I'm sorry she's not doing better."

"Look at the clock, Pop. It's almost time I'd be getting my bath. Then, I lay out my school clothes, and get ready for bed. I don't know what to do." She snuggled into an even smaller bundle on his lap.

"Little girl, you're doing exactly what you should be doing. Gram and I will make sure everything's all right."

Gram joined them in the living room, doing that eye-contact thing with Pop. She put quiet music on the turntable, sat on the sofa, and took up her book. A turned-down page marked her place, and she remembered how the action was building. Hopefully, she could get in some pages before the action built in her own home.

Gram tried to concentrate on the book, but sad memories began their assault – nights when her daughter repeatedly broke curfew. The notice that the girl hadn't been at school in a month, and was being expelled. Gram couldn't forget the nights that her only child failed to come home at all. Then there was the positive pregnancy test. The hurried marriage, and the not unexpected divorce that followed. The responsibility of motherhood only minimally altered the ongoing bad behavior. The only blessing that came from the turmoil was the beautiful baby girl who now sat on her grandfather's lap. Gram smiled at Graciella, and returned to her book.

This time it really was a car door slamming shut. Everyone jumped up. Pop flipped on the bright porch light. Gracie pushed past him to the screen door.

Mom emerged from a shiny, fancy, black car. She was all dressed up. Gracie had never seen her mother so glamorous. But Mom tripped, and stumbled in regaining her balance. She must have thought it was funny because she giggled before righting herself. She bent over, hands on her thighs to support the boisterous laughter that came next.

"Mom's acting crazy. What's wrong with her?"

"Missus, take the girl to the kitchen, and keep her there. I'll tend to this." Pop's face was red; his jaw set firmly. Gram took hold of Graciella's shoulders, and turned her around while Gracie struggled to look out the front door.

"No, child. Turn around. I'm certain there's some brownies left for us."

"Stop! I want my Mom! What's going on?"

"Pop's going to talk to your mother. We're going to the kitchen. C'mon."

Gram managed to get the girl into the kitchen despite the tears they both shed. There was no interest in brownies, but there *were* loud voices from the front yard. Gram imagined porch lights going on at all their neighbors' houses. Wouldn't be the first time. Finally, it was quiet. Car doors slammed, and a car's engine noise faded as it drove away. Pop entered the kitchen.

"Graciella, I need you to go to your room for a bit," he said.

"No! Where's my mother? Did she leave me again?"

"Gram and I will talk to you in just a few minutes. I promise. And I promise that everything will be all right. But right now, I need a little time with Gram."

Graciella stomped down the hall, and slammed her door.

Gram sobbed in Pop's arms.

"It's my fault – all my fault. I know it is. I was a terrible mother. I did so many things wrong, and now we have this. Now, our daughter is hurting *her* daughter. And it all started with me."

Pop held her, and let her cry for a while. "You're going to be all right," he said. "We're all going to be all right. This doesn't all fall at your feet. A lot went on back then, and we both struggled to find a way to help her get on the right path. We did the best we could. For any mistakes we made, we'll make amends by ensuring that Gracie is all right."

They walked hand-in-hand to Gracie's room. Pop knocked, and they went in.

Pop spoke. "Sweetie, you're going to stay here tonight, and we'll take you to school in the morning. Then, we'll see what needs to happen next."

"Doesn't she want to take me home?" Gracie's voice was quiet.

Gram sat next to her on the bed, and put her arm around the child. Pop thought long before answering.

"Your Mom loves you, baby. She loves you with all her heart, but she's having a rough patch right now. We'll try to help her get through it, and while she's working on it, you'll be with us as long as that takes. It may be a while, but everything's going to work out. Most important – Gram and I will see to it that you're safe and comfortable here with us."

"I want to see Mom. I'm afraid."

Pop sat on the bed on her other side, making bookends of grandparent love. "You'll see her for a while in just a few days. But remember, Gram and I are going to see to it that you're never afraid again."

JUVIE HALL

Just past the reception counter were three rows of small lockers like there used to be in bus or train stations. The stacks of lockers were about six feet tall, and most had keys still stuck in their locks. Must not be many visitors today.

"And when you've finished signing the form, put your purse and jacket in a locker. You'll lock it, and take the key with you. When you're done, an aide will buzz you through the door. Any questions?"

She'd barely listened to the receptionist.

"No, no questions."

Lily looked beyond the lockers to a metal door featuring a small section of reinforced glass, the crisscross network of metal wire reminding her of a spider's web. Was it to keep someone in or out? There was a faint scent of body odor in the cramped waiting room. No one still waiting looked pleased to be there. Her belongings stashed in a locker, Lily slipped the key into her skirt pocket.

She approached the door, and followed the directions of a hand-written sign above a button worn concave by the pressings of hundreds of fingers. "Press here for entry."

She waited until a young, but tired-looking face appeared at the window to examine her. A metallic voice screeched from the intercom.

"Who are you here to see?"

"My daughter, Virginia Bodette."

A louder buzzer startled Lily. She flinched.

"Open the door now." The young attendant was impatient. "Follow me."

Lily trailed her down a white hallway that gleamed so brightly that she nearly expected celestial choirs. But that would have been unlikely here in Juvenile Hall. The attendant extracted a fistful of keys from her pocket, and unlocked a door.

"In here. I'll get her."

Lily wondered how many times a day the young woman had to repeat the same, monotonous tasks and instructions.

It was a small conference room with one outside window, no curtains, but more reinforced glass. The window in the door to the hall also included metal-webbed glass. Lily wondered if they'd gotten a deal on the bulk purchase. The walls were institutional green. The floor, brown linoleum. There were no pictures on the walls. There appeared to be nothing save the table, ashtray, and chairs that might be launched by an angry internee or visitor. Lily chose a chair in the middle of the long side of the table. She wanted to convey accessibility. It probably wouldn't make any difference, though, to her daughter.

The door opened. Her daughter walked in dressed in pink scrubs, and hair pulled back in a ponytail. With her fresh-scrubbed face, the girl looked so much younger than her sixteen years. It made Lily's heart ache.

Virginia looked at her mother indifferently, and turned to the emotionless aide. "Smoke." The aide produced a cigarette, lit it, returned the lighter to her pocket, and stepped out, closing the door behind her. She stayed at the door's window.

"They always watch us, no matter what we're doing or where we are," said Virginia. "I don't know what that idiot at the window thinks I'm going to do in here. But, you get a visitor; you get a cigarette. Makes you want more company even if you don't give a damn about them."

"You've always looked so pretty in pink," said Lily.

"It's the color that inmates wear. Helps them spot us in a crowd."

"I'm sorry, but still, you look good."

"I doubt that. Took you long enough to get here."

"They don't allow visits or phone calls for a month, and then I had to save money for the bus ticket, and get the time off work. I'm sorry."

"Sure."

"Baby, you know I hadn't heard from you in several months before you landed here, but, since you're still a minor, I finally got a phone call. It took a while for them to locate me. They said you'd been in the middle of the street, taking off your clothes, but hanging onto a bag of drugs and credit cards. They told me you were high or drunk. So, all told, they arrested you. They said multiple charges."

Virginia rose and walked to the outside window, flicking ashes on the floor.

"Yeah. And you weren't anywhere around to bail me out. Why are you really here today? Not so I can get an extra cigarette, I'm guessing."

"I'm your mother. I love you. You'd run away months before your arrest, so I knew nothing about where you were or if you were safe. At least the arrest told me you're alive and mostly well. I've been worried sick about you."

"Your boyfriend still in the house, Mom?"

"He doesn't live there, never has, and I don't see him much anyway. I'm taking a night class, so I can get a better job."

"Yeah, too busy to wonder where I was."

"That's not true. I looked and looked for you. I looked everywhere. Called all your friends. Walked the neighborhoods. Put out flyers. Nothing worked. The police didn't help. They called you a runaway."

"And I cried. You didn't have to be out there, Virginia. You know. You could have come home any time. We didn't have a fancy house, but it's our home – *your* home. I kept praying for you to come home."

"Without Daddy?"

"It wasn't your fault, Virginia. You were only twelve."

It was seven in the morning, and Mom was already out of the house. She was a school cafeteria worker for breakfast and lunch, and, in the late afternoon, she went to her second job as a kitchen helper in a nursing home. Virginia was to get herself up, eat some cereal, dress, and go to school. Daddy also got up in that time frame, and readied himself for work at the construction site. Family schedules didn't always mesh, but that's the way it had to be.

Young Virginia was washing her breakfast dishes when Daddy entered the kitchen. He walked slowly, and his countenance was as gray as summer storm clouds.

"Daddy, what's wrong? You look awful. You should go back to bed. Stay home today. I can skip school, and stay home with you. How 'bout that?"

"I'd never lose a day's pay, and neither would your mother. You skipping school is the same thing as skipping work. School's your job right now, little girl. I'm fine. Just a little tired. Gotta go. Can't be late."

Virginia protested, but lost. She thought: *Grown-ups rarely listen to kids*. Daddy's sickly looking appearance stayed with her all day. Geography and sentence diagrams made no impact. She ran home after school faster than ever. Daddy wasn't there. Mom would be at her second job. Virginia was alone, and afraid. She sat on the front stoop, and waited for someone to show up. Eventually, an unfamiliar car parked in front of their bungalow, and a man in work clothes approached. He called her by name.

"Virginia Bodette? Is your mother here?"

"She's at work. Who are *you*, and why do you want her?"

"I'm from your dad's job. He's had an accident. He's at Mercy Hospital."

Virginia flew to her feet. "Oh my God! What happened? Is he bad hurt? We have to go! I have to get Mama. Yes, we have to get Mama and go to Daddy. Hurry!" Her words tripped over each other.

The stranger motioned to the car. "I'll take you."

They drove to the nursing home where Virginia jumped out of the car almost before it stopped and raced inside, unseeing except for the route to the kitchen where she crashed into her mother's arms.

"He's dying; Daddy's dying. I know he's dying. We have to go. Fast!"

"What on earth are you talking about? Slow down," said Lilly.

"Daddy! He had an accident. The man told me. He's from Daddy's work. C'mon." Virginia pulled on her mother's arm. "He'll take us to the hospital."

They reached the emergency room, and were told that someone would be with them soon. A nurse finally summoned Lily and Virginia to an empty treatment room. After another interminable wait, a doctor joined them. Lily's feeling of foreboding proved tragically true.

"I'm sorry."

The doctor said more, but neither woman caught much of it. They cried too hard and loud. The only thing they knew was that he was dead. He'd been working on an upper floor of the building's frame. Appeared to faint. Fell eleven stories down. Died on impact. The doctor offered condolences.

"Daddy was sick when he got up. I should have made him stay home. I *could* have made him stay. I know I could have. But I didn't, and then he died. I did it. I killed him."

"Baby, you didn't. You were a kid, and he was a grown man," said Lily. "He was set on going to work, and that's what he did. He didn't know how sick he was. Please don't blame yourself."

Virginia knocked on the hall door, and shouted to the waiting attendant. "Smoke!"

The woman answered just as loudly. "Only one."

Virginia banged her fists against the interfering door, and kicked it until the attendant pushed the door open, and Virginia away from it.

"Sit down and behave, or your visit is over. This is no fun for me either. Sit down now!"

Virginia sat. The attendant left.

The first chair Virginia pulled away from the table was yanked so angrily that it crashed to the floor. Virginia ignored it, and sat in a different chair.

Lily said, "Are you all right now?"

"Do I look all right? Am I having fun in here?"

"It will only be a few more months, right?" asked Lily.

"I guess." Virginia settled down. "You know, I wasn't running up charges on the credit cards I had. That would have cost me more time in here. I was just going to sell them. I needed money. But I got high and crazy, and got busted."

"Since you're a juvenile, they have school, and groups in here, don't they?"

"Oh yeah. They're *rehabilitating* us. I actually don't mind the school work, but they try to mess with our heads in group."

"Like how?"

"They say it's Daddy's fault, not mine that I messed up."

"Well, I don't think that's what they mean. Daddy had an accident and died. He's not at fault for dying, but his death is when you began changing."

"They say his dying made me start acting out. I did what I did. It's not Daddy's fault."

Lily looked at her watch.

"You ready to leave? Too much time with me? Too hard talking?"

"Virginia, I'm not the enemy," said Lily, finally exasperated. "I think the only enemy you have is yourself. Stop blaming yourself."

"You're full of crap." Virginia got up, and kicked the chair she'd turned over. The attendant banged on the door, and shook her head when Virginia turned to look. The girl walked to look out the exterior window.

"I'm just freakin' mad. I'm mad at being here. I'm mad at smartass people trying to change me. I'm mad for acting stupid for so long. I'm mad at you for not being here with me, and for having a boyfriend."

Lily knew her daughter was crying despite Virginia's turned back. She went to her. Quietly, she asked, "May I hold you?"

Virginia turned quickly into her mother's arms, and cried like she did at Daddy's funeral.

"Everything's wrong, Mom," the girl sobbed.

"I can't say I know how it felt being out there so long on your own, or being locked up in here," said Lily. "But all I really know is how bad you're hurting right now, and I wish more than anything that I could make it go away."

Virginia took a step back, and wiped her face.

"Am I just bad? Have I been just awful forever?"

"No, darlin'. Of course not. You're not bad. I'm not one of those people who know that kind of thing, but I think you've just stuffed down all your feelings about your Daddy dying, and the girl who was left without recognizing those hurts just set about hurting herself. *You're* the one who's been hurt the most since you ran away. You've been punishing yourself."

Virginia went back to the table and sat.

"So why do you have a boyfriend? Don't you miss Daddy? Don't you love Daddy anymore?"

"My sweet girl, I miss your Daddy every day. Roy is a good man. I enjoy spending time with him – but not so much time. I'm working hard to make a better life for you and me. Roy understands that. Your Daddy would want me to have a good friend in my life."

"I don't like it."

"I understand that, but he's still a good friend."

The door opened, and the attendant cleared her throat. "You need to wrap up now."

"Will you come back?" Virginia asked her mom.

"Yes, I will, darlin'. Thank you for wanting me back. I know you can have phone privileges. Call me collect. When you get out, will you come home?"

"I've done things."

"I know. That's in the past. I very much want you home."

"I'm thinking about it. I'm thinking real hard."

NEARLY DEPARTED

Living on the edge of town was the best thing in Tildie's young life. Their home was a respectable three acres, a measurement she couldn't picture, but it felt like the whole wide world. There were large, mowed front and back lawns, nearby trees to climb, a pond to jump in, and, surrounding it all, the mysterious woods with a twist of a lightly flowing stream. The best part was that Tildie was free to wander and explore as long as she could still hear her name called. Sometimes she simply lay sprawled out on the warm grass, absorbing the heat of the Mississippi sun and the smell of earth beneath her.

The house was roomy with many windows to tempt scented breezes. Mom and Dad didn't yell at each other so much since the move, but sometimes she could still hear angry voices in the night. How did kids live in town with nowhere to play or hide from parental discord? She'd lived in town and only remembered feeling confined. Or whatever similar word fit an eight-year-old's vocabulary.

School had been out for three weeks, and cousin Brucie had been there a week. His family lived, not in town, but in the big city, and he'd been sent to stay for most of the summer. He was only seven, but an acceptable playmate, though sometimes whiney. He generally did what she told him, though, and that counted for a lot. Some people thought Tildie was bossy, but clearly someone had to be in charge.

The cousins spent the morning building a makeshift house in the back yard, using fallen tree limbs and patio furniture. At lunch, Mom filled a tea glass with ice and strong-smelling brown liquid for herself and gave the children grilled cheese sandwiches and pickles. She put cookies for each in paper napkins and said she needed to lie down to vanquish her headache. It was the cue for the children to take off to explore the woods when no one would be calling for them.

At first, they tiptoed quietly, holding hands, looking around for wild animals that might devour them. Maybe there would be bears or lions. Surely snakes. When they relaxed, they began running, hiding from each other behind trees, jumping out and yelling when one scared the other. Brucie was such a sissy. Then, Tildie got serious.

"You know, don't you, that Indians lived around here a long time ago. I bet we could find Indian bones or skulls or at least some arrowheads if we look for them. Walk carefully, Brucie. Look down. Don't squash what might be history. You're probably too young to get the point. Just watch out."

"No, I'm not too young. You think you're so smart, but I know stuff, too." Brucie looked at his feet and crept farther into the trees.

They moved quietly and watched the ground for ten minutes before Brucie spotted it.

"Look! It's a baby bird. It fell from its nest."

"Where? Show me. Oh no. Look at its little self."

Tildie saw the shattered egg nearly invisible in the weeds and tall grass. In the midst of the clutter was a bird-like creature. It was fully formed with legs, stubby wings, head, beak, and what would become eyes. But it was not mature, not birth-ready. There were no feathers. The transparent eyelids were never going to open. The skin was translucent. It was still an embryo, but what do children know of an embryo?

"It looks sick," said Brucie.

"I know. It needs bottle-feeding. All babies taken from their mothers need bottle-feeding. We can do that. I'll watch it. Run to the back porch and get that old box of Mom's crap. Dump out the crap and bring the box back here. Hurry."

"You said crap. Two times."

"Crap, crap, crap! Grow up, Brucie! Go get the box."

Brucie ran, then slipped up on the spacious back porch so his aunt wouldn't hear him. He heard her upstairs, singing and laughing at things he didn't understand. He found the box, dumped out some junk, and started running back to the injured bird.

Tildie scooped up the bird thing with a large magnolia leaf. She gently rested her charge in the box that Brucie proffered, then marched solemnly back to the big house. Tildie looked for her mother and, finding her upstairs in bed, shook her and called her attention to what might have become a bird some day.

"Jesus Christ, child! Why are you bringing that abomination to me?" Mom struggled to sit upright. She looked bleary.

"It's a baby bird, Mom, and it's sick. What do I do to take care of it?"

Mom stood up and swayed. "I'm going to the kitchen."

In Tildie's experience, that wasn't a good idea, but she and the birdie followed. The girl hoped she wouldn't need to grab for Mom if she stumbled on the stairs. Sometimes Tildie worried whether she was big enough to stop Mom from toppling down the stairs. Sometimes she wondered if toppling might be the best thing. Then she was ashamed.

In the kitchen, Mom refilled her ice tea glass.

"Please tell me what to do with the baby."

Mom took another sip and glanced at the thing in the box.

"There's nothing to do. It's just barely alive. It won't live. Throw it in the trash. Dump it somewhere that I can't see. It can't live, Tildie." She took another sip and scrunched her face. "Get it out of here. I can't look at that non-dead, non-alive thing. It gives me the heebie-jeebies." Mom staggered as she headed upstairs.

Tildie studied the thing in the box and slowly made her way back to Brucie.

"Mom says it won't live. That it can't live and that we should dump it in the trash."

"In the trash? That's where you put garbage. We can't just throw it away. It's alive." Brucie took the box from Tildie who sat on the grass and looked pained. She thoughtfully scratched a mosquito bite on her sweaty leg.

"See. It's breathing. Look, Tildie. I can tell. What would it do in the trash?" Brucie hugged the box to his thin chest.

"Okay," Tildie sighed. "Awful. It would be the worst kind of slow, awful dying in there with supper scraps and used Kleenex and what Mom calls woman stuff that she throws away. It would be the worst thing ever for the little birdie. So we have to put it out of its misery. If it can't live, we should end it fast. Don't you think it's hurting right now?"

"You mean kill it? You want us to kill it?"

"Mom says there's no way it can live. How long would it take the birdie to die by itself? Wouldn't that be awful? Do we let it suffer or do we help it go?"

"I don't understand."

"Rusty, he was my dog. Him and Mom and Daddy were the first things I knew. I remember when I was little and new to walking. Most kids don't remember that far back, but I do. I remember because Rusty was always there like he was going to catch me if I fell. Of course he couldn't. He was just a dog. But I loved him. He slept next to my bed. He was always there. I don't know how old he was, but he was lots older than me."

Tildie looked around at the trees and snuffled back some nose drippings.

"When I started kindergarten, he got really slow. He tried to be at the door when I got home, but he couldn't always get there. When I was going back to school after Christmas holiday, Mom and Daddy told me how sick

Rusty was and that he hurt all over and that it wouldn't be kind to let him keep on hurting. They said the dog doctor could help Rusty go to sleep and go to doggy heaven where he'd feel good again and run and chase rabbits – but probably never catch one. Daddy took Rusty away. Me and Mom stayed home and cried. I cried for a long time, but Mom told me that Rusty would thank us. She said that the doctor would put Rusty out of his misery. Those were the words she used." Tildie wiped her nose on her arm. "I guess that's sort of what we need to do for this itty baby."

"I'm sorry about your dog. What do we do for the bird?"

"I don't know. Let me think."

Tildie studied everything around her except the nearly-bird. Brucie, on the other hand, continued holding the box to his chest and making cooing sounds to the pathetic creature.

"The stream. I guess that's it," said Tildie. "We can drown it fast."

"Tildie! *Would* it be fast? Don't make the baby scared."

"It won't be scared. I don't know if it *can* be scared, and it will be over fast. I'm not going to smash it with something hard. I couldn't do that. Gimme the box."

Brucie reluctantly handed it over and followed Tildie to the wisp of a stream that barely moved since there hadn't been much rain that summer. They got down on their knees next to the water. Tildie lifted the magnolia leaf that still held the barely formed birdling. Brucie started whining quietly.

"Shut up, Brucie. We have to do this to make it easy."

She ignored that Brucie was probably crying. He was such a child. Tildie held the leaf just above the water for what seemed like an hour. She finally lowered the magnolia leaf until it rested on the water's surface like a little boat carrying the embryo, and then she tilted the leaf. The bird baby slipped into the water. Both children held their breath. And then the birdie popped up to the surface. Brucie screamed, scrambled to his feet, and ran ten feet away. Tildie choked, thinking she might upchuck, but used the magnolia leaf again to scoop the featherless baby from the water.

"Is it still alive?" moaned Brucie.

"I don't know, crybaby. I don't know. Let's look and do something before ... oh, you know. Oh crap, crap. It's still breathing." Tildie put down the bird and leaf, and walked away, snuffling and kicking a rock.

"Are you just gonna let it hurt? Do something, Tildie!"

"All right! Shut up. If you don't like this, you should do it yourself or go home. I'm doing the best I can. This thing is gonna be put out of its misery one way or another."

"You said you'd help it. Not make it drag on. Come on, Tildie. Fix this."

"Crap! I think I hate you, and I know I hate what I have to do. Crap!"

"You're gonna get in trouble for cussing," said Brucie.

"Oh, shut up. I'll drown you in the stream if you don't shut up. Then I'll get in trouble for more than cussing. How much can you ask me to do?"

Tildie knelt again next to the stream. She felt pebbles sticking into her bare knees. She studied the bird thing and the nearly still water.

"We'll weigh it down. That should do it."

She looked around until she spotted a large rock, one bigger than the bird.

"Okay," said Tildie. "You're gonna dump the bird into the water, and I'll push the rock on top of it."

"I can't!"

"Yes, you can. You have to. I can't do all this by my own self, and you have to stop being a baby. Right now."

Brucie sniveled and began crying again. He took the magnolia leaf and looked to Tildie who held the big rock. She nodded. He tipped the leaf. The baby bird slipped into the water. Tildie shoved the rock into the stream with a slap and onto the bird, but the bird slipped out again. Brucie ran, but

Tildie managed to get the rock firmly on top of it for sure this time before she crawled away and threw up. She spit four or six times to get the taste of vomit out of her mouth. She finally looked at the stream and the rock, and saw no evidence of the birdling. As she left the murderous stream, she heard Brucie keening, then saw him hiding behind a tree as if the baby bird might come after him.

The next noise she heard began so quietly that she thought it was her imagination. But the siren grew louder and closer. She thought how odd it was to hear a siren way out here on the town's edge. Then, she was quickly aware that it must have stopped at her house.

"Run, Brucie. Something's wrong at home!"

They ran as fast as they could, but when they crossed Tildie's back yard, the ambulance was pulling onto the road toward town. Auntie Lou, who lived with her family in the sharecropper's house, was in the side yard looking like she'd been crying. Tildie ran to her.

"What's happening? Where's Mom? Where's my mother?"

"Come here, babies. I came to bring squash from my garden to the Missus and found her flat out at the bottom of the stairs. I called for the help, and they was going to call your Daddy. I'm to stay here with you'uns."

Tildie could barely breathe.

"Mom fell on the stairs? Is she bad hurt? What do we do?" Tildie didn't know she was crying.

"We jes stay here till we be told diff'rent. I fear your Mama's plenty hurt. Come inside."

Tildie didn't know what to feel. All she could think of was rocks, lots of really big rocks.

THE ENVELOPE

The envelope, stuck in between letters, bills, and ads remained invisible until Lorene returned to the house, and stood at the entry hall table to sort the fistful of mail. She stopped looking when she reached that envelope. She thought her heart might have stopped beating for a moment. She'd been expecting it for years, but it was still a shock. She'd always believed that maybe it wouldn't come after all. Lorene put the other mail on the table, and carefully examined the envelope. She ran her fingers across the typed address: "Mrs. Lorene Witherspoon." She pressed her fingers against the logo in the return address section, and slid them down to the lower left corner: "Personal and Confidential." She turned the envelope from front to back, and back again. She squeezed it between her fingers and thumb, estimating the number of pages inside. Probably just one. She smelled the good stationery scent of the envelope, then put it in the table's drawer. She gathered the rest of the mail, and took the stack to her small desk in the kitchen.

Thanksgiving is next week. Brady will come home from Vanderbilt on Wednesday evening, and he's bringing home a fraternity brother. Lorene's mother-in-law would also be there in addition to the three of them still living in the house: Husband Clarence, high school daughter, Polly, and herself. Lorene would give the housekeeper the day off on Thanksgiving, so there would be much to do in advance to ensure a perfect holiday. She didn't like slip-ups.

Lorene heard the heavy front door slam shut. They lived in the big, old Witherspoon home on historical Belvedere in mid-town. Lorene loved the big house, but always pretended to take its elegance for granted as if she'd always lived in such wealth, which she certainly hadn't. The imposing residence became home to the senior Mrs. Witherspoon when she moved in as a young bride, and took on household responsibilities. After the death of her husband, and marriage of her son, she continued to live in the house with Clarence's family for as long as they could reasonably maintain her declining health. That's when she was moved to the most luxurious nursing home in Memphis. She was brought to the house frequently for family activities. Lorene saw it as a loving duty to the aging doyenne.

Clarence approved, and appreciated Lorene's goals and activities. She was beautiful, charming, educated, reasonably well-bred, and completely supportive of his professional ambitions. She was an excellent wife and mother. As a hostess, she produced seamlessly perfect events while glowing and glittering, apparently unencumbered by managerial details. He was awed by her on a daily basis. His professional associates and clients also regarded her as an asset to Clarence's career.

As the door thunked heavily, Polly called out. "Where are you? I'm home, but I'm leaving."

"Kitchen desk. Come on back."

The girl bounded into the room. "Mommy!" Polly giggled, and hugged her more reserved mother while standing behind her. Polly was Lorene's most exuberant child. Always had been. She had never given her parents any trouble.

"Oh look," Polly laughed. "You're making your lists for Thanksgiving. You'll need a table of contents like a book before you're through. Mom, I'm going to change out of my school uniform, and meet Eunice at the library. We might hang out on the lawn. That's okay if I'm home by dinner, right?

Then, I can tell the nuns that I went to the library after school. They'll be so impressed."

"Sure. You can go, but check your watch. I want you home by 5:30. Scoot."

Lorene and Clarence had a good marriage, good children, and a comfortable lifestyle. She was grateful for a charmed life, at least for now.

Thanksgiving was a combination of elegance and homeyness – neither of which was accidental.

In mid-December, Lorene passed the entry hall table with an armful of Christmas decorations. Most of the first floor of the house was already filled with the perfume of the towering fir tree currently residing in the formal living room. The scent reminded her of her youth. Lorene stood, looking at the table's drawer. Shifting the bundles in her arms, she pulled open the drawer, and looked at the envelope. Still there. Still waiting. Lorene slipped the drawer back into its casing and continued decorating.

She was excited about the upcoming Christmas holidays. The senior Mrs. Witherspoon would be with them for four days, so Lorene arranged for a caregiver from the nursing home to stay with them as well. This time, Brady would be bringing home a girl. Lorene prayed they weren't serious. Hoped they wouldn't press her to stay in the same room. He was just too young. Young people don't always make good decisions. Her widowed, older sister agreed to spend Christmas week with them, so she wouldn't be alone. In addition to those staying at the house, Clarence was still deciding whether to invite any of the bachelors at his bank to come for Christmas Day, as was frequently his custom. It was good for the young men, and it built camaraderie.

Lorene's first Christmas in the imposing house was six months after her marriage to Clarence. There were seven houseguests that year, and five more invited for Christmas Day. Mother Witherspoon was still in complete control of the house at that time. Some women in her position might make it difficult for the young bride, but Mrs. W could see the future in Lorene's hazel eyes. Lorene was devoted to Clarence, and would one day become the lady of the house, so Mrs. Witherspoon took the girl under her wing, lovingly teaching her the necessary skills and demeanor. Clarence was proud of both women, and delighted at the bond that grew between them.

First Brady, then Polly was born. The three-generations slipped into their appointed roles. Conflict rarely intruded. It was almost a storybook household without a Rumpelstiltskin to threaten disaster.

As they sat for this Christmas dinner, Clarence toasted his wife for bringing them all together, and creating their perfect home and holiday. The gathered friends and family applauded, and Lorene blushed.

New Year's would be relaxing for Lorene because the Witherspoons weren't hosting any activities. The kids had parties to attend, and Lorene and Clarence would go to the country club. New Year's Day would be just for football, lasagna, and the family.

Three days before New Year's Eve, there was a dust-up between Lorene and Polly.

"All my friends are wearing dresses like this!"

"I've told you before. I'm not *their* mother. I'm yours, and that dress just isn't appropriate for a girl your age. You can't wear it."

The slamming of Polly's bedroom door temporarily terminated the conversation. Polly pleaded her case to Clarence when he got home, but to no avail. Naturally, he backed Lorene. Yes, there would be plenty of time for dresses like that.

The holiday hubbub was over by January 2 when Polly and Brady were back in their respective schools, and Clarence was once again overworking. Lorene took the envelope from the drawer, went upstairs to her bedroom, and locked the door. She sat on the chaise for five minutes before she could cautiously slit open the waiting envelope. It was from the Department of Human Services.

Dear Mrs. Witherspoon,

Our office would like to speak with you regarding an event that took place December 19, 1964. Please call our representative, Mrs. Janice Moore, at the number listed below. We would enjoy speaking with you at your earliest convenience."

Lorene's breath grew ragged as she re-read the letter three times. She stared at herself in the vanity mirror, and imagined all of the family standing behind her scowling, and pointing fingers at her. Temporarily composed, Lorene returned the letter to the entry table drawer downstairs. She'd get around to the phone call. She knew she needed to.

It was nearly Valentine's Day when Lorene, once again locked in her bedroom, dialed the DHS number for Mrs. Janice Moore.

"Mrs. Witherspoon, I'm glad to hear from you. I was concerned that you might not call, but I understand that the letter was a surprise – I hope not a bad one."

"I've wondered when this call might come," said Lorene. "You must understand, though, that neither my husband nor my children know anything about this."

"I do understand. It's not unusual. Depending on how you plan to move forward, however, you'll need to think about how you'll tell them. With respect for your privacy, we compose the letter you received in most vague terms. But here we are now, and I'm sure you've surmised that the daughter you put up for adoption has asked our agency to contact you with a goal of reunification. I presume you've been thinking about that subsequent to receiving our letter."

Desperation was what Lorene felt most of all. She'd hoped never to be in this position, but knew it was a responsibility she couldn't escape. "Yes, I think we should meet. How does that work? Who calls who? I would prefer to meet her at a restaurant – neutral territory, you know. Does she live here in Memphis?"

A daughter, she was thinking. I had a little girl.

"One thing at a time," Mrs. Moore said. "She's not in Memphis, but she goes to school in the vicinity. I'll let her tell you where. I'm sure she could come to town on a Saturday or Sunday."

"That would be difficult since I don't know yet when or what I'll tell my family. Isn't there a weekday when she doesn't have class that she could come?"

"Mrs. Witherspoon, considering the effort she put forth to find you, and then the delay since we sent you the letter, you might consider accommodating *her* schedule."

That hurt, but it was justified. "Okay. You're right. I'm sorry. I could concoct a reason to be away from the house alone for a Saturday lunch. I'll identify a discreet restaurant in east Memphis, and give you the name and address later. In the meantime, I suppose you'll let her know that I want to see her, and let her choose a date."

"I'll certainly talk with her, and ask for a convenient date. I would urge you, Mrs. Witherspoon, to think carefully before creating more secrecy. It could be more disruptive down the road than clearing the air now."

"I appreciate your input. I'll think about it. What's her name? What's my daughter's name?"

"It's Theedy Tomlinson."

"Theedy." The name rolled sweetly off her lips. "All right, Mrs. Moore, so thank you. The next step will be for you to call me back after you speak with her, with Theedy, right?"

"That's what we'll do."

"Mrs. Moore, I'm sure you'll not speak to anyone other than me here at the house – or not leave suspicious messages."

"Of course not, Mrs. Witherspoon. I'm very discreet."

"Mid-day is probably the best time to call. No one will be here. Yes, mid-day." Lorene nervously listened to the approaching sound of her world falling apart.

"I'll call mid-day, Mrs. Witherspoon. I assure you that I've done this work for thirteen years, and I'm cautious in the way I proceed."

"I don't mean to question your professionalism. I apologize. I look forward to your call." That was almost true.

Again returning the letter to the drawer and, noting the whereabouts of the housekeeper, Lorene went to their bar, and poured a large shot of whiskey. She'd frequently wondered over the years about the baby. Nobody even told her back then whether it was a girl or boy. That was policy for unwed mothers at the time. She'd had both regrets and curiosity, but, along with her parents and older sister, they survived, and she moved on to build a good, proper life. Now she wondered if this good life would survive. She poured a second shot.

It took a week for Mrs. Moore to call. Although Lorene shuddered each time the phone rang when everyone was at home, she also felt a growing anticipation at the prospect of meeting this girl – Theedy. Clarence noticed that Lorene's usual serenity was tattered around the edges. She'd had many social obligations and activities to coordinate, and, with typical concern for her well-being, he suggested that she might want a vacation. Dear Clarence was always sensitive to her needs. She brushed off his concern, blaming her anxiety only on lady problems. And she waited for the call.

On a Tuesday just after lunch, Mrs. Moore called. Lorene took the telephone call in her bedroom, and closed the door.

"Theedy is pleased that you're willing to meet her, and to accommodate her schedule," said Mrs. Moore. "She agreed to the place and time you suggested. These meetings can be very stressful for both parties. It will feel awkward. As the adult, you'll be the one to put her at ease. Doing that will help put yourself in a more comfortable place."

"I understand. I agree." With the arrangements made, Lorene just wanted off the phone.

"Mrs. Witherspoon, you've probably already thought of it, but Theedy will probably ask you difficult questions. You might want to start thinking about your answers. It's better to plan this kind of thing in advance, but I'm sure a woman of your position is more than aware of that."

"My position?"

"In the name of full disclosure, surely you know that your family name is well-known in this city. I've seen your names and photographs in the newspaper for years. I'm only telling you this so that we aren't hiding anything. I would never, ever breach my professional code of ethics, or divulge sensitive information about a client."

"I understand," Lorene said frostily. "After our meeting Saturday, do either of us owe you a report?"

"No ma'am. It's entirely up to the two of you now. I wish you both well, and I hope I didn't upset you with my knowledge of your family."

"Everything's fine. Good-bye." But, of course, it wasn't fine. Now there was an additional threat. Somewhere near the back of their property, Lorene heard creeping disaster. Armageddon was surely coming, and it was all her fault.

Friday night at the dinner table, Lorene casually mentioned that she planned some shopping the next day.

"Oh, Mom, take me. The spring lines are in stores, and I'm *dying* for new clothes!"

Clarence quickly stepped in. "With some birthdays on the horizon, your mother might want solo shopping time. Can you dig it?" He winked at Polly.

"Oh, Daddy, nobody says that!" She winked back. "Well, all right, Mom, but you better come home with something for me."

Lorene tried to appear nonchalant on Saturday morning, but she spent an inordinate amount of time in her closet. A suit? Dress? Slacks? Perhaps jeans, sweater, and vest to look low-key, cool, and yet fashionable. What would Theedy wear? What outfit would make Theedy comfortable, and would convey, "I'm an adult, but not a fuddy-duddy." She settled on gray wool slacks, a white sweater – not the cashmere – and a gray and black vest with brass beading. She wore low-heeled shoes, and a black leather jacket. Temperatures were still crisp in late February.

Lorene arrived thirty minutes early at the small restaurant. She chose a table where she could watch the door. She'd had two cups of coffee when Theedy entered. Lorene recognized her immediately, and stood, smiling. Of course, Theedy would look like that. Just exactly like that. The exquisite cheekbones, the deep pools of knowledge behind the dark eyes. Lorene didn't think she remembered what the father looked like, but immediately saw his image in his daughter's face. Theedy walked directly to Lorene. There was the awkward moment when they must decide to hug or not. They did not.

"I looked up old photos of you and your husband in the society sections of *The Commercial Appeal* archives. You're as beautiful as the photographs depict you," said Theedy.

She wasn't gushing, simply reporting. Her dark hair was pulled back to a ponytail at the nape of her neck, and draped to the mid-point of her back. She wore a white linen, button-down collar shirt and a navy wool pantsuit. She didn't look at all nervous. She was elegantly beautiful and composed. Lorene wondered how she'd made such an amazing young woman. Lorene felt intimidated, agitated.

"Mrs. Witherspoon ... "

"Could you call me Lorene?"

"I can do that. You look tense, so I'll start. Did you give me away because my father's black?"

Lorene was momentarily speechless.

"No ... and maybe. I was so young. It was hard back then. You may not understand. May I just tell you what happened? I know you might never forgive me. I might not forgive myself. And I don't know that my thinking of you so much over the years could make any difference to you now."

"Actually not, but go ahead. I'm here to find out how I came to be."

Lorene wanted to cry. She hadn't talked about this to anyone in twenty-six years. She was suddenly ashamed of her perfect life that had never included this girl.

"Of course you have a right to know. I'll tell you the whole story, and pray that you can understand."

Theedy, impassive and much like an Egyptian sculpture, sat and waited.

"I was just barely eighteen. It was spring break of my senior year at Miss Hutchinson's. A dozen of us girls went down to Pensacola. I don't know why our parents didn't insist on a chaperone. We were only high school kids; I would insist on that for *my* daughter – my younger daughter. We piled into two cheap motel rooms at the beach. It was exciting. There were kids everywhere – high school seniors, college students, maybe some other kids who just wanted to be there. You couldn't take two steps without falling into a party. There were sunbathers, swimmers, surfers, and just partygoers. I took three bikinis and little else. It was total freedom, and a bit of chaos.

"I met your father the second day we were there. He was a college student down from Amherst with a bunch of his friends – white and black. He might have been the most handsome man I'd ever seen. The civil rights movement was making positive changes, but it was harder in the South. I honestly didn't know many black people, so there was initial awkwardness between Jerry and me – at least on my part. He was completely comfortable with himself and of our being together. He gave me confidence. He was so smart and funny and cultured. We talked about everything, and he always had insights that were new to me. I felt inferior to him, and yet drawn into and accepted into his sphere. If I didn't love him, I at least was entranced with everything that he was and might possibly become. He was my first lover, and I was grateful that he was the one.

"As those things go, we made romantic promises to each other at the end of the week. The intensity and freedom had been divine, but it was time to return to the real world. We exchanged telephone numbers and addresses. I received one sweet, but distant letter from him. There's no fault to be assigned, Theedy. Our lives were just going in such different directions. I was glad to have known him. High school graduation, and the realization of my pregnancy occurred about the same time. I was relieved to get through the graduation ceremony without throwing up. I couldn't imagine telling him about the baby I was expecting. There was no love, no relationship. It was my ... issue to deal with."

"You mean *burden*, don't you, Lorene?"

She was so cold. Lorene couldn't think of any way to get through to her. Maybe she shouldn't. Maybe she deserved Theedy's scorn.

"Let's be honest. It was not a *burden*, but it was a problem. I was single and eighteen with many expectations from my family and circle of friends. It would have shamed my family greatly back then for me to openly produce a child out of wedlock."

"Particularly if I was half black."

Lorene's back stiffened. "Yes, Theedy. Particularly if you were racially mixed. I'm not talking about my feelings or my love for the baby I carried, but for the social constructs of the time. I felt strongly obligated to protect my family as well as you."

They paused and looked up.

"Hi, my name is Annie, and I'll be your server today. What can I get you girls?"

Lorene gestured to Theedy.

"I'll have sweet tea, and can we get chips and salsa?"

"Yes ma'am, you surely can. And you?"

"I'll just have a coffee refill, please. Maybe some more cream."

Theedy lit a cigarette, exhaled and looked at her mother without expression. "So, you find out you're pregnant. What next?"

Lorene continued. "I had to confess most of the story to my parents, and beg their forgiveness ... "

Theedy interrupted. "You said *most* of the story. You didn't tell them the father was black, did you?"

"No, I didn't. It would have been pointless. There was already anger and a lot of tears – theirs and mine. Your father's race wasn't relevant to determining what to do. The final decision was that my older sister and I would go visit our aunt in Vicksburg for a while. With both of us gone, there would be no suspicions. Jeannie, my sister, went back to MSCW in the fall. Auntie took me to an attorney, and arrangements were made that, upon delivery, DHS would take custody of you, and find an adoptive family. You were born that December. I went into labor while Auntie and I were trimming the tree. You were born the next morning. They took you away immediately without letting me see you. They didn't even tell me if the baby was a boy or girl.

"I entered Sophie Newcomb in New Orleans in what should have been my second semester. No one at home ever suspected the truth about my absence. I knew that you'd go to a wonderful family who could give you so much more than I ever could alone. That was my comfort."

"Did you tell my father?"

Annie provided the tea, coffee, chips and salsa. Lorene waited until her daughter munched on some chips, and took a sip of her tea. She needed a moment to think.

"I'm afraid I did not tell him. I'm embarrassed, but, by the time you were born, I didn't know how to contact him, and, as I said, we had no ongoing relationship. Spring break had been all there was. I couldn't imagine telling him. So I gave you up. If it matters, I sobbed for days. In my heart, I've acknowledged your birthday every year. And each year as I start decorating the tree, I remember the Christmas I went into labor with you. I was really scared on that day."

"Actually, Lorene, it doesn't matter much. So, you don't know who or where my father is? Maybe his name."

"No, baby. I don't. His name was Chasen, but two letters were exchanged, then nothing."

"His last name?"

"I'm sorry. I don't remember."

"When I found out you were the one who was white, I hoped I'd find out who my father was. I guess I'm not surprised that you don't know, him, being black and all. Here's what I want you to know, Lorene. I was adopted by a wonderful couple, Lois and Henry. They were white, but they already had a bi-racial child, a boy, and after me, they adopted another mixed-race girl. It was an amazing family. Lois and Henry were committed to making us all feel welcome, valued, and loved. They knew we'd face obstacles, and they prepared us for them. They helped us gain self-confidence and self-love. I owe everything to them.

"You should also know that I graduated high school magna cum laude. I worked for a while as a paralegal, and now I'm nearly through with law school at Ole Miss. I know I should give some credit to the genes you and my father contributed, but mostly I credit Mom and Dad. I've already accepted a good position with a firm in Atlanta. I'll be moving over there right after graduation, and I'll sit for the bar in Georgia."

"I think you're incredible, and I'm so proud," said Lorene.

For the first time, Theedy's face softened. She reached her delicate hand across the table, and rested it on Lorene's arm.

"Don't worry, Lorene. I don't expect to be invited to Easter dinner." She smiled. "I don't intend to complicate your life. Your family doesn't need to know anything about me. My life is complete as it is. I don't need to intrude into yours to make mine work. I wanted to see you, to look for a part of me in you. Thank you for being honest with me, but we don't ever need to meet again."

"But, if you're agreeable, maybe we could write," said Lorene. "I'd like to know how your new job goes."

Theedy looked sympathetic.

"You're a nice lady, Lorene. I'm glad you agreed to this meeting. I could say 'maybe' that we'd write, but 'maybe' is hard to count on, isn't it?"

Theedy put down a ten dollar bill on the table, and walked away.

END OF DAYS

His illness had been long, but the funeral seemed even longer. Worth Maloney had been a leader, a force of nature, a star in the small community. He'd done so much for so many that every pastor in the little town wanted, needed his time to regale Worth's contributions. He'd been the loan officer of the town's only bank, the man who manipulated rules to give probably bad loans to townspeople of questionable credit, but distinct need. Worth knew they'd make good, and he knew they needed the money that only he could provide. He was a deacon in the church, a member and sometimes president of every local fuzzy animal men's club, chairman of the little food bank, founder of the housing project for local lost souls, a long-time member of the Jubilee, Mississippi City Council where he regularly and humbly declined offers of the mayoral position, and, instead, received the implied crown of leadership without official vote or boring minutia. Worth was the go-to guy for everything in Jubilee.

Then, he died.

Izzy, the only child of Worth and Mabel, was reluctantly drawn back to Jubilee to manage all the funeral arrangements and her mother's uncertain future.

After the interminable funeral, after the mournful graveside service, the herd of regional mourners descended on the Maloney mansion for free refreshments, to eyeball the interior, and to strut themselves as sorrowful friends – whether or not they actually were. Other fake mourners were there for networking and to see and be seen with the county's elite. Here and there were the few, sad people who really cared for Worth.

Izzy put on, like a coat, the local customs she'd nearly forgotten. She circulated through the rooms in her appropriate, Vera Wang black dress. The obvious expense of it would feed Jubilee gossip for weeks. She accepted condolences, smiled mechanically, and dabbed her eyes whenever the circumstance required.

She'd been raised for public decorum, escaped it, and now was thrown back to do her Southern duty. When she couldn't stand it any longer, she searched for her mother and found her missing.

Entering the master suite, Izzy found her mother sitting in one of the brocade Queen Anne chairs in the sitting area. Mom was staring fixedly at some invisible spot across the room. She didn't seem to blink. Izzy noted the Valium bottle on the end table.

"Mom, hey – *Mom*. Look at me, please."

The older woman, perfectly dressed, coiffed, made up, and wearing her best pearl chocker along with the pearl and diamond earrings, continued to ignore Izzy.

"Mom, dear Mom, I know you're distressed about Daddy, but there are so many people out there who need to see you. It would be a really good thing – the polite, royal thing in this town – if you could just walk through some of the rooms. Consider your position, Mom. Today you must stand in for Daddy's status. I've been away a long time, and this crap is pretty tedious, but I've been doing it, and I'll go with you. Right by your side. How 'bout that? We have to, Mom. It's your job. Mine, too, unfortunately."

Mom turned her head slightly in Izzy's direction, but neither spoke nor focused. She returned to staring at the presumably significant spot on the far wall.

"Well, all righty then," said Izzy. "I'll make your apologies. Grief and all that."

Izzy circulated, comforted those who sincerely mourned, and mentally discarded requests for her mother's future political endorsements. As guests were finally clearing out, she slipped into the kitchen, waited for the caterer's help to leave for the receiving rooms' cleanup. She reached into the private liquor cabinet. She'd locked the more public one in hopes of keeping the wake under control. They weren't Irish, after all. She opened a bottle of Crown Royal and took a deep, long sip straight from the bottle. She waited for the warmth to glide into her stomach to calm her nerves if only a bit.

When she'd escorted the last mourner to the front door and paid the caterers, she returned to her mother.

"Everyone's gone, Mom. You need to come to the kitchen with me. It's time to have something to eat. No conversation about it. Just get up and come with me."

Eula was the only house servant who remained. It had been Eula who mostly raised Izzy. She watched the women entering the kitchen and filled plates for them of the best reception leftovers. She exchanged looks with Izzy who nodded and nearly smiled. It was Eula's cue to leave. Eula, invisible as all servants in Jubilee, stepped into the back mudroom where she hung her apron and gathered her personal belongings to head home. Before she touched the exit doorknob, Izzy appeared and went to her, arms open.

"Precious Eula. I've missed you. You're a saint to stay this long with them," said Izzy. "How have you survived my parents?"

Eula gave the younger woman another hug and stroked her face. "Miss Izzy, it's a job, a good job, and I need it. It's not a happy house like when you was here, but I know your Mama needs me as much as I need to work here. It's not out of love no more. The riptides in this house are as wicked as them in the big Mississippi River. You watch yourself. Now, you get back in there." She smiled at Izzy. "You've grown up just fine."

"I'm more grateful to you than you can imagine," Izzy said.

As she stepped out the back door, Eula turned and spoke quietly. "Watch yourself."

Back in the kitchen, Mom sat ramrod straight. She used her fork to scoot the food here and there into modernist, abstract piles. She rarely ate, but, with every other occasional bite, lifted her linen napkin and patted her mouth twice, left then right. Izzy watched. Mother represented everything about Jubilee society that Izzy had fled. She longed to see her mother relax, let go, shove a piled-high fork of food into her mouth and let it dribble down her chin. She wanted to see her mother belly laugh. Izzy returned to the liquor cabinet, took a gulp, observed the bottle, and took it out to make a respectable drink. It seemed the only way.

"How much do you drink?" asked Mom.

"What? We buried Daddy today. Everyone in three counties has been here to give you their sympathies, and the first thing you say to me is how much do I drink? Good God, Mom. And the answer today is not nearly enough."

"Don't take the Lord's name in vain."

"I escaped this life for college above the Mason-Dixon line and have done my very best not to come back into this craziness. Please don't try to pull me into your quagmire of rigidity, polite lies, and phoniness. I'll be gone soon, and you can make up whatever story suits you. Between now and then, I just might swear again."

"You were always a difficult child."

"Yeah, because my parents were cardboard stick figures. I was happier down in darky town with Eula, but you wouldn't let me stay there. I had a destiny, you said. Bullshit. I was never meant to live your cold, unyielding life."

"Daughter, you're trying my patience. You've been a great disappointment to us."

"Here's how I disappointed you: I graduated Vassar magna cum laude, and I've had an impressive career in magazine writing and editorships in New

York and Los Angeles. What a disappointment to my parents. Oh right, I refused to do the debutante thing, and I wouldn't enter your beauty pageants. Is that what turned you against me? This is all so mindless."

"You haven't been here. You haven't represented the family properly. You didn't marry the man your father and I chose. It was a good match, an appropriate one. And now, you haven't married anyone and you have no babies. You're drying up."

"A charming characterization." Izzy worked on the stiff drink. "Mom, this conversation about my perceived failings isn't really useful, and it's making me tired. Have you nothing to say about my Daddy? He's dead, you know. Don't you care? Don't we need to discuss the steps we should start taking tomorrow to wrap up his business dealings? Jesus Christ! He made you and me – mostly you – the big time ladies of the region. You now have tons of money. Shouldn't you plan something in his sweet memory? Maybe a foundation or ongoing support of the food bank – in his name, of course. He'd like that."

"You're a fool. His business, the bank ... you have no idea who your father was."

"Of course I do. He was loved by everyone. He was involved in every good venture in the county. He set the example for my public contributions. He loved us. He was everything."

"He was nothing. He loved himself. Everything he did was to enhance his reputation and make sure that everyone treated him like the king he wanted to be. "

"Mom, that's cruel and so wrong. He was a shrewd businessman and bank officer. Maybe he cut some corners, but look at all the good works he did. Don't talk badly about my father." Izzy thought she might cry, and she didn't want to give her mother the satisfaction.

Another drink called Izzy. Her mother frowned in distaste.

"Any *good* he did was outside – for show. It was rarely in his home or his heart."

"I won't believe you. Can't believe you. He was my father, and I loved him. I'm not naïve. Are you telling me that he wasn't a faithful husband? That he had an affair? I'm sure women were attracted to him. You should have put down your foot. That's not what women these days have to accept, Mom. You should have taken your power."

"Summa cum laude be damned. You're as much a fool as he was."

"I can't take any more of this. I'm going to bed. I'll stay here three more days to help you get things in order, then I'm out – unmarried, un-babied me."

"Sit back down. Maybe get your drunken self more liquor. That is, if you want to know your family."

"In publishing, that's what we'd call a very good tease. And I'm far from drunk. Just give me a little time."

She sat back down at the table.

"Okay. Go. Tell me whatever you want."

"Your father, my late husband, and I kept you so protected. For a long time, he kept me that sheltered, ignorant. Only since he's been sick did I discover the whole truth. Our wealth? He played a shell game with our money. Everything's mortgaged to the hilt. I'll probably lose this big house and live in some bug-infested slum. The finances – a sham. None of this is real."

"Oh, Mom, you're being dramatic."

"No, you'll see tomorrow when we go to the attorney. The 'big man' is broke, and so am I."

"God, I'm sorry. I don't quite know what to say. I guess we could sell what we can, and I could bring you up ... or I could find you an appropriate apartment around here that we could afford. Something that wouldn't embarrass you. I'll help with the money, of course. You can say that the house was just too big for you by yourself."

"You're such a child. Do you think that's all?"

"Did he have a mistress or a side family?"

Mom actually laughed. Of course she lifted her napkin to her mouth to disguise the outburst just like a proper Southern lady. But she really did laugh.

"Not even close. Your father with another woman? Oh no. Hell no, if I might say. You see, being the widow of the most important man in three counties carries an abundance of pressure as well as prestige. He is viewed as nearly the messiah. Despite whatever financial issues come to light, he will be forgiven. But not this.

"There was no other woman," continued Mom. "So, what a disappointment on our honeymoon to discover that he was impotent ... at least with a woman. But I loved him, and he was a good catch. So I held his secret all these thirty-six years. He provided a proper surrogate for me, a lovely man. We had a husband-approved, extremely secret affair for fifteen years. We were very discreet as was my husband in his private life. The South nearly suffocates under layer upon onion-like layer of lies and secrets. My assigned lover and I grew to love one another very much."

"What the hell story is this? You expect me to believe this craziness? It's a soap opera plot. I'm going to bed."

Izzy stood, paced around the kitchen, poured a shot, started out of the room, and was stopped by her mother.

"Sit back down and calm yourself, missy. The man I'm telling you about was your true father. Take that in. Worth had wanted us to conceive a child, an heir for him. But, as time went on, he became irrationally jealous. My husband had the dearest love of my life banished to a worthy position in Memphis. I should have gone with him. He asked, but I lacked the courage."

Izzy found no words

Mom said, "Do you remember Uncle Beau lunching with us at The Little Tea Shop in Memphis when we went to shop?"

"Sort of," Izzy puzzled. "He was there more than once when we went to town. He was nice enough."

"That was your true father, and he cared very much for you," said Mom. "That first publishing job you got in New York? He called in a favor. Now, do you feel so fancy?

"And now, after all this, I'm required to act like the grieving widow. I wish Worth had died twenty years ago. Stop looking shocked. You know you don't belong here. Now you know why. None of this will affect you except that you will receive no inheritance. Don't worry. I won't be a burden on you. I'm not sure I like you very much. So take the bottle back out of the cabinet. You want it, and you're going to need the rest of it tonight. The house of cards starts collapsing tomorrow."

VANISHED

I remember exactly when she disappeared. It was the day after my first day of school – my very first. She and Daddy rushed into the house when they got off work. The baby-sitter left, and Mom scooped me up and twirled me around, calling me her little scholar, her school girl, her six-year-old genius, her brainchild. I laughed so hard that I nearly peed my panties. She and Daddy just sort of nodded to each other as Mom went in to change into jeans and that old, green pullover sweater.

Mom wanted to hear all about school, but Daddy told us to come to the table for dinner. It was his turn to cook. I just remember being a chatterbox. Mom laughed at me, and Daddy reminded me to eat. I helped her clear the table, then we ran into the living room.

Cuddling up with Mom on the sofa was so warm and perfect. Her smell was a bit of her perfume and sometime the funny scent of the cigarettes she occasionally smoked in the back yard. Tonight, the sweater smelled a lot like the spaghetti sauce she'd spilled.

I told her that I could recognize more words than most of the other kids. I also tattled on the stupid boys who made fart noises when the teacher left the room. And then, told her about those super pretty girls. I asked if I'd ever get that pretty and if I could have a new dress. She listened to me, really listened. Daddy watched TV and smiled at us now and then. I was big enough to do my own bath, but it was Mom who tucked me into bed and read me a story. She said that pretty soon, I'd be reading the stories to her. She kissed me on the forehead and told me how much she loved me.

The next morning, she was gone. Disappeared. That was twenty years ago.

I asked Daddy over and over and over again what had happened, but he didn't have a real answer. He just said she'd decided to leave. On that first morning, I sobbed as I ran to her closet, only to find it empty. I opened drawers and cabinets. There was no trace of her.

I cried for weeks. Daddy tried to comfort me, but I didn't want to be comforted. Daddy had to force me to go to school, but he couldn't make me learn. I did nothing but sit at my desk. At recess and lunch, I found nearly private places where I could cry with little intrusion. At home, Daddy tried to be the one to tuck me in and read stories, but I rolled over and turned my back to him.

He finally took me to a child psychologist. On the first visit, he sniffled his sadness, but I didn't. The therapist excused him to the waiting room so he could speak with me privately. His office had bright colors and pretty curtains. There were dolls, small tables and chairs, toys, and puppets. He smoked a pipe, but it wasn't as good as Mom's funny cigarettes. I didn't feel like I fit in that happy-happy room. I was angry. I was always angry back then.

"Sweetie, how do you think I can help you feel better?" he asked.

"Give me back my Mom," I said.

"Baby, I'm sorry. You know I can't do that," he said in syrupy tones. "But I can help you accept her absence ... if you let me."

"I'm not your baby, and if you can't give me back my Mom, then I don't want you."

I kicked him on the shin and ran into the waiting room. Daddy dragged me back there two more times, but I wouldn't cooperate. I didn't kick him again, though.

Gradually, my extreme anger morphed into sadness and eventually into a state of numb abandonment. I could never make sense of it, and I still can't. That's why I thought it was a bad joke when she called yesterday. I don't know how she found me. I'd graduated from the University of Memphis, found good work, and been on my own for years. But she had found me. Did she really love me after all? I asked her trick questions to prove that she was real. She was. And she wanted to see me. To explain or try to. She told me that she'd be at Court Square today at three o'clock. She'd be sitting on the bench to the southwest of the fountain. I told her I'd try to be there.

I didn't know how to feel. I was ecstatic. I was furious. I wanted to see her, but I was afraid to. If anything, I wanted to be in the first grade, snuggled next to her. It had been twenty years for God's sake. What possible excuse could she have?

I got to Court Square twenty minutes ahead of time. She was already there. It was her back, but it was her back. Her hair was pretty gray, but she was wearing that same green sweater. How could she have kept it all these years? She must have worn it just for me.

My feet had turned to granite. I thought I couldn't take a single step toward her, and now I wanted to.

She stood. My stomach clinched. Then, the stranger in the green sweater turned and walked away.

It took me two hours before I gave up and walked away, too.

HIGH TIDE

When the temperature and humidity collide at 97, even native Memphians seek refuge at swimming pools, movie theaters, department stores, or other air-conditioned buildings. When Lena Armstead stepped from her air-conditioned office building into the damp gauze of heavy summer air, her breath caught involuntarily, and she opened the top two buttons of her nurse's uniform. Having to work half-day on Saturdays was not her first choice, but at least it was cool inside. Now the hot weekend lay ahead.

"I'm home," she called out when she arrived.

"Back here, Mom."

Lena walked through the small front rooms of the duplex to her daughter's room.

She stopped at the door and shook her head. "You're actually doing homework on a hot Saturday afternoon? Did I raise you wrong?"

Julia sat cross-legged on her bed next to the open windows and across from a tabletop fan.

"Make fun if you will, but I'm afraid of getting behind in summer school. It goes so fast, and there's so much to learn. Maybe I should have waited to take it in the fall. Tenth grade is when everybody else takes biology, but I'd probably be afraid of it then, too. It's hard."

"Jules, you always worry, and you always do fine. Sometimes I think you're a little old lady. Do what you want. I'm changing clothes. And I'm opening more windows. It's like an oven in here."

"Sure, Mom. That's what it's like for some people who can't go to an air-conditioned office," Julia mumbled. She wiped her forehead with her shirttail.

Minutes later, Lena reappeared. When the white uniform was discarded, the bun at the nape of her neck became a ponytail. Her pedal pushers and snug pullover dropped ten years from her already attractive appearance. She liked it when people thought she and Julia were sisters. Married, pregnant and divorced young made their financial situation sometimes precarious, but as soon as she found a suitable husband, everything would be perfect. Decent husband material was out there somewhere, and her quest continued despite some bad choices here and there.

Boys were coming around the house these days, and Julia always suspected they were actually there to see her vivacious mother. Lena was drawn by nature to center stage. She couldn't help it.

"So how much longer are you going to keep at the books?"

"I don't know. Maybe an hour or so. Why?"

"I don't know," said Lena. "I'm restless. Want me to get you a coke?"

"Sure. Thanks." What did restless mean today?

Julia's concentration turned piecemeal from Lena's busy-ness. Cabinets and drawers banged open and closed in the kitchen. The television came on, then the station changed through its three channels and back again. Lena walked up and down the hall. There was rummaging in dresser drawers in Lena's bedroom.

She returned to Julia's door.

"Jules, here's what's going to happen. It's three o'clock now. I'm going to take a short nap. You'll wake me at four. We'll eat a cold dinner. And you'll be through with homework. You're going to be dull, dull, dull if you sit in here all weekend. Instead, we're going to the beach."

"The beach? Maywood?"

"No, you silly. The *real* beach – at the Gulf Coast."

When Lena was like this, Julia always remembered The Party. Julia was in the seventh grade and giving her first boy-girl party. There were chips and dips and soft drinks, and a stack of 45s to play on her hi-fi. Her mother's girlfriend, Ruth, came over to keep Lena company. The sort-of chaperones moved the television into Lena's room. They agreed that Julia's partygoers would be well behaved, and Lena would greet the guests, then watch TV in her room with Ruth. She promised to be good.

Julia was in the kitchen pouring another Coke for someone when all the chatter in the living room stopped. A wide-eyed girlfriend stepped into the kitchen.

"You need to come out here."

Julia's friends were backed away from the center of the room because that's where Lena and Ruth had seated themselves on the floor. Lena's long hair was parted in the middle and hung straight over her shoulders. They both wore black eye makeup and white lipstick. They wore oversized sweatshirts, tights, and short shorts. Ruth gently tapped on a bongo drum. Lena read from a poetry book. Beatniks.

None of the junior high guests knew what to do or think. Julia returned to the kitchen without speaking. She stayed there until she was certain the two women had retreated to Lena's bedroom. They thought their joke was just too funny. None of Julia's classmates laughed or asked questions. Julia's best friend put on another dance record. Julia was humiliated. She never had another party. A suggested Saturday trip to the beach, hundreds of miles away, couldn't be as bad as the party had been.

"Mom, you have to go to work Monday morning. I have to go to school. This is Saturday afternoon. This trip can't possibly work."

"Of course it will. I'll drive us down tonight, and drive back up tomorrow night. We'll have a day at the beach. We'll be tired Monday, but we'll have such fun. Now, I'm off for my nap. Finish your school work."

At 4:15 p.m., Lena mixed a salad with tuna, cottage cheese, cold green peas, and a little chopped onion. It was tasty and didn't heat up the already steamy house.

"Baby, go take a cold bath and put on some fresh clothes. You're all sweaty sticky." Lena patted Julia on the head and cleared the table with unnerving glee.

When Julia re-appeared, she looked like an only slightly younger version of her mother.

"What's going on with the paper sacks?" asked Julia.

Three of them, apparently full, crowded the small kitchen counter. Lena beamed.

"You need to get some things together for yourself. Swimsuit, change of clothes, that sort of thing. I've already packed this bag with snacks and sandwich fixings so we won't have to buy any food, just cokes and coffee. The drive will be cooler after dark, and that makes this the best idea."

Lena's energy level was familiar and not always a good thing.

"I put towels in this bag – for beach blankets and others for drying off. Oh, maybe I should just get a blanket instead. That's what I'll do. And in this bag I put my bathing suit and clothes, toothbrush, that stuff. You need to get your things together. Here. They'll fit in the bag with mine. I'll pull out these beach towels and pack a blanket instead."

"Mother, I don't think this is a good idea. It's just too far. I don't even know if our old car will make it."

"You're always worried about something. Stop being an old lady and get your things." Lena frowned hard enough to make the wrinkles between her eyebrows reveal themselves. "Trust me, okay? We need to pack the car and get on the road. It won't be dark for a couple of hours, but we should get going anyway."

And she was off, beach towels in hand, on her way for a blanket and pillows. It was always this way. Julia might have been the voice of reason, but at least this time, she was talking to herself.

About midnight, as they drove south, the road noise grew quieter. Bright, colored lights replaced the funereal darkness of the open road. The two-lane highway had run through rural Mississippi and only encountered a handful of small towns. Now, it blossomed into four lanes and entered the state capitol's city limits. The changes in light and sound woke Julia from an accidental nap. She wiped away the slender line of drool sliding toward her chin.

"Hello, sleeping beauty. So who is it who couldn't stay awake after all?" Lena winked at her daughter. "This is Jackson. I want to fill up here. Don't know how long it will be till we have another chance. There's just not much going on down here. I think the station up there on the left looks open."

While the gas station attendant filled the car and cleaned bug-spattered windows, the women made restroom, candy bar, and coffee stops inside.

Back on highway 51 headed toward the Gulf, Julia found a radio station and sang along loudly. She was off-key, but no matter. She was just trying to keep her mother (and herself) awake. They were in darkness again. Few cars kept them company. When the candy bars were gone, Julia dug into the snack sack in the back seat for other treats to keep Lena alert in the tedium of the dark, monotonous road. Two hours later Julia struggled to stay awake and felt the old car lose speed.

"Nothing's wrong," said Lena. "I just need to get out and walk around somewhere. I have to shake myself awake. Gawd, coffee would be good. Help me look for something – anything – a wide place in the road will do."

They both opened their windows all the way so the assaulting wind would keep Lena's senses alert. It was thirty-five minutes before they spotted a single bright light on the side of the road, probably a half-mile ahead. It was high above the road like a streetlight, but more likely it was a farm's security light.

"Look! It's a little store with gas pumps out front," said Julia with disbelief. "How crazy way out here in the middle of nowhere."

Lena slowed more to look for the driveway. "There are probably farm houses around here, back off the road. For sure, there's never a store where there aren't people to shop."

Their headlights and the security light unveiled a small, old, wooden building with a closed sign hanging in a window. The two gas pumps were tired and outdated. The Armstead women gratefully jumped out of the car almost before Lena turned off the ignition. They stretched this way and that to ease their stiff backs. Julia mimicked a crazy dance, and Lena laughed at her. The hour and the drive made them silly. They were so intent on each other that they didn't hear the man step around the corner of the building until he racked his shotgun.

"Hold it right there! Hands in the air!"

The women wheeled around toward the voice, screamed at the sight of his gun, and clung to each other.

"Hands in the air, dammit! Can't you hear?"

Lena stepped in front of Julia, raised her hands and started talking fast. She started by saying they had no money to steal and were not there to steal anything either. She blurted out that they were just driving from Memphis to the coast for a day trip to the beach. They only stopped there because she feared going to sleep at the wheel.

"We mean no harm, sir. Honest, no harm at all and pray that no harm comes to us. We'll leave right now if that's okay with you. We'll just get right back in the car and be on our way."

He bought it. He lowered the gun and explained that he lived in the back of his store. Their headlights and then their voices woke him. He had to be careful out here.

"You sure don't look very dangerous," he said.

He apologized for frightening them. Lena offered again to leave, but he had a better offer. He unlocked the store and flipped on the inside lights. The musty smell was somehow comforting to Julia.

His name was Hank, and he'd owned his little store for a long time. Didn't get much company. "Coffee?" He started a pot before making sandwiches and cutting slices of pie from the baked goods delivered daily by one of his neighbors. Julia noticed her mother casually slip off the ponytail holder and fluff her hair about her shoulders. Hank expressed concern that the two women were on the road alone in the middle of the night. *Why wasn't her husband driving them*, he wondered aloud and expressed surprise that such a lovely lady might be alone in the world. As Lena helped him pick up their trash at the end of their most welcome meal, Hank wrote his telephone number on a scrap of paper and gave it to her. If there's trouble of *any* kind on their trip, Lena should call him.

Julia could have written the script. Men just did things for Lena – except stick around. When the end of the world approached, Julia hoped she'd be with her mother and that the man with the keys to the escape craft was within range of Lena's scent.

That's what it was. Pheromones, Julia thought. Lena must exude that mysterious, sexual scent that mesmerized men – at least for a while.

Hank turned on his gas pumps and filled the car's tank. He checked under the hood, added water and oil, and gently chided Lena for poor car maintenance. Naturally, he refused payment. Which was good because they probably didn't have enough money. The women were refreshed. The car was ready. Hank was disappointed that he had to keep the station open Sunday afternoon or he'd drive them down to the beach. That wasn't in Lena's plan anyway.

"Honey, you're gonna need to be special watchful for the next fifty miles or so," Hank warned. "Highway fifty-one runs through swamp for a while, and gators like to cross the road along the way. You need to give them the right'a way. If you hit one, it'll flip your car, and I don't want to be hearin' about that. You be careful and stop by here on your way back. I'll stay open."

He opened the door to help Lena into the car.

She pushed her dark hair away from her face and gave him one of those smiles that a man could live on for a month. She squeezed his hand that rested on the window frame. Her touch was soft and warm. He might have blushed. Julia wondered if Lena was aware of her gift.

"He sure was a nice man," said Julia.

"Yeah. I wonder how he survives way out here in the boonies," said Lena. "So boring."

Worried about the gator warning, the two were hyper-alert for nearly one hundred miles. They could smell the swamp, and the humidity frizzed Julia's hair. Her sleep-starved eyes stung from the strain. They saw nary a single reptile crosswalk. When the car clock circled the five o'clock hour, the women were pulling into Pass Christian, a small beach town less commercial than some of its neighbors. The sun had not yet decided to make an appearance so Lena looked for a place to wait it out. She pulled onto the side of a gas station that was just across the highway from the beach. She took the back seat with her pillow, pushing paper grocery sacks onto the floor. Julia curled up in the front. The sun would wake them.

"We're burning daylight. Let's go, girl." Lena's energy was back to supersonic level.

"Yes ma'am." Julia's head slowly surfaced from a peaceful dream. Although it was early, she was already sweaty. They hadn't rolled down the windows enough to get much sea breeze.

"I'm going to see if the restrooms are unlocked," said Lena. "We'll change into our bathing suits, leave the car here behind the station, and just walk across the highway. We can make sandwiches for our breakfast. Surely there's somewhere around here to get a cup of coffee."

The women's restroom was unlocked. That usually meant dirty, but they did their best not to contract any fatal diseases. They emerged ready for surf and sand.

"Early aren't you, ladies?"

Lena laughed at the man standing in front of the building as they rounded the corner. At least he didn't have a shotgun.

"Yes, sir. We don't want to miss a minute of this beautiful day," said Lena, her face flushing as it sometimes did when flirting. "We just drove down from Memphis to splash in your waves. I do hope my car won't be in the way if I leave it behind your building."

It was open season on gas station owners.

Bud allowed as how the car was just fine where it was. He studied Lena and politely acknowledged Julia. He excused himself to open up. Before locking the car, Lena shoved the snack sack at Julia. Lena got the blanket and towels.

"Bud, we're going to make some breakfast sandwiches for ourselves, but I would surely kill nearly anything for a cup of coffee. Anywhere around open yet?"

"You're lookin' at it, Lena. I always make coffee when I open up the place. If you're just across the road, I'll bring you some."

Lena grinned and shot the look at Julia. They raced across the empty highway to the sand and staked out their territory. They made a breakfast from odd combinations that Lena packed. They shed their cover-up shirts and were basking in the early sun when Bud appeared with two cups of coffee.

"I might have overstepped, little lady. I didn't know if you wanted coffee, too," he said to Julia.

He brought packets of Cremora and sugar. They talked and laughed. Lena told about being on gator watch as they drove through swampland.

She didn't mention Hank. Bud went back to his station with a promise to return. Lena kissed her daughter's forehead and took her on a walk. They splashed each other in shallow water. They picked up seashells and avoided the skeleton of a small fish. These were the good times. If only it could be this way forever.

When they returned to their blanket, a young, redheaded man in shorts and tee shirt awaited them. He said that he worked for Bud and that he brought cokes and cheese crackers from the machine if they wanted a snack. For once, someone actually saw Julia instead of her mother. She saw him appraising her long legs and slender body. It made her tingle. Is this how her mother feels?

Lena accepted the gifts and ordered the teenagers out of her presence.

"I'm going to get a rest now. You two, go do something," she said.

Ralph kicked off his shoes next to the blanket. When the boy turned away, Lena wiggled her eyebrows and grinned at Jules.

The kids walked to the edge of the sand and sloshed through water that barely covered their feet. There were awkward silences that finally disappeared into teenage chatter. Ralph played football at the local Catholic high school. He didn't care much for the classes, but was involved in most school activities. He couldn't believe that Julia was going to summer school voluntarily. He worked for Bud in the summer to earn spending money. He thought it was funny that Catholic education separated boys and girls.

"I guess they think we'll stay pure if we don't sit in the same classrooms." He laughed and took Julia's hand. "C'mon. Let's get that bathing suit wet."

Ralph trotted into deeper water pulling Julia along with him. He looked awfully cute when he laughed.

"You'll get your clothes wet. You have to go back to work," warned Julia as she tripped into an unexpected swell of warm, Gulf water.

"Who cares?" Ralph wrapped his arms around her and launched the two of them into a wave. They emerged on the other side, laughing and spitting salt water. Ralph held her tightly and helped her jump, keeping both their heads above the next wave. His hands slid down her back and cupped her butt. He kissed her before the next wave knocked them down. They were apart now, and Julia was afraid of being close again.

"I have to go back. Mother will get worried," she said.

Ralph tried to pull her close again. Julia squirmed away.

"Don't do that." She walked back to the sand. Ralph didn't hold her hand on the way back. He looked disgusted. They were still a distance from the blanket when Julia realized that Lena wasn't there. Julia walked faster, and the football player reluctantly kept up.

Back at the blanket, Julia made a 360 degree turn, but couldn't see her mother anywhere.

"Where is she? Can you see her?" She unconsciously began chewing on the inside of her cheek.

"Jesus, girl. She probably just took a walk. Or maybe she went back to the station to pee. Look at this. One of them left us burgers and fries." He dug into the McDonald's sack and spread food on the blanket.

For the first time, Julia noticed the small, one-story motel a block west of the gas station. "I saw that red truck at the service station right after we got there. It's Bud's, isn't it?"

"Yeah. Bud owns the motel, too. Did I mention that he's my uncle?"

"Well, *she's my* mother, and she doesn't need to be over there."

"Who put you in charge? She's the adult, not you. Sit down and eat or just be quiet."

Ralph's charm apparently washed off in the surf. He was gruff, insensitive. Is this what happens when boys don't get their way?

Julia was embarrassed that her worry didn't erase her appetite. She grabbed one of the burgers and ate it standing up, staring at the red truck. She finished another burger and some fries. Finally as the sun began setting and marking the count down to their departure, Julia saw her mother and

Bud walking out of a motel room hand-in-hand. Ralph maintained his sulking silence.

"Baby, have you had a great afternoon? Bud let me take a nap over there. He owns the motel, too. How about that?" She and Bud still held hands.

Julia was embarrassed again, but not about her appetite.

Bud looked at Ralph's damp clothes. "Well, it looks like you've been a lot of help today at the station. Pack up the girls' stuff. They're going to change clothes and head back to Memphis."

Ralph disappeared after he hauled the Armsteads' gear to their car. When the women emerged in dry clothes, Bud helped Lena into the car and handed her a fresh cup of coffee. They didn't kiss, but Julia could see that they wanted to. She might be young, but that look was unmistakable.

Driving back toward the swamplands, the women were quiet. Julia listened to her mother hum some song.

"So, tell me," said Lena. "Is Ralph just as nice as he is cute? When should I expect him to show up at our doorstep?"

"I'm not going to see him again. Don't want to."

"Why on earth not?"

"Oh, Mother. For one thing, he's a jerk. Besides that, we live hundreds of miles apart. It's just not practical."

"Well, I'm going to see Bud again. We really hit it off."

"You have a visit planned already?"

"Not exactly, but we exchanged phone numbers. I'll be hearing from him. And I can always call him if I want."

"So you have his home telephone number?" Julia already had a bad feeling.

"No. He said that with the hours he puts in at the service station and the motel, I'd never catch him at home, so he just gave me his work numbers. I thought it made sense."

Julia looked long at the enduring hopefulness of her mother.

Finally, she spoke. "I love you very much, Mom."

SISTERHOOD

Wedding bells for the middle-aged bride and groom actually rang. The bride had hired a group of professional bell ringers to play as the minister, groom, best man and bridesmaids entered the small chapel. The cue for the bride's entry was the traditional wedding march played by three violins. The wedding was a small, but elegant affair. Exactly as the bride had ordered, detail by excruciating detail. The two bridesmaids were teenage daughters – one from the bride; one from the groom. The bride made it clear that neither was the maid of honor. They were co-equal. One carried the ring that the bride would present to her husband. The other would, at the proper moment, take the bride's nosegay of gardenias and baby's breath. Equal. No partiality. That was Eunice's plan for mothering both girls.

Initially, Eunice and Stanton thought it was good that the girls were the same age. They could trade clothes and secrets. They would be best friends, and delight in finally having a sister. But then, expectations and reality don't always mesh.

Molly Milligan was pretty, popular, an excellent student, and a born leader. Her step-sister, Twyla, was plump in a fluffy sort of way. She'd not been given the gift of beauty. Her top teeth should have had braces years ago, and there was no striking feature to induce a second look. Nevertheless, she presented herself to others with a congenial personality, but that wouldn't get her passing grades. She was what they used to call "slow." When people described Twyla, they generally called her sweet and shy. Molly was ready to welcome her new sister.

Eunice persuaded Stanton that they should both sell their homes, and buy a new one, so neither would be moving into the other's territory. The three-bedroom model was perfect – separate bedrooms for the girls. Each room had a window to welcome the morning sun. Each had an ample closet. Eunice decorated them in similar themes, but Molly put out her trophies and a few certificates of achievement. Eunice was irritated, but decided to let it go this time.

Stanton was an executive overseeing operations at several manufacturing plants. He traveled frequently. He loved his new wife, and was grateful and confident in leaving the household and maternal oversight to her.

After settling into the new house, Twyla and Molly enjoyed late summer afternoons at their club's pool, movie nights with Molly's friends, and beauty shop manicures. With permission from Eunice, Molly hosted a slumber party, and introduced her new sister to all her girlfriends. Twyla was shy, but enjoyed being included.

The only thing Eunice didn't do was, thank goodness, dress the girls alike. But she was careful to buy two blouses here; two blouses there; a pair of loafers; another pair of loafers. Molly began to tire of the inevitable sameness that Eunice dished out. Molly had also noticed that all the pictures of her deceased mother had disappeared.

In Memphis, it never cooled off much by Labor Day, but school started anyway. The girls walked to school together in their new back-to-school clothes. They were both in the eleventh grade, but different classes. Few classmates knew they were step-sisters because it hadn't occurred to Stanton to adopt Twyla, and give her his name. Eunice probably had a plan to get around to that.

Molly looked for her new sister at lunch.

"Hey, Twyla, I found you," said Molly. She didn't notice that Twyla was at a lunch table with strangers. "I'm going to stay after school and join the Thespian Club. Why don't you do it with me?"

"I don't know what that is," said Twyla.

"Oh, they put on plays, and do the scenery and costumes and stuff. There are things to do for everyone who wants to join. What about it? In the auditorium after dismissal bell. See ya then." And Molly went off with friends finishing their lunches nearby.

Twyla showed up that afternoon, and became a member of the Thespian Club. She sat next to Molly. The advisor described plans for the year, and the play they would produce in second semester. She also described the need for students to put together scenery, work the lights, act as prompters, and collect props and costumes. There was work for everyone. Scripts were distributed with the announcement that try-outs would be in two weeks.

Report cards for the first six weeks came out before Thespian try-outs. Molly was thrilled that she made honor roll with straight A's except for a B in a required class that she hated. Twyla wouldn't show Molly her card, and wouldn't tell her what it said. Molly hurried home, but couldn't get Twyla to catch up. Trees had begun putting on their gold and red fall cloaks. Twyla pretended to be intent on studying them.

"Eunice! Where are you? Look at my report card," Molly cried out as she ran through the house. Her step-mother was quietly pleased until Twyla made it into the house, and had to produce her report card. Eunice managed to keep her smile intact, and complimented Twyla. She signed both cards as required.

"Will Daddy be home tonight so I can show him? Or can I call him? He'll be so excited," babbled Molly.

"I'm not certain, Molly. He's so preoccupied right now with business that I think we should leave him be. You can tell him another time. As I'm thinking about it, girls, I think these reports are actually only needed by the two of you in order to guide your attention to studies. I don't want you to bring them home any more. Just sign my name for me."

"No!" said Molly. "Daddy always wants to see my report card, and I want to show it to him. He's proud of my grades. He won't understand why I'm keeping it from him."

"That won't be a problem," said Eunice. "I'll explain it to him. Now, you two go upstairs, and get out of your school clothes."

Eunice always kept an even tone, an impassive face, but Molly had learned that when Eunice was up to no good, her left eye twitched. Before turning toward the stairs, Molly stared at her father's wife. The woman's left eyelid quivered.

As slowly as Molly dragged her feet climbing the stairs, Twyla's step was light and quick.

"I guess Daddy won't get to brag this time," sneered Twyla.

"He's not *your* Daddy," said Molly. "Don't push it."

It was soon time for each high school grade to elect its class officers. Groups of students had been campaigning in the halls, lunchroom, and study hall for a week for their favorite classmates. On election day, students cast paper ballots in morning homeroom per their grade level. There was an assembly during the day's last class period to announce the newly elected class officers for each grade. Molly entered the cavernous auditorium surrounded by her best friends. They were excited; they were nervous. As they passed Twyla, Molly offered a conciliatory smile. She received none in return.

The announcements began with the freshmen. Applause and screams of victory went up as winners' names were called. The four officers took their seats on stage. The sophomore announcements followed the same pattern. Time for the junior class. Molly and her group held hands in a daisy chain along their assigned auditorium row. Secretary. Treasurer. Vice President. Junior class President – Molly Milligan! Screams, applause, foot stomping, and cheers filled the room from both the junior and senior classes as she walked to the stage. Molly's face nearly hurt from grinning so broadly. The juniors barely heard the senior class announcements.

Molly was still receiving congratulations as she left school that afternoon. Twyla brushed by her, deliberately bumping her shoulder as she passed. "I voted for the other guy," she whispered.

Stanton was home when the girls arrived. Molly found him in his home office. With the stacks of books and file cabinets and piles of folders, it always had the smell of the school library. It was Molly's favorite room in the house.

"I won, Daddy! I'm junior class president!"

Stanton stood from his desk, and bowed ceremoniously. "Madam President." He hugged her, and kissed the top of her head. "I'm so proud of you. I'd love to say that you're a chip off the old block," he laughed, "but you already exceed anything I've ever done."

Eunice followed the voices, and entered the room.

"We should celebrate, don't you think, Eunice? Let's all go out to dinner."

"That would be lovely, wouldn't it, but I'm afraid I already have a pot roast nearly ready to serve."

For the first time, Molly saw Daddy give a stern look to his wife. "I'm sure it can be put up. It will be even better tomorrow, don't you agree?"

"Of course. I should have thought of that," she answered. "We should celebrate Molly's election." Her left eyelid fluttered.

Molly got to choose the restaurant, and the special dessert. It was almost like old times. It was a night when the loss of her mother was a physical presence at the table. She thought she could see it on Daddy's face, too.

Molly's school year was the best ever, and she tried again to be pleasant to Tywla. Molly caught up with her step-sister on the way to play try-outs.

"Twyla, are you going to try out for a part? You really should. I'm going to."

"Of course you are. I don't think I need to," said Twyla. "I don't think that acting is for me."

"I'm sure there's a part for you, and, even if there's not, there are a lot of important jobs to be done to put on the play. C'mon. I know you'll be on one of the teams."

Most of the club members went to the stage one at a time to read for a part. Twyla did her best. She and Molly took their time walking home.

"Twyla, I was so nervous when I tried out. My knees were actually shaking. I mean *really* shaking," laughed Molly.

"Don't lie. You did great. You'll get a part like you get everything." Twyla picked up her pace, and put the length of a block between them.

It only took a week for the list of cast members to be posted next to the club sponsor's classroom door. Molly won the part of the second female lead. Some students who crowded around the list, yelled out in happiness. Others quietly turned, and walked away. Molly spotted Twyla down the hall.

"Hey, I got pushed out of the way before I could see what you got," said Molly. "What's your part?"

Twyla grimaced. "I saw that you're one of the leads. Do you just get everything? I'm on the props committee. Big flippin' deal."

"Twyla, there *is* no play without props. It's important. Don't be so glum. We'll have fun going to rehearsals together."

"Sure."

At home, Eunice met them in the foyer before they could head to their rooms. "Lovely ladies, how was your day?"

Twyla answered immediately. "Assignments for the play were posted. The golden girl there got one of the leads, of course. I'm supposed to find props. Big whoop."

"Props? You have greater skills than that. You have just as much right to a part as that one does." Eunice shot a look at Molly. "That's it. You're not going scrounging about for useless pieces of junk. Just quit. You're better than that."

Twyla looked smug. Molly didn't bother to say anything.

After changing clothes, Molly took a schoolbook to the front porch, and did her reading while waiting for her father to get home. Eunice and Twyla left her alone. She threw down the book, and ran to the driveway when Daddy pulled in. Out of breath, she jumped in the passenger seat.

"Take me for a drive – right now. It's important."

Stanton put the car in reverse. He drove a few blocks to a neighborhood park, and pulled in.

"Okay, no one can interrupt. Tell me what's wrong."

"Daddy, they hate me. They both hate me. Eunice belittles everything I do, and doesn't want you to know when I do something good. She won't even let us bring home report cards because I get better grades than Twyla. I don't know what to do. I feel like I just shouldn't get good grades or chosen for anything at school. I think life would be easier then."

Daddy reached across the front seat and squeezed her hand. "Baby, I think you might be feeling too sensitive. Twyla isn't you, and never will be. She's bound to be a little jealous, but she's a lovely girl. She's successful in her own way. Have you tried to include her in your activities? Give her a position in some of your clubs?"

"I have! She turns up her nose, and is mean to me. And Eunice encourages her. I don't know what to do."

"Oh, Molly, you're being dramatic. Eunice wants very much for the two of you to get along. You just keep being yourself. You make us all proud."

The house was at peace for a while, but Molly cringed when she was elected to the homecoming court. Although Twyla said nothing to her on the way home, Molly knew that her step-sister was aware and angry. On that Friday afternoon, Molly avoided Eunice when they got home. Daddy was out of town. She didn't call him. Instead, she dug out her stash of savings from its secret place, and called a girlfriend. They quietly made plans to shop on Saturday for a formal gown that Molly could wear as junior class princess in homecoming court. Eunice tried to involve the girls in dinner table conversation that night, but failed. Frosty silence matched the late fall weather.

On Saturday morning, Molly made appropriate excuses and darted out the door to meet up for shopping. When she returned home with the large bundle, Eunice confronted her.

"Have you been shopping by yourself? Your sister or I would have gone with you. What on earth did you buy anyway?"

Now she had to tell.

"It's an evening gown," Molly said reluctantly. "I was elected to the homecoming court, and I needed a formal gown. Bitsy went with me. I used money that I've saved. It didn't cost you and Daddy anything."

"Unwrap it. Let me see," commanded Eunice. Twyla had joined them by that time.

Slowly, Molly unwrapped the dress. It was electric blue with a satin bodice, and chiffon overlays on the skirt. The modest neckline featured a border of faux crystals.

"Very extravagant," said Eunice with pursed lips.

"I think it's beautiful," said Molly.

"Of course. Twyla, did you know about this?"

"I told you about Homecoming, Mother. I didn't know about the dress."

"Take it to your room, Molly. We don't need to discuss this any further," said Eunice.

Molly didn't show the dress to her father when he got home. She was sure that Eunice would tell him some story about it.

The next week, Molly went into her father's office. "Homecoming is a week from Friday night. I'm the junior class princess, and I have a beautiful dress to wear. I really, really want you to be at the football game. There will be a big presentation at half time. Please, Daddy."

"Of course, I will. Wild horses, and all that," he joked. "You bet I'll be there. The whole family will. Can I wear a sign saying I'm the father of the prettiest girl in school?"

"Oh, Daddy." Molly loved it when he teased. When he did, he felt like *her* Daddy, not anyone else's.

Molly's escort arrived at the appointed time to take her to the football stadium where they would have special seating. Eunice and Stanton greeted the young man at the door, and waited. Stanton's eyes misted as he watched his beautiful daughter descend the staircase. She looked grown up. Her mother would have been so proud. He noticed that her escort was properly awestruck. Photographs were taken, and the couple departed. Stanton couldn't wipe the silly, proud grin from his face.

The three remaining Milligans arrived at the stadium, as there was much commotion around the homecoming court. Photographs were being taken. Well-wishers crowded around. Stanton tried, but couldn't spot Molly for all the people bustling about the student royalty. The family was climbing the steep stairs to a higher section when the accident happened. Eunice slipped and screamed. She went down on her hands and knees, but was able to roll over to a sitting position. Her hands were skinned, and one knee had a cut.

"Sweetheart," said Stanton. "Here. Let me help you up, and we'll get those scrapes cleaned."

Eunice tried to stand, but yelled again.

"It's my ankle!" she sobbed. "It's broken. I know it's broken."

Stanton knelt, and examined it.

"I don't think it's broken. I think you just twisted it, but I guess we should take you to the emergency room to make sure. Twyla, there are always paramedics near the field. Go see if we can get some help. I don't know if your mother can walk just yet."

Molly saw something going on at the next aisle, but was having fun, and it surely had nothing to do with her.

After the game, the royal court went to the homecoming dance where they would again be presented. After the dance, they went out as a group for burgers and to show off their finery. It had been a fantasy in which Molly actually felt like a real, princess. Her date took her home, and gave her a sweet kiss before watching her step inside the front door. Twyla was sitting on the stairs, smiling.

"They're in the living room," she said.

Molly saw her father first. "Daddy, I never saw you. I thought you'd get to me when we left the field after half time."

"Baby, I'm so sorry. Eunice had an accident almost as soon as we got to the stadium. We had to take her to the emergency room. Fortunately, it's just a sprain. I hate that we missed your big night. We'll get to see pictures, though, won't we?"

Molly saw Eunice on the sofa, her foot elevated, and covered with what was probably an ice pack. Eunice didn't look at all pained. Her eye twitched.

"I guess there was nothing else for you to do. I'm tired, so I'll just go to bed."

"First, tell me about it," said Stanton. "Was it great? Did you have fun? How was the dance?"

"It was okay. Good night."

Twyla was still sitting on the stairs grinning like the Cheshire cat as Molly swished past in her evening gown.

Christmas holidays were good. Daddy took vacation time to be with the family, and everyone seemed happy. They worked together putting up Christmas decorations, and occasionally bursting into off-key holiday songs. They laughed at each other, and felt like a family. The girls received nearly identical Christmas presents in equal amounts. Molly and Twyla exchanged sentimental gifts. Stanton and Eunice planned to go to a friend's house for a New Year's Eve party. Molly had a date for a New Year's dance at the local YMCA. That left Twyla.

"Stanton, Twyla still doesn't have anything for New Year's Eve. We can't leave her home alone," insisted Eunice. "It would just be so sad."

"Well, we can't take her with us. There won't be any children there," said Stanton.

"Molly needs to take her."

"Molly has a date, Eunice. Do you really think Twyla wants to be a third wheel? Isn't there a church activity she could attend?"

Voices were raised. Tears were shed. Stanton finally, and sheepishly, went to Molly's room.

"I'm sorry, sweetie," he said. "Twyla is kind of left out of New Year's plans. That is, she doesn't have any plans."

"I'm sorry," said Molly. "Isn't something going on at church?"

"That's not going to work. I'm afraid you'll need to take her with you to the dance."

"Are you kidding? I have a date! No way."

"I know. I'm sorry. I'm really sorry, but there's no other way."

"It's not fair! Leave my room. Just get out!"

Molly didn't come down to dinner. The next morning, she gave in, and called her date to explain that they'd have a chaperone. She apologized, and tried to settle him down.

Twyla pretended that everything was fine. "Molly, what are we going to wear for New Year's? Won't we have a ball!"

The spring's Thespian Club play was scheduled for a performance during the school day for the student body. There would also be performances Friday and Saturday nights for fundraising.

Friday morning, Molly gathered her two costumes, and saw Daddy as she went downstairs.

"What's all that, kiddo?" he asked.

"Daddy, you know. The play starts today. Are y'all coming tonight or tomorrow night?"

"This is news to me. What's going on? Eunice and I are leaving this afternoon for a weekend trip."

Molly said, "You can't! I told her. I told her a long time ago, and I saw her put it on the calendar. You can't go."

Eunice came in from the kitchen, wiping her hands on a dish towel.

"What's going on, Eunice? We need to be here for Molly's play."

"I'm so sorry, but we have non-refundable reservations, and our friends are counting on us to share expenses for the cabin and river guide. It would be hard for us to pull out now, and cause them to pay a lot more. I don't know how I could have missed Molly's play being this weekend. I just feel awful."

Molly watched Eunice's left eye twitch.

"I'm sorry, baby," said Stanton. "I don't guess we can get out of this. I'm really sorry. I'll make it up to you next time."

"Next time, right." Molly slammed out the front door.

The play was a grand success. Molly was flawless in her performance. She was swept up with the excitement, but found herself looking around to see if Daddy had shown up after all.

In the spring semester, Molly made the honor roll three times. The yearbook staff chose outstanding seniors and juniors for a special display in the book, and Molly was one of the honorees. Twyla heard the announcements, but Molly didn't tell anyone at home. She no longer invited Twyla to join her in anything. She decided not to go to the junior/senior prom, but somehow Daddy learned that prom was on the horizon.

"What do you mean you're not going?" he asked Molly.

She finally rattled off all the recognitions she'd received that year. "I didn't tell you because I knew it would just cause trouble," said Molly. "I've told you that Eunice only wants to drag me down. If I accept a date to the prom, you'll probably make me take Twyla with me, and I just won't do it. I won't. I'd rather stay home."

"I didn't realize that things were this hard for you. I can't tell you how bad I feel about it. About not paying enough attention," said Stanton. "You go ahead, and accept a prom date. Twyla will *not* go with you. She'll go if a boy asks her. She'll stay home if she doesn't have a date. I promise. No one will interfere with this special event for you. You're going to need a new gown. Take this credit card, and go shopping with Bitsy this weekend. Take her to lunch someplace good. Do it up right. I'll take care of the rest."

"Thank you, Daddy. Thank you so much."

Molly wiped tears from her face, and, after giving Stanton a huge hug, ran upstairs to carefully hide the card so it wouldn't be found before the weekend.

She came home from shopping with an exquisite, gold brocade gown. She took it straight to Stanton's office to show him. The other women in the house were obviously cool to Molly as prom approached. On the day of the big dance, Molly took out her dress and assembled undergarments, shoes and accessories. When she returned from getting a manicure, she went immediately to her dress. It was almost time to start getting ready. The cap sleeve on the left shoulder drooped loosely away from its seam. It wasn't an accident. She burst into tears, and ran to Daddy.

Eunice said, "I wish I weren't so clumsy at sewing or I could fix that."

Twyla shook her head, and slipped a small pair of scissors under a couch cushion.

Stanton was, at last, angry. "I'll take care of this." He called a long-time neighbor who came to the house immediately. She gave Molly a sweet hug, and set about repairing the gown. She'd been a good friend of Molly's mother, and had no affection for Eunice.

As she left, Eunice closed the door, and turned to Stanton. "That was kind of her to come straight over, but then, she doesn't have anything taking up her time, does she? Being divorced and all."

Molly's date had to spend a few minutes with Eunice while waiting for Molly. Twyla sulked in her room. Daddy knocked on Molly's door, and she called for him to enter. She was even more beautiful than her homecoming evening.

"You look just like your mother," he said with a catch in his throat. "I've brought you something."

He opened a jewelry box, and showed her a treasured necklace that Molly remembered. It was gold, topaz, and pearls. "It was your mother's," he said. "I thought it was perfect for your gown. She'd want you to have this. Let me fasten it."

"I don't know what to say, Daddy. Thank you. It's wonderful. You're wonderful. If I say more, I'll cry."

"And so will I. Don't ruin your makeup." He stood back to look at her again. "Your mother and I couldn't have asked for a more perfect daughter. Now, let's go downstairs. There's a young gentleman waiting for you."

Prom meant that the school year was almost over. After finals, Molly defiantly brought home her report card, and presented it to Daddy at dinner. There were straight A's for the entire semester, and she'd been inducted into the junior class Honor Society. As Daddy congratulated her enthusiastically, Molly stared hard at Eunice.

"I'd have done something special if I'd known we were celebrating," Eunice said insincerely.

"There's even more to celebrate." Stanton and Molly grinned at each other. "Because of her outstanding grades and achievements, Molly has been accepted to an exclusive girls' boarding school in the northeast. I'll miss her awfully, but it will be an amazing experience, and give her a chance to spread her wings. And provide a leg up for her future. The school's graduates are almost guaranteed admission to one of the Ivy League women's colleges. She worked hard to achieve this, and I lift my iced tea glass to salute her."

Eunice and Twyla did the same, but with less exuberance.

As the girls were getting ready for bed that night, Twyla went to Molly's room.

"So, you're being kicked out. I get to stay here with your *Daddy*. Too bad for you."

"You don't get it, do you, Twyla?" said Molly. "I'm being freed from the awfulness of you and your mother. I'm going to have a great life. Daddy sees through the two of you now. You might need to pack your bags for a different reason."